THE CASSATT SISTERS

A NOVEL OF LOVE AND ART

LISA GROEN

Black Rose Writing | Texas

This is a work of fiction. Names, characters, businesses, places, events, and incidents are either the products of the author's imagination or used in a fictitious manner. Any resemblance to actual persons, living or dead, or actual events is purely coincidental.

ISBN: 978-1-68513-659-8
LIBRARY OF CONGRESS CONTROL NUMBER: 2025935729
PUBLISHED BY BLACK ROSE WRITING
www.blackrosewriting.com

Printed in the United States of America
Suggested Retail Price (SRP) $21.95

The Cassatt Sisters is printed in Book Antiqua

*As a planet-friendly publisher, Black Rose Writing does its best to eliminate unnecessary waste to reduce paper usage and energy costs, while never compromising the reading experience. As a result, the final word count vs. page count may not meet common expectations.

PRAISE FOR
THE CASSATT SISTERS

"Replete with emotional interactions that bring the sisters and their world to life, *The Cassatt Sisters* is hard to put down, intensely revealing, and a work of art itself."
–Midwest Book Review

"A well-crafted portrait of two famous artists, their suffering, and their joys."
–Kirkus Reviews

"*The Cassatt Sisters* brings alive La Belle Époque, making us feel Degas, Pissarro, Morisot, Cassatt, and other artistic luminaries are our good friends. A touching and engaging read."
–Louella Bryant, author of *Sheltering Angel, A Novel Based on a True Story of the Titanic*

"Readers who love historical fiction will revel in the storytelling of Lisa Groen as she captures the passion of the Impressionists and the two amazing Cassatt sisters."
–Joan Donaldson, *Ae Fond Kiss: Love Blossoms in Tennessee*

For Aaron,
who opened our first conversation
with Impressionist art.

THE
CASSATT
SISTERS

"The door which you have opened to me will not be closed behind me and a whole legion shall follow me."
–Marie Deraismes, French feminist, 1828–1894

Impression

Edgar stepped toward me and stopped. We stared at each other, not speaking. Our silence amplified ambient sounds—the pop of a log in the fireplace, the clop of hooves pulling a carriage, the hush of a lamp next to his bed. My breath quickened.

He took another step toward me and, standing close, kissed me. He pulled away to look into my eyes. I felt weak, an ache rising in me, and he leaned forward to kiss me again. His fingertips felt the back of my head, unpinning my hair until it unraveled into his hands. He moved to stand behind me, and I could feel his chest rise and fall. Edgar placed his palms on my shoulders. Shivery, I turned to face him. He stared at me, concentrating, as if imprinting my form to memory.

In dreams, the past comes back to me. My life loops in snippets while I sleep. That night. Long days printmaking in his studio. And a question—are love affairs merely an opportunity to see the way we mislead ourselves?

Camille Pissarro worked with us in the afternoons. My sister Lydia brought lunch often. To hear us laugh! To feel Edgar's eyes on me. To sense life and art and love coalescing.

At the easel, my hands are young again. They grasp brushes easily. My eyesight no longer fails me. Edgar lost his vision, too, at the end. I want to remember everything before my days turn dark.

–Mary Stevenson Cassatt, January 1920

1.

In the seventh decade of the 1800s, Paris became the City of Light. A sense of progress accompanied the time like a traveling current. Gas lamps gave way to incandescent bulbs burning so brightly, lovers searched for darker shadows in which to embrace. The newly lit grand boulevards surrounding the Paris Opéra bustled with people and carriages. I strolled along the rue Laffitte one evening, a charming cobblestone street lined with stone-colored buildings—the center of Parisian art. One fine gallery after another vied for the attention of passersby, but my favorite belonged to Paul Durand-Ruel, a second-generation dealer known for collecting avant-garde paintings.

Les avant-gardes, the breakaway artists Durand-Ruel supported, openly defied the Salon, a juried exhibition that for centuries set standards and shaped careers. I, too, had set my sights on the Salon when I'd arrived by steamer from Philadelphia thirteen years prior. The jury had accepted one of my paintings when I was only twenty-four. I remember thinking, *surely my career will flourish.*

The gallery's large picture window sparkled in reflected streetlight, and I pressed my nose against the glass to peer at the paintings inside. Three pastel ballerinas glowed in a gilded frame on the far wall. Miniature dancers dressed in silk and tulle waited in the wings before a performance. As my rose-scented perfume gathered against the glass, I imagined the large bouquets they'd hold in their arms after the performance while taking their bows.

I don't remember how long I stared at the painting, only the thrill of color and light, and I felt a shift within—away from the Salon and its fickle approval of my paintings. And toward a new path lit by artists who longed for progress. Not since I'd run my fingers over my first metal tubes of oil paint had I experienced this kind of certainty. I forgot about the years I'd watched students from Académie des Beaux-Arts, which barred women, advance beyond me. I didn't think about my auditions to gain instruction from Académie professors during off-hours. Or how my ambitions had been dismissed by my father—even when the Salon exhibited my paintings.

The portrait of ballet dancers thrilled me. I hadn't yet met the artist, but I whispered to myself while standing at that window. *Je suis arrivée.* In Edgar Degas' work, I saw my future. I pledged to find as many of his paintings as I could.

I found Degas' work in galleries and, when I was lucky, at a private residence. I came upon his self-portrait one afternoon, displayed next to a large oil portrait for sale, of a jockey and his horse. More movement, color, and surprising composition, but my eyes returned to the artist. I memorized and carried the angles of his face with me, secretly searching for him while going about my days in the city. If Degas were to cross my path, I'd recognize those dark, sad eyes and offer my hand. I came to know quite a few of his paintings during that time, but I did not meet him in the public places where artists mingle. The fates were trickier than that.

"Where are you going, Mary?" Father asked.

After years of study and toil and independence, I shared a home again with my newly retired parents and sister Lydia. Mother leapt at the chance to live in Paris again after Father transferred the helm of his business to my brother. Our sunny residence in Montmartre cheered me after living alone in boarding houses and tiny apartments.

The skirt of my cornflower silk dress filled half the width of our hallway, and Father dramatically turned to his side to let me pass. Delighted as I was to have my parents with me, at thirty-three, I was not accustomed to questions about my comings and goings in the evenings.

"Thomas Couture has traveled from Écouen to sell some paintings and has asked me to a dinner party."

Father looked at me blankly.

"My former teacher."

"Ah yes. And does he know you've turned coat on his tutelage?"

"Not yet," I said, smiling and shaking my head. My father could get to the point faster than most. I had told no one outside my family I was longing to break with the academic tradition, the style the Salon prized.

"A hearty conversation to be held over dinner, I assume?" Father asked.

"I thought I'd tell him in the carriage."

"Ruin his evening quickly, then?"

Mother stepped into the hallway behind Father. "Are you going out tonight?"

Before I snapped, Lydia opened the door from her bedroom, sewing basket in hand. "Are we taking tea in the hallway tonight?" she asked, walking toward the library.

I laughed and followed my sister, grateful for her timing. Our maid Anna's heels clicked toward us on the wood floor. She was coming to announce my teacher had arrived. When I met him in the foyer, Lydia had already extended her hand in welcome.

Couture, thirty years my senior, seemed charmed by Lydia's kindness. He also looked far better dressed in his charcoal suit and vermillion pocket square than he ever was in his studio. In the heat of the summer, he taught with his shirt untucked and unbuttoned, belly out. This startled some of his young students, as it did me when I first arrived. He could pull himself together when necessary for an exhibit or day in the city, but the man shunned decorum like a silver-haired child. More than once we saw him napping under shade trees as we walked down the gravel path to his studio. He was inclined toward daydreaming too, probably the quality that helped him paint *Daydreams*, a schoolboy at his desk observing a soap bubble. Couture was a man who could become mesmerized by minor distractions. If soap bubbles had appeared in his studio, I felt sure he'd stop teaching to watch them.

"Mary!" he said, seeing me. Lydia nodded and left us.

"Monsieur Couture. Don't you look nice?"

"My dear. It's been too long. I can't wait to hear how things are with you."

Something about the way he spoke made me pause. The art world was small. The Salon's exhibit had come and gone. Couture would know my paintings had been rejected. Did he extend the evening's invitation out of concern?

"Shall we?" I asked.

He fidgeted in his suit the entire carriage ride, speaking only of our party's host, Jean-Baptiste Faure, the celebrated baritone opera singer. Couture knew I'd loved Faure's rousing performance as Hamlet. Faure was a beloved performer, *la coqueluche de Paris*! As we stepped out of the carriage and into his stylish home, Couture told me the singer was also a keen collector of paintings. No wonder he'd dressed for the occasion.

Ladies and gentlemen of all ages gathered in the grand living room, surely expecting a song or two later in the evening. Young waiters in crisp suits passed through the room with trays of champagne and *canapés*. On the piano was Faure's wife, singer Constance-Caroline Lefebvre, playing Mozart for friends who gathered around the upright.

We settled into a green velvet sofa, watching people in fine attire circle in and around us.

"I was sorry not to see your work at the Salon this year, Mary. I'm sure you realize you're not the only one."

"The judges do seem to be taking a stand."

"Courbet and Manet refuse to paint in the academic style, and for that, they're being punished," said Couture.

"Are Courbet and Manet refusing one style, or building upon what they've already learned?" I asked, seeing an opening. "Because I—"

"They're artists not revolutionaries," he interrupted. "But there is a clear movement toward something more modern," said Couture, continuing his previous thought. "I'm especially interested in the work of Edgar Degas, who hasn't abandoned the tradition entirely. He seems to push it forward."

If I had been half listening to our conversation—the topic of artistic rebellion had become dull—the mention of Degas snapped me alert. I began to speak and was interrupted again.

"Did I hear you mention my friend M. Degas?" asked the baritone Faure himself, leaning over the sofa. Wearing a claret silk jacket, our host extended his hand toward me, and Couture made the introduction.

"I've begun collecting his paintings—*très original*," the singer said, enunciating every syllable as if notes on a score.

"May I see them?" I asked urgently, scanning the walls of the room.

Couture remembered his manners for both of us and thanked the singer for hosting us.

"Yes, pardon me," I said, before offering a simple explanation. "I admire his work, too."

"He comes to my shows, a most enthusiastic fan."

I opened my mouth to ask when Faure would perform next—

"Mademoiselle Cassatt was just telling me how much she enjoyed your performance as Hamlet," said Couture, saving me again.

I chastised myself for not complimenting him first.

"You may not know Mary is also an artist," Couture continued, "my exemplary student who graduated to have her own paintings at the Salon."

Faure pretended he remembered my name and paintings before agreeing to show the new pictures to us. He led us to a music room with tall ceilings and a wall of doors opening onto a courtyard of well-trimmed lindens. A grand piano sat on one side of the room, next to a carved walnut music stand. I imagined Faure and his wife rehearsing in the room and wondered if they would perform here later in the evening. On a facing wall hung several large paintings, including two by Degas.

"*A Woman Ironing* and *The Dance Class*," the virtuoso said with stage-like gestures. "I commissioned the ballet picture, which he painted in a classroom of the Opéra."

Ambitious, the painting featured twenty-four women. A single ballerina dances while others stretch and their mothers wait. A conductor stands in the painting too.

"*Merveilleux*," I said immediately, struck by the depth of field Degas achieved by using a diagonal perspective. This was a scene one might come upon walking into a rehearsal.

"And this painting," Faure continued, "I bought on the same day because it also captivated me."

Here was another oil portrait, simpler but more striking. Degas rendered the dark silhouette of a laundress against a light background. His hurried strokes mirrored the woman's industry.

"May we study them a few minutes longer?" I asked.

My interest in his acquisitions flattered him. Degas' work, precise yet modern, was everything I aspired to accomplish. I'd be grateful to receive a commission for something other than a portrait. I longed for my work to stand on its own, to entice a collector like Faure.

Couture then examined other paintings. Next to *A Woman Ironing* was an outdoor scene in the country, a woman herding a cow.

"Pissarro," he said when I joined him. "Faure has excellent taste."

Faure had become an avid collector of avant-garde paintings, befriending many of the artists whose work I admired. He had two portraits of himself Manet had painted. Though Manet continued to submit paintings to the Salon, he also pushed against tradition.

"I'm tired of painting the same way I always have," I said, turning to Couture.

He stared at me, wide-eyed. I knew what he was thinking. I was already swimming against the tide as an American woman in Paris. Why reject Salon dictates now?

"It's a risk, but I'm not sure the Salon has helped me like it has you. I'd like to try something different."

Couture, to his credit and despite his age, nodded silently. We turned again toward Pissarro's pastoral painting featuring a working-class farm woman.

I stood back, taking in the astounding collection an opera singer had curated. The arts were coming together in ways no one expected. Painters, musicians, composers, writers. Paris was a fulcrum of culture, the center of creativity. I could sense it happening all around, but rather than rejoicing, I felt an urgency to tap into the current, to work more imaginatively. I knew I could not paint fast enough.

As I gathered my composure to reenter the party, inside I teemed with ambition. Couture and I watched the crowd from the doorway. How long would it be before I'd meet the man whose art so captivated me?

A new musician had taken a seat at the piano, selecting a Strauss waltz for his first piece. Within moments and fueled by multiple flutes of champagne, guests pushed furniture against the walls for a makeshift dance floor. Couples came together and waltzed in circles wide and narrow around the room, including Faure and his wife, who seemed delighted by the impromptu space.

"S'il-vous-plaît?" a gentleman asked. He extended his hand, requesting a dance. "I heard you complimented my paintings."

My heart jumped as I turned toward him. His black eyes rested on me easily. Dark hair framed his face. His hand was still outstretched as he raised his eyebrows, waiting for an answer.

"Monsieur Degas."

"Will you dance with me, Mademoiselle Cassatt?" he asked. My cheeks flushed.

He knows my name. Taking his hand, I reminded myself to breathe as he led me around the room, keeping time with the dance's triple count. Why hadn't I paid more attention in finishing school? I tried not to think about his hand on my low back or how dizzy I felt. My cheek brushed his chin. He smelled like citrus and sandalwood.

And the dance was over as quickly as it had begun. I'd barely caught my breath. I hoped to sit with him on the sofa and discuss the novelty of his paintings. I yearned to ask what he was working on, which of Faure's performances he loved most, and where he imagined the artistic revolt would lead. I wanted to sit close to him and lean into a long conversation.

He bowed to me after the dance, still holding my hand. As quickly as he appeared, Degas was gone. When would I see him again? Seeing the time, I knew Couture would want to return home soon. He was older than my father, not fond of late nights. He hadn't seen me on the dance floor and was surprised to learn Degas was at the party.

"I wish I'd been able to meet him," he said.

"I wish I had too."

11.

The day after our meeting, I stood at the window of my studio and watched the rain fall. Under the eaves and protected from the storm, a cluster of yellow and white daffodils reached for the sky. Their cheery blossoms amplified my resolve to begin again. How many years had I trained with teachers who mentored me in the academic style Salon judges looked kindly upon? I longed to work with total independence, without worrying about the opinions of a jury.

The wind blew, rattling the glass in the panes, and I pulled the shawl my sister, Lydia, had knitted tighter around my shoulders. My eyes moved to my easel and an unfinished portrait of Madame Aubert, the financial necessity of the moment. I gazed at two paintings I'd unwrapped the night before, my Salon rejections — *Portrait of a Little Girl in a Blue Armchair* and *The Reader*. I eyed the little girl, her plaid school skirt pushed up, white petticoat exposed. Did the judges mistake the girl's insouciance as my own? The kettle whistled from the stove.

Lydia had saved me. Before she and my parents came, I'd felt as low as I could remember. This was the first time in seven years my work would not show at the Salon. I'd given my life to painting. Though my art had found some acclaim outside of France, in Spain and Italy, Paris eluded me. I watched with avid attention the pictures that received the most interest at the Salon's exhibits and the ones selling quickly. But as I looked to what was happening beyond my easel, I felt less sure of my creative instincts. If suddenly ocean scenes sold well, did it mean I should change my subject? Sometimes trends influenced artists, but they did not inspire me.

Edgar Degas had moved beyond pure imitation in his pictures. He composed his subjects imaginatively, from fascinating viewpoints. I itched to do the same, in my way, but how? My paintings seemed to ask a question more urgently with each passing day. *Do you like me?*

I held my breath, waiting for the answer from other artists, friends, teachers. What kept me going after completing a painting, especially when others didn't seem to respond as I'd hoped, was my own answer. *Yes.* Perhaps this was all any artist could hope for—an inner compass to point me to my truest work—beyond copies and commissioned portraits.

Would Degas agree?

I imagined his hand, outstretched for mine, and poured myself tea. Warming my palms on the porcelain cup, I stared again at the unfinished portrait. Commissions like this had paid for my rent, travel, and art supplies. I needed to work on Mme. Aubert's elaborate brocade gown that showed her wealth and personality—one who was not shy of bright colors and fashion. She stood next to a tall window and looked out onto a garden terrace. On the table next to her sat a bowl of deep red cherries that complemented her emerald dress.

She sat for me in the evenings. During the day, I enhanced details I roughed in earlier. This allowed me to work faster. So far, she liked the portrait and hadn't asked me to make her eyes larger or slim her waist like other patrons.

She was probably forty years old, and this painting would hang in her home before being passed down to one of her children's homes, then to one of her grandchildren's homes. A portrait must satisfy how people want to be remembered, not necessarily how they are. I always kept this in mind while gazing at old paintings. People present the face they want others to see. For those who could not afford such a rendering, stories must suffice instead. A painting was like a story.

I calculated the time it would take to finish, three, maybe four days, and how long the commission would cover my expenses before I'd need to paint another. The thought of finishing faster inspired me enough to fold the shawl and pick up my smock. I dug through the art box for the right tubes of paint and retrieved my palette. Perhaps I'd ask Mme. Aubert to lengthen her sittings in the evenings.

The lamp had nearly run out of oil when I completed the detail of her gown and added highlights to the crystal bowl. Satisfied with my progress, I stood back to examine the portrait. Her face and hair required more work. As my eyes fell to the cherries piled in the bowl, I thought about our trees in Pennsylvania.

"After breakfast, I'd like you to harvest the cherries, Mary."

My mother, Katherine, was a blur in the mornings, helping the cook harvest food from the garden and plan the meals for the week. She liked hard work as much as Father, believing it to be a balm for most everything. When fruits or vegetables ripened, Mother would cancel her plans so she could put up stores for winter. I tried to stay out of her sight as an adolescent, for fear I'd be called to help, but some mornings it was unavoidable.

I ate slowly, lingering over the last bites of toast, sipping my tea. And when I finished, I poured myself another cup. I had my own work to do, a series of family portraits. I dedicated myself to improving my technique, asking my parents for more paint, instruction, and art books. Everyone grew tired of my requests to pose, except Lydia, who engaged in needlepoint and embroidery while she sat.

My parents knew they would need to make a choice about my education, deciding whether to continue my traditional instruction or send me to the school I'd begged to attend since I learned of it — the Philadelphia Academy of Fine Arts.

"Mary," said Mother sternly, leaning into the room.

Grumbling, I left the table, fetched an apron, and went outside. I pulled the ladder to the base of the first tree, hooked the tin pail over my arm, and climbed the rungs. It was early enough that the flies wouldn't bother me, but the thought of them made me pluck the fruit faster. The cherries stained my fingers, and the pail grew heavy. Sweet cherries on the first tree. Sour pie cherries on the other two trees. My late brother Robbie's favorite pie was cherry.

Mother stood below me as I lowered the first bucket of fruit. She disappeared into the house, then returned it empty. I searched her face, wondering if she thought about my brother. She rarely spoke his name anymore.

As children, we'd moved to France then Germany because of Robbie, on the chance European doctors could help harden his bones. Despite the effort, and our family's highest hopes, Robbie's health worsened, and he died in Germany.

The flies eventually found my juice-stained hands and fruit-filled bucket. Fat, black and buzzing, I swatted them. "Could we have a cherry pie for dessert this week, Mother?" I asked, regretting it as the words left my mouth. The spiteful urge to see Robbie register in her expression was impetuous, and I knew it.

Mother gazed up at me wistfully, and my cheeks flushed with shame. She nodded and gathered her apron in her hands to wipe them, twisting the fabric a few seconds longer than necessary before disappearing again into the house.

In my studio, I gathered brushes to soak them in the basin. Early memories came unbidden. Why is sadness easiest to recollect? This nature of mine—to blurt before thinking, to push rather than ask, grated on me as much as anyone. Once when we were young, Robbie called me selfish for refusing to play one of his games. Even now, I pursued my own interests ahead of everything else. Lydia would never put herself before others. She'd always possessed an innate instinct for diplomacy and patience. I refilled the teakettle and set it back on the stove.

I wanted to rekindle the delight of meeting of Edgar Degas, but remorse had settled in. Gathering my coat, hat, and umbrella, I set off for a walk to the bakery. I'd finished the work on Mme. Aubert's portrait sooner than expected and wanted something sweet to nibble with my tea. A tart perhaps, the closest I'd find to cherry pie in Paris. The walk would clear my mind so I could turn my attention to a new painting. *We danced.* I still found it difficult to believe.

111.

Months later, in early May 1877, Degas sent word that he wanted to visit my studio. When I read his signature, the note trembled in my hands. I'd attended the last Impressionist exhibit, lingering especially in the rooms with his paintings. I'd secretly hoped to run into him, curious if he'd remember me from Faure's party.

Lydia had agreed to join me for his visit. She busied herself by arranging a table for tea. We caught each other's eyes when we heard the rap at the door. Lydia smoothed her skirt as I went to greet our guest.

Before I could welcome him properly or express my regard for his work, Degas handed me his hat.

"Mademoiselle Cassatt," he said, waving a hand in the air to avoid pleasantries. "I'm quite eager to see more of your paintings."

My stomach fluttering, I could hardly believe he was there, let alone asking to see my art. I smiled, said, "*Merci*," and gestured to the pictures I'd selected for display.

At forty-two, Edgar Degas was a panther in human form, his gait and gaze so deliberate the hair on the back of my neck stood tall when he came near. The precise tailoring of his suit made his body appear sharp, cutting through my studio like a blade. Carrying a black valise, he walked the length of the room, narrowing his eyes as he studied my canvases. Was this the man I'd danced with? Did I imagine the charm?

Standing by the row of windows, I clasped my hands to stop from fidgeting. Lydia bustled at the stove, boiling water and arranging fruit and pastries on a serving dish. Daylight slanted over the herringbone oak floor. Degas' shoes gleamed as he turned from one canvas to the next. His fingertips touched the edges of my paintings. Minutes passed before he spoke.

"I told a friend yesterday I could not imagine such fine painting coming from the hand of a woman."

Lydia's activity at the table ceased. She clasped her hands at her waist as she waited nervously for me to speak. She knew my quick temper and inability to suffer foolish opinions about female artists.

"Monsieur Degas, I will only take your words as the sincerest of compliments. I have admired your paintings for many years."

My sister exhaled and resumed her arranging. Degas stopped to watch her quietly place each dish on the table.

"I haven't yet introduced you to my sister."

"Pleasure," he said, taking her hand kindly before turning back to me. "I seem to keep hearing your name. And I remember a picture of a Spanish woman you had at the Salon—"

"Ida."

"She wore a mantilla." He paused and glanced back again at my paintings. "I'm here to ask you to exhibit your work with our group next year—"

"The Impressionists?"

"Well, if you insist on calling us that. I consider myself a realist. But the newspapers have given us the vile name, and I believe we're stuck with it."

I loved the name, and the other title the press used, the Independents—artists who were refused by, then refused to take part in, the Salon. I attended each of the rogue artists' three exhibits and watched as their audience grew. The newspaper tallied fifteen thousand people at the most recent show.

Gustave Caillebotte's brilliant painting *Les Raboteurs de Parquet* flashed in my mind—shirtless workmen stripping varnish from a hardwood floor. Caillebotte showed the toil of the working class, a theme Degas presented too. But it was Claude Monet who unintentionally offered the name "Impressionist" through his painting *Impression, Solei Levant*. One in a series, the painting featured the port of Le Havre at sunrise. Monet's quick brush strokes, capturing a moment of color and light, caused critics to deem the work unfinished. But some saw beauty in the hazy approach.

Degas' invitation hung in the air unanswered. I didn't hide my conspiratorial smile. To cast my lot with him and his friends, to give up trying to please the traditionalists at the Salon was a dream. Blond light spilled into the room. Birds twittered from the bushes outside, their wings flapping against the branches.

"I'd be glad to join you." I extended my hand, and he took it, holding my gaze with an intensity that startled me.

"Would you like some tea, M. Degas?" Lydia asked, arm outstretched toward the table. Degas bowed slightly to my sister, showing his upbringing finally.

"*Je serais honoré,*" he said courteously.

He drank his tea quickly but showed little interest in our attempts at conversation until the subject of the Salon came up again.

"An exhibition past its prime, if you ask me," he said.

"They passed on both of my submissions this year," I said, not hiding the sting of rejection.

"My point, exactly," Degas noted.

Lydia smiled. I felt lightheaded in his presence.

When he left, Lydia and I stood with our backs against the door until we were sure he was gone.

"May," Lydia whispered, "the Impressionists!"

I shook my head in disbelief. "Edgar Degas likes my work."

"I think you've found a new friend. He was nothing like his reputation."

"You mean he wasn't cantankerous? Did you find him friendly?"

Lydia walked back to the table and refilled our teacups. She had purchased croissants and sweets at the *patisserie* earlier that morning. Degas had touched none of them. I followed her to the table and tore a corner from a croissant, waiting for her answer.

"I find him charismatic," she said finally. "Do you think he sleeps with his models? He paints so many women."

"He wouldn't be the first. I'm not interested in his exploits. I'm interested in his art. By affiliating with his group, my paintings may garner more attention, and at least they won't be subject to the rigors of the old judges."

"What do we know of him, apart from his talent?" my sister asked, passing me a small porcelain pitcher of milk. I stared at its curved form, the pink floral design and gold edging.

"That he's a better dancer than a conversationalist."

Lydia laughed. "Well, the great artist believes talent exists in the hands of a woman. That's a start."

IV.

I paced the length of my studio and back again. One might imagine painting with an eye toward a well-attended exhibit would make the work easier. On the contrary, especially at first, I folded under the weight of my own expectations. The stakes felt higher, and for the first few weeks, I could not sit still long enough to paint. There is the creation of art and the reception of art, and the two should not commingle. Worrying about how the public might perceive my paintings before putting a hand on the canvas was vain. How could I release this compelling need to produce work that would impress even my peers at the first exhibit, especially Degas? To be a part of the Impressionists compelled me to be more imaginative, productive, and responsible for creating the best pictures I could. A sense of duty pressed on me in ways I hadn't known before.

When Lydia came to the studio and suggested a walk, I felt relieved to escape the place and my fretting. Taking my sister's arm, we set off toward l'île de la Cité, the island in the Seine, the center of Paris.

Lydia had arrived in Paris when I'd run out of companions. Friends with whom I'd worked, traveled, and lived had all given up art to return home. While my friends' parents had encouraged their daughters' artistic hobbies, my father did not, primarily because neither of us saw art as a hobby to fill time before marriage. I did not want marriage. Art was my career, and therefore he insisted I pay my way.

Not that he couldn't afford to support me. Father had made his fortune investing in businesses that paid him handsome returns. He achieved his wealth in part because of the hard work of his father, and his father's father, back to our Dutch relatives who sacrificed the comfort of their homeland for the promise of America. Now that he owned a successful investment bank, he did not want his children to squander the opportunities his station provided. He wanted my sister and me to marry well, to be educated, and to begin families with gentlemen of property and means.

Yet here we were, unmarried women in our thirties. Our heels clicked along the cobblestones, newly cleaned by street sweepers. The sun, still low in the sky, flashed between buildings. Lydia and I felt its warmth for a few steps at a time.

Lydia had lost her fiancé in the war, but there was no excuse for me. Why, Father asked, after generations of sacrifice, could I not see the advantages he'd worked all his life to give me? He was certain other women less fortunate would jump at the opportunity of my life. I had heard him tell his friends his youngest daughter had an infuriating passion for art. He tried to discourage it during my adolescence when he realized I never planned to give it up. How often Father would remind me there was more to life than imitating it through paint.

When he retired from his investment position and moved to Paris, I wondered if Father had finally accepted me. After sending letters home for more than a decade, maybe he knew I'd never return to a conventional life. Whatever his reasons, I was elated to have them close. I'd been lonely before they arrived, and I no longer had to work as a copyist at the Louvre to cover my expenses. I needed only to pay for my studio and art supplies, which gave me more time to paint freely.

Lydia slowed her pace and came to a stop. We stood in front of église Saint-Eustache, a grand medieval church. A line formed at the side of the building—mothers, mostly, and children. Coming closer, we saw a well-organized assembly for food distribution. Church workers had set up tables with fresh produce, milk, eggs, fish, meat, and other staples. Members of the Catholic parish hurried guests through a line, making sure each had all they needed. After filling their baskets with food, the women walked past us, holding the hands of their children.

"This isn't just a walk. You brought me here intentionally."

"I did," said Lydia.

I sighed. Her attempt to distract me from talking about painting irritated me. I wanted to lay my anxieties at her feet, for her to comfort me, not assign me a time-consuming chore. The sight was familiar. The War Between the States created hardship for families and Lydia had dedicated herself to feeding them, volunteering at a church in Philadelphia. Her work intensified after her fiancé's death.

"How did you find it?"

"Missions are easy to find when you're looking for them. Let's see if they need food or supplies."

I sighed, shook my head, and tried not to think about the blank canvasses in my studio. A woman in a navy wool cape who led the effort gave Lydia a list of items the pantry needed. Soon we were off to buy enough bread and milk to get them through the day. We bought a tray of *mignardises* too, tiny dessert pastries for the children.

This was Lydia's way. And despite my initial resistance, I noticed my irritation fading with simple errands that fed families in need.

"It took more than one hundred years to build this church," Lydia said. "The masonry and building crafts were passed down through generations. Great grandfathers, grandfathers, fathers, and sons. They gave their lives to creating this beautiful structure."

A year's worth of painting seemed too short to change much of anything. I felt exposed, and the persistent chase of my career above everything else felt petty and small. We walked back to my studio in silence. The air was breezy. Tiny clouds covered and uncovered the sun. Lydia stopped as I pulled the old iron key from my skirt pocket to open the heavy door—a large one-room apartment on the corner of rue Duperré.

"Painting is work you love, but it's still work," she said before turning to walk home.

My flustered thoughts quieted at last. Only those who know us deeply can utter truths that still the heart and mind. Lydia brought me this kind of clarity. I looked around the studio, opened the windows, straightened the table with art supplies, and began the work of selecting canvases for my next paintings—grateful for the simple task. I settled into the work in front of me.

V.

New pastels rattled in the wooden box I carried the next morning. The buildings at dawn appeared blue and the air pink. My heels echoed along the stone streets. While Paris slept, I plotted the painting I'd begin that morning. I could not afford to waste time when my career had moved, finally, in the direction I wanted. I understood better than anyone what it meant to exhibit with the Impressionists. The opportunity came with one requirement—utter dedication, something I'd felt since the first day I'd held a paintbrush. I only ever wanted to be an artist.

When I first came to France, Mother accompanied me on the steamer. She helped me settle into my boarding house, a tiny room with a single bed, desk, chair, and a small bureau with scarcely enough space for my clothes. I went to work immediately, finding tutors, applying to be a copyist to pay my way, establishing myself in a profession few women chanced.

As I walked, the birds woke in the trees above. The world stirred—street sweepers, a milk wagon, children walking to school. I pulled the key from my satchel. Inside, I unlatched the windows and drew them open, unbuttoned my jacket, rolled my sleeves, and stretched my arms into a clean white smock. Tilted against the wall next to the stove stood a board covered in light blue paper. On its textured surface, I envisioned my first pastel in a series — women in their finest clothing attending the theater.

The Opéra Garnier was the premier venue for performing arts — opera, symphony, ballet, and plays. Parisians loved them all; a night spent at the Opéra was a celebration. The stage and orchestra pit were Degas' domain, along with the rehearsal halls and backstage views. What did I know about the intimacies of dancers? But I knew what it was like to dress for a performance, to climb the grand staircase of France's finest theater. How might I capture the thrill a young woman feels taking a seat in a *loge*? Or the way the light plays in her hair, reflecting the gilded décor?

The night before, Lydia had agreed to sit in a lemon silk gown while I sketched a study in charcoal. It was late and she was tired, but she did it knowing I was too stubborn to accept her refusal. My sister gave in, chuckling with resignation. "May," she called from the chair. "Will you ever change?"

No. My hands flew through my supplies, searching for the right colors while squares of sunlight warmed the floor.

My body always seemed sturdy compared to Lydia's. Nothing about me was frail, nor was I traditionally beautiful. Any appeal I possessed was hard-earned through study or work. Lydia's beauty emanated from within and shined even when she was tired.

Time disappeared. My attention mixed with colors as I shaped scenes, form, and light. Something mysterious lies beneath art. A benevolent spirit entered my paintings and inhabited images almost without my bidding. I knew a piece was good when the subject surprised me, when a person's expression emerged suddenly. I did the work, of course, but I couldn't ignore how images seemed to reveal themselves in their own time.

The next morning in the studio, as initial forms took shape — the outline of a chair, Lydia's silhouette, the room behind her—I heard a knock at the door. I stood stiffly, bumping the easel and scattering pastels on the floor. Irritated by the interruption, I strode to the door and threw it open.

"*Oui?*" I asked the *préposé* in a blue uniform. He took a step backward and raised an envelope with my name in a small script.

"Mademoiselle Cassatt?"

I nodded, took the envelope and bid him a hasty good day before closing the door. Inside were a card and two tickets to the ballet. A shiver rolled down my spine as I read the note.

Dear Mlle. Cassatt,

Please accept these tickets to the Opéra as a gift for you and your sister. My colleagues and I are eager to exhibit your fine work with ours. Thank you for joining us.

Amitiés,
Edgar Degas

I stared at the tickets. Such serendipity. My family had not yet secured seats for the season. A rush of joy rose from my feet to my face. The painter I'd admired, the one whose work thrilled me to the core with its skill and modernism, had invited me into his circle. I felt lightheaded, forgetful of everything I had done five minutes earlier.

I don't know how long this reverie lasted, but my attention only returned to the painting as the midday sun faded into the willow's dark green leaves outside the windows. "Enough," I said aloud, standing to begin again. I couldn't afford to bask in something I hadn't yet achieved. I pledged to guard against swooning over an unformed future and stood squarely in front of my painting.

Lydia's form returned, not the lines on the canvas but the curve of her left shoulder and the light that bounced in her hair. I layered colors for her flesh and time slipped sideways.

I remembered my sister in her ballgown, dancing with the young men we knew in Philadelphia. She attended dances every weekend, her sights set on marriage. I was fifteen, and she was twenty-two, but those seven years between us were a century. Though Father commented often on the cadre of male suitors sending letters and leaving flowers, I knew her secret. I found his letters inside her lap desk. She liked Thomas Houghton best.

As if she were remembering him on my canvas, an expression emerged on Lydia's face. My sister leans forward, hands clasped, sleeves snug against her shoulders. She is poised and engaged. She possesses no self-consciousness, delighting in the moment.

My studio grew dark before I stopped. I cleaned my hands by lamplight while oolong tea steeped on the stove. I wondered what Mother and Lydia had planned for dinner. Life had become more comfortable since their arrival. I almost took their presence for granted. My parents and sister stood with me as I chased my dreams. They accepted me as I was, caught up in my own purposes, and believed I had something valuable to offer the world through my art. They included my dreams among their own. These are gifts I'd never be able to repay.

But then, I was merely tidying up and after, sipping tea. Sitting in the high-backed Bergère, I let my dreams resurface while staring at the unfinished painting. Imagining my Opéra series lining a wall at the next Impressionist exhibit, I reached into the pocket of my smock and drew out Degas' card and the tickets. I'd take my sketchpad.

VI.

"I could imagine spending my life here," said Lydia, before the Louvre's grand stone doorway. We stood together under an enormous umbrella as the rain fell steadily, gathering in growing puddles reflecting the gray sky.

"It's true we could spend a lifetime at this museum and not see everything."

"I meant Paris," said Lydia, turning to face me.

"You don't miss Pennsylvania?"

"I don't miss the memories of him there, or the war. The land, the dirt itself seems soaked with sadness. I know France had its own wars, but I'm new here. My life feels new here."

The thought of us aging together in Paris, becoming old women in the Montmartre apartment, comforted us both. Fat drops of rain rolled off the edge of our umbrella, wetting the surface of our coats.

"With your help, we will always remain stylish, even when we're old," I said, glancing at the covered doorway. Lydia didn't budge.

"Will I still model for you, then? Will you paint a series of old women at the Opéra?"

We both laughed. I couldn't imagine how my art would change in that much time. But to imagine Lydia by my side for the duration of my career gave me a deep sense of peace. I threaded my arm in hers and we walked in together.

Lydia shook off the umbrella and handed it, still sopping, to the doorman. I needed some time to roam, to be away from my studio for an afternoon. My inspiration and motivation had run dry. No matter how many times I walked through the front gate to wander the museum's tall, arched corridors and rooms, the old palace inspired me. The stone stairs were well worn. How many people had walked the hallways, traveling backward in time through the windows of paintings — observing earlier people and places? How many aspiring artists had set up their easels on the oak parquet floors to learn from the masters?

Lydia and I walked arm-in-arm and stopped to watch a copyist paint Diego Velázquez's popular *Portrait de l'infante Marguerite Thérèse*. One of the family portraits the Spanish master painted for King Philip IV, the painting features his three-year-old daughter in a white dress trimmed with black lace and pink bows. The copyist did not glance up while we watched. He kept working, lost in concentration, imitating Velázquez's color, brushwork, and composition. The odor of linseed oil and paint filled the room.

Young artists flocked to the Louvre to be copyists. This, alongside a formal education, was the entry gate to the profession. Art is built on the shoulders of previous generations. The man stepped close to the painting to view the bodice of the girl's dress. How many brush strokes comprised Marguerite Thérèse's small waist? How did the light play on the white fabric?

"You can observe the way an artist creates with his strokes," said one of my first teachers in Philadelphia. "But until you try them yourself, attempt to recreate them, you don't internalize the practice. Your hand doesn't know the feeling of them."

The artist stepped close to his easel and mixed a creamier white with his palette knife. Lydia squeezed my arm before walking away to view sculptures and other paintings.

As a student, I'd sought paintings to copy, even in private collections, to practice new techniques. I set up my easel often in museum hallways, even as I studied with tutors. In Paris, I had access to the world's foremost art collection. When I arrived, the question I asked was—which artist would grow me in the right direction? At first, I looked for the gaps in my knowledge. And sometimes I followed my curiosity—copying a historical painting or portrait of a person whose expression delighted me. These were the studies I practiced between copies.

This artist had chosen a painting popular with tourists. Americans especially were traveling to Europe in greater number. They wanted to take home something to remember France. The copyist touched the tip of his brush in the cream paint and applied it precisely to the girl's waist on his canvas.

The reproduction followed the rules of copies. The canvas was one-fifth smaller than Velázquez's so no one could mistake it for the original. Once his painting was complete, the copyist would submit it to the Louvre for an official stamp of approval on the back of the canvas. Then he could sell it to the highest bidder. No signature—neither his nor a copy of Velázquez's— was permitted. The artist stood back from his easel, apprising the new color, and acknowledged my presence.

"*Joli travail,*" I said, complimenting him. I knew how important the sale of a copy could be, and how much time it could buy the artist to work on his own paintings. He nodded without saying *merci.* I was one of many observers in his day, and a woman at that.

A man behind me cleared his throat. "This is quite a compliment to you, sir," rang a familiar voice. "Mlle. Cassatt is a fine artist."

A shiver ran down my spine. When I turned, he was there, extending his hand toward me again and smiling. I reached to clasp it.

The copyist seemed embarrassed then and bowed his head to acknowledge Degas and, as an afterthought, me.

"M. Degas," I said. "What a pleasant surprise."

"My day has turned brighter," he said. A tall, bearded man in a rumpled suit stood next to him. "Have you met Camille Pissarro?"

"Only through his beautiful paintings. I'm glad to meet you."

"Pleasure," Pissarro said, also offering his hand. "I understand we're colleagues now, Mlle. Cassatt. Thanks for bringing some class to our ragtag group."

I liked him at once.

"Is that your sister, sitting in front of Lady Liberty?" asked Degas.

I nodded. Lydia sat on a wooden bench, gazing at *Liberty Leading the People* by Eugène Delacroix. The massive painting—eight by ten feet—commemorated the French Revolution. The Louvre had only recently displayed the work following the artist's death. Eyeing the soldiers in the painting, I knew she was searching for Thomas in their faces.

"She lost her fiancé in our last war."

"*Mon Dieu*," said Pissarro. Degas' expression grew soft.

"Thank you for your gift of Opéra tickets," I said, trying to lighten the mood.

"I thought you and your sister might like a night at the theater."

"So kind. I'm very lucky to have her in France with me now."

"Indeed," said Degas. "I don't wish to disturb her, but wish her my best. I wonder if I could visit soon to see what you've been working on?"

"Of course," I said, my mind rushing back to my canvases. Which of them would I feel ready to share?

"I will send a note," he said, before walking away.

"*À bientôt*," said Pissarro, tipping his hat.

I walked to Lydia and sat next to her, looping my arm again in hers.

"M. Degas says hello."

"He was here?"

"He didn't want to interrupt you. You were so lost in thought. He wants to come again to the studio to see my progress." I smiled at the prospect. "I met another Impressionist—M. Pissarro."

"I'm happy for you, May."

She understood that apart from my time in museums or ateliers, I socialized little with artists. My relationships were with family friends and private art collectors. Bohemian circles were not societies women entered easily. I needed a companion to get around town. My community was populated by friends in the safety of homes, public spaces, and restaurants when accompanied by friends. Only on rare occasion would I intersect with other artists. And though I came to belong to the Impressionists, societal rules for women meant I felt somewhat isolated from the very world I wished to inhabit.

The collegial nature of meeting Degas and Pissarro at the Louvre was an experience I craved daily. Fortunately, the Opéra, like museums, was a venue where I could freely socialize with whomever I pleased.

VII.

On that late-summer night, I wore a robin's egg blue silk gown with gathered Normandy lace along the *décolleté*. The gown's short sleeves, edged in the same lace, sat off-the-shoulder. Lydia surprised me by presenting me with the finished dress the previous afternoon, bringing it to my studio straight from the hands of a seamstress. Lydia's new gown was made of peach silk, also off-the-shoulder, with flat bows that sat on her upper arms. She wore a white gardenia in her hair and on her chest.

Our carriage rolled through the streets of Montmartre before descending on rue de Rivoli to avenue de l'Opéra. Sunlight faded to twilight. We rode in silence as lamplighters illuminated streetlamps that flickered on the crisp forms of buildings. As we approached the theater, electric lamps shined more brightly.

To enter the Opéra Garnier is to walk into a world of make-believe. Here one arrives to be admired and to admire others, to see society at large dressed in their finest. We ascended the marble staircase in the grand foyer, which was akin to the red curtain opening before a performance. The chandeliers flickered, light bouncing off crystal, casting a golden glow upon the crowd. The social spectacle of the venue was nearly as important as the entertainment itself. Women and men mingled freely in the theater.

Originally commissioned by Napoleon III but completed after France returned to a Republic, the Opéra was a portrait of opulence mixed with practicality. In the most public areas of the theater, the first to be constructed, only the finest materials were used. The grand staircase, constructed of rose, green, and white marble, stood in contrast to the lesser frequented hallways and dining rooms.

That night, the opera Carmen, by the late composer Bizet, was presented to Paris for a second time. The controversy the opera stirred when it first opened, ten years prior, had disappeared. The French had once shunned the production, which the press had condemned for its "vulgar" female protagonist. But in a decade since, Carmen had gained acceptance, especially in Austria, where the country's love for music allowed people to embrace the production whole-heartedly. Like most of Paris, I hadn't yet seen the opera and the atmosphere among patrons assembled and chatting in the rotunda and on the staircase was one of anticipation.

Lydia and I claimed our seats in the red velvet loges. The luxurious vantage point gave us a bird's-eye view of the entire theater. Each loge was a small stage itself. Other audience members met my gaze, but there was only one person I truly desired to see.

For his own theater paintings, Degas would seek a short man playing a cello, sweating through concert scales. Or he'd focus on a stagehand, pulling ropes to lift and lower actors above the stage. His curiosity for mundane machinations made him unique among the Impressionists. In his art, Degas, like the author Émile Zola, had taken on the cause of ordinary men and women.

He'd connected with an aesthetic shift in Paris, away from art as inspiration or mere illustration. He'd joined a social revolution. Degas would likely never admit or talk about it, but he recorded the ordinary lives of the proletariat. This, I came to believe, infused his paintings with a deep compassion. Pissarro did the same for farm laborers in the French countryside where he lived. They both portrayed nobility in working-class people. Rarely had lower classes been given equal time in paintings. Artists came from a life of privilege, yet despite this—maybe because of it—Degas and Pissarro felt a responsibility to capture real people. Images of the working-class pervaded their paintings as strongly as any theme attributed to our group. While art critics classified us as Impressionists, our subject matter differed.

I sketched the beautiful architecture, the decor, the heavenly painted ceiling by Jules-Eugène Lenepvea, including the gigantic bronze and crystal chandelier designed by Garnier himself. Opulence surrounded us, which filled me with a sense of possibility.

"It's stunning," said Lydia, looking at the fresco through her opera glasses.

My sister's silk dress shimmered with light. I drew her admiring the theater. I sketched audience members and imagined Degas backstage or in the orchestra pit. Though Degas fixed his attention on performers, I was more interested in the audience—women wearing their finest dresses, waving fans, wanting to be seen. The expectation in their faces mirrored my own. I loved my work, and I wanted other people to love it as well.

After a new opera opened, patrons attended often—even consecutive evenings—to learn and hum along with the music. The lights did not dim in the theater as the show began. Performers looked into the eyes of the audience, nearly two thousand in attendance, and the audience looked back. Parisian theater was a social event, not merely entertainment.

As the opening bars of the opera filled the hall, I felt a hand on my shoulder. I turned to see Degas motioning me to join him. Whispering quickly to Lydia, I gathered my skirt and followed him through empty hallways until we were inside of a wide fold of a stage curtain, the wings of the performance. Being hidden on stage with him thrilled me. The sound of the orchestra floated up to us. Carbon-arc lights carved the set—a village square—in bright relief against a pale blue sky. Being so close to the production, experiencing the singers' voices filling the theater and vibrating beneath our feet, was a gift. I felt as if I had entered the playwright's imagination. I smiled at Edgar, to express my awe and thanks.

"I thought you might like it here," he whispered, his lips brushing the top of my ear, sending a thrill down my back.

Up close, I heard the actors breathing and saw their expressions accentuated with bright makeup. The heads of the orchestra bobbed with the tempo, the tips of the musicians' bows moving in unison over strings.

"*L'amour est un oiseau rebelle*," Carmen sang to the men in the square, who taunted her and asked when she would love them. "Love is a rebellious bird," she replied, flirting with them in a soprano melody, slipping the stem of an open pink rose into the top of her dress. The large blossom bounced over her breasts as she walked from one man to another. Bizet's score rose and fell, a seduction of notes drawing the audience in and pushing them away, mirroring Carmen's power over the men and foreshadowing their doom. Beware the siren who would entice then take your life away.

When the audience broke into applause, Degas turned to me. "You're glowing tonight, Mary." He offered his arm to escort me back to my seat. I felt courted by my colleague, and this confused me. Could our art and attraction coexist? When we returned to the empty hallway together, I could find no other words than *merci*.

I slipped back into the red velvet chair next to Lydia. My sister clasped my hand and fluttered her eyelashes in imitation of Carmen. I batted my eyes in response and reached for her opera glasses. Focusing them on the stage, I wished instead to scan the audience for him. Was he gazing at me? I flushed with the thought.

I couldn't remember the last time I'd felt admired. Had I ever known the deep sense of belonging I felt in Degas' presence? He'd invited me backstage, a place where his paintings had found their inspiration. He knew I would understand. To be in his confidence, to feel his regard, left me breathless.

That was the evening our initial acquaintance faded. Soon after, he asked me to stop calling him Monsieur and start calling him Edgar.

VIII.

Autumn came with its crisp air and golden light, intensifying the rose-colored view I'd gained since meeting Edgar. How strange to utter his name so casually. He was coming for a visit, and Lydia would join after a trip to the post, a daily errand since she and Mother kept copious correspondence with family and friends back home.

With a basket of bread, pears, and brie over my arm and a hundred questions to ask him, I set the table with a cloth printed with lemons and leaves I'd bought from a street vendor in Provence. I had selected three pictures to share, two from the new Opéra series, and a rejection from the Salon. Surely *Portrait of a Little Girl in a Blue Armchair* would find a place with the Impressionists.

He came with yellow-tipped red dahlias wrapped in paper and tied with string.

"*Bon matin,*" he said almost bashfully.

"How lovely," I said, as he handed them to me.

Edgar took off his hat and walked in.

As I arranged the flowers in a vase, he saw my canvases and walked to the little girl.

"That's one of my rejected Salon entries."

"You've rendered her mood very well," he said. Turning toward me, his eyes fell on the flowers I'd placed in the table's center.

"May I move them to the windowsill so we can admire them in the light?"

"*Bien sûr*," I said, moving them myself while he watched. Did he often stage a room when not painting?

We sat together, drinking tea and talking. Edgar rubbed his eyes. A few strands of silver wove through his dark hair and curled over his collar. I refilled his cup, taking extra care not to spill the hot water into his saucer. My hands were less steady in his presence. He took milk in his tea, no sugar. I sliced the bread, pears, and cheese on the cutting board and carried them to the table. Lydia would arrive shortly.

"Please tell me how you came to paint. I'm curious to hear how an American girl dreamt of this vocation."

"I'm sure my story is not much different from yours. It probably came down to an aptitude and fondness for color."

"Ah, but if it were that simple, we would have more artists descending on Paris, wouldn't we?" he said. "My father saw it in me. When I dropped out of law school, he knew I would become an artist. Tell me your story. I want to hear it."

I demurred, but my breath quickened. I was ten years younger and hadn't come close to achieving what he had. Could he really be interested?

"Lydia saw it first in me."

He nodded, waiting. He rested his chin on his hand, eager for more.

"When I was twelve, she gave me a gift. She made me follow her into the field behind our house one morning before sunrise. It was summer, and the birds were singing—red cardinals, brown and orange robins, yellow finches."

He smiled at the detail. I told him how I followed Lydia barefoot into a dewy field. My sister lifted her skirt to keep the hem dry. I ignored the hem of my dress to keep up with her long strides. A sailcloth bag, stuffed with the gift, swung across Lydia's back. When we arrived at our favorite stand of trees, the sun rose and sparkled on the field we'd walked.

Lydia was nineteen and, in every way, presentable—courteous, meticulous in her manners, and thoughtful of other people. She was more comfortable standing on the side than in the center and had a gift of observation that allowed her to see straight into people's hearts. I often felt Lydia understood me in a way our parents could not.

We sat together on a fallen oak. Soft moss covered its bark from years of rain, and I brushed my hand over it, trying not to be impatient as Lydia pulled the bag into her lap.

For nearly a year, Lydia had tutored me in French grammar after school. Mother insisted I keep up with my languages since moving back from Europe. Lydia would have rather picked up her knitting, but she sat with me while I conjugated verbs aloud and wrote them at the kitchen table. In the margins of the paper, I sketched what was around—the dog, a vase of flowers, my pile of schoolbooks. Lydia didn't stop me from drawing, as my teachers did.

One afternoon, I drew the outlines of my sister's face and hair. I'd learned from a visiting art teacher how to look for light and shadows. He taught me not to see features, like her eyes and nose, but to picture them as shapes. Before long, Lydia's face and knowing expression peered back at me from the notebook paper, and again a few feet away. This was the first time I'd sketched a person. I looked at Lydia, then back at my paper, astonished. Lydia stood to look at her likeness and blinked.

"She told me I had a gift," I said.

"Yes," he said. "How fortunate she saw it in you."

I told him about the artistic fervor that followed, and how it surprised everyone but Lydia. Our father, who was entertained at first by my passion, soon grew tired of my single-minded interest. In his mind, I was on the brink of young womanhood, a time to expand my education, travel, and hobbies so I could become a poised young woman who would eventually marry and have a family of my own.

In the meadow behind our house, the sun climbed past the horizon and stirred the insects into a steady buzz. The horses neighed from the barn. Everyone would dress soon for breakfast. Finally, Lydia pulled at the drawstring on the bag in her lap and drew out a package wrapped in newspaper. Inside was a wooden box containing twelve metal tubes of oil paint.

She told me to paint. She said our parents would have no choice but to enroll me in art school when they saw my dedication and talent.

I'd learned from my art tutor that artists had always mixed their own pigments for paint or hired others to do it for them. Only in my lifetime could oil paints be purchased pre-mixed and ready. And my sister had placed this expensive purchase into my hands. I ran my fingers over the cool metal tubes and opened the caps. I showed Lydia the colors, like summer birds, and felt a shiver rise from my hands into my body.

It took every ounce of discipline not to run home to paint that very moment. I wanted nothing more than to enter a real art studio, to study the master paintings I'd seen at the World Fair when I was a little girl in Paris. I vowed to capture the world as precisely as I could.

"You're right," I said. "Her fascination with my talent was transformative."

Edgar placed his hand on top of mine, his expression wistful.

"How lucky to have her close still," he said.

My attraction to him pulled at me like a magnet, as if my will and mind were of little consequence. His palm was warm.

His eyes held mine with kindness and regard. He seemed to understand me fully. I sipped the air, unable to fill my lungs.

The clank of the latch startled us, and Lydia pushed open the heavy door. Edgar pulled his hand from mine and placed it on the handle of his teacup. My sister walked into the studio carrying a package and letters from home.

"*Bonjour*—" she said, hesitating.

Could she feel the ripple in the air between us?

"Mlle. Cassatt," he said, standing. "I was listening to stories about your childhood in Pennsylvania."

Lydia set down her things. Edgar pulled out a chair for her to join us, and I poured another cup of tea.

"*Merci*," she said, catching her breath. "Have you been to America?"

"Yes, my mother was from New Orleans. I visited relatives in Louisiana a few years ago. I stayed for five months and enjoyed it very much."

"You're half-American then?" I asked.

"Yes. My mother's family was Creole, and she moved to France after marrying my father. She told many stories of her home, and I was eager to visit."

New Orleans was a bustling international city. The port was one of the country's busiest for shipping and immigration, second only to New York. I had a difficult time imagining him anywhere but France, but New Orleans was easier.

"Everything there fascinated me," he said. "Black women of all shades, holding little white babies in houses with fluted columns surrounded by orange-trees and magnolia gardens. Ladies in muslin sitting in front of their little houses. Steamboats with two smokestacks, as high as the twin chimneys of factories. Fruit merchants with shops full to overflowing. And the beautifully planted quadroons."

"What a vivid recollection," said Lydia.

"I found the city so vibrant and when I returned, I sought equally interesting subjects in Paris."

"So the dancers?" I asked.

He laughed. "And the laundresses, and the stagehands, and anyone who might bring something new to my tired eyes. I find working, everyday people more captivating."

"They're captivating for us all," I said.

"I've come here to see and talk about your paintings, and I've derailed that conversation, asking for your stories instead," he said. "I hope you'll allow me to return soon."

"M. Degas," said Lydia, "We welcome you any time."

"Please, call me Edgar," he said.

He kissed our cheeks before leaving. Lydia stayed for another hour reading while I cleared the table and set out my supplies. I moved the vase of dahlias to the tiny side table beside me. Hours later, at my easel, I shivered, remembering the weight of his hand on mine.

IX.

I'm not sure how long Edgar stood in front of *Portrait of a Little Girl in a Blue Armchair*. I walked away to thumb through sketches I'd made at the Opéra, looking for the subject of my next painting.

"Have you considered reworking the background?" he asked.

Lydia looked up from the wool scarf she was crocheting. I walked over to the canvas.

The painting featured the girl in one chair and her dog in another. In the background was the room, a few sticks of furniture, and sunlight reflecting through French doors onto the floor. I shared the painting with him because he asked to see it. I didn't imagine he would advise me on improving it, but of course I listened. Though he admired the way I'd portrayed the girl's sassiness and wasn't recommending I change her, he questioned my composition. I couldn't see how changing the background would improve it.

"I wonder if adding asymmetry to the room might accentuate the girl," he said.

Edgar drew a rudimentary sketch of my painting, adding two more armchairs to the top of the canvas — one in the center, and another on the left. The tops of both chairs were outside the frame, cropped at the top. He also angled the back wall as it intersected with the floor. The effect of these changes, which I could see immediately, was to bring the eye straight to the girl. I'd painted her off-center in the foreground, but the chairs now created a way for the eye to move through the painting. The jumbled arrangement of armchairs—as if she'd pushed and played on each of them—created a directional flow. The simple change made a meaningful difference.

"Ah!" I said, grabbing my palette to mix more aquamarine. Lydia walked over to watch.

As I painted over the small table in the background to block in a chair, Lydia began fidgeting. She didn't like to watch me make changes once a painting was complete. She trusted me but fretted as I painted over hours of previous work. I narrowed the floor space by adding the second chair to the canvas, like the sketch. Edgar stood watching. His suggestion had widened my perspective, so I could see the scene anew.

"Yes," he said. "I think the one in the center should be turned, though." He picked up a brush.

"Wait, what are you doing?"

Lydia straightened her back. He stopped.

"This is my painting."

I snatched the brush from his hand. I didn't care how talented he was. No one would paint for me. He glared at me, then turned to fetch his hat. He walked out without saying goodbye.

"He didn't ask my permission," I said, turning to Lydia.

"He probably thought you were ungrateful, but that was an unnecessary tantrum. I dare say he won't pick up one of your brushes again." Lydia, like our mother, had no tolerance for bad manners.

I looked at the painting, his sketch, my palette. Any gratitude I'd felt evaporated.

"The change will improve it but—"

"He should have asked," Lydia said. "Would you raise a brush to one of his canvases?"

"Never." Still, I felt troubled.

Lydia resumed her crocheting in the sunlight by the windows while I despaired over Edgar's abrupt exit. I wanted access to the wider community of Impressionists and wondered when I might get to know the other artists. I was one of three women. Berthe Morisot was the most active female Impressionist. She'd taken part in the exhibits from the beginning. Marie Bracquemond had also been invited to show her work. The artists, male and female, were scattered in and outside the city.

When would I see him again?

I suddenly envied the Impressionists who painted *en plein air*, where the immediacy of changing light helped to shape their compositions. Being outdoors compelled quick decisions and brushwork on every part of the canvas until the work was finished. Working in a studio, a painting's completion comes when the artist decides it's done. I glanced at the little girl in my painting. It could take an entire day to finesse the details of the new chairs I'd added.

I pulled the stool to my easel and dug through my art box for the right colors. Resuming the work on the background, I saw the brilliance of Edgar's suggestions again. The more I worked on the composition, the sharper the girl came into focus.

He shouldn't have presumed to paint on my canvas, but I could learn from him. I longed again to be near him. I tried to imagine the feeling of his hand on mine.

Lydia stood to stretch. "I have a bit of a headache. I think I'll walk home," she said. "Coming soon?"

"Yes."

She stood before my painting. "I see what you're talking about now," she said. "The arrangement's unconventional, not something you would typically paint."

"You're right. I wonder what else I'll pick up from him. His revisions have turned my sense of proportion and space upside down. I'm still trying to make sense of them."

"Remember you were a fine artist before you met him, May." My sister gathered the mail in her arms and left me to clean my brushes before locking up for the night.

X.

I passed a fountain as I walked through the Jardin des Tuileries on my way to the Louvre. Afternoon sunlight shimmered upon the water as it fell through the air, splashing into the large marble basin. A schoolboy in a navy-blue jacket pushed a sailboat along the surface of the pool, steering it along the perimeter with a long stick while running close by to avoid capsize. He reached far over the water when the sail suddenly caught wind. I pulled out my sketch pad, outlining and shading the water and the boat, then the boy's hands and face, trying to reveal his determined expression as he chased it. He reminded me of my brother, Robbie. The boat listed and fell to the side, but the boy threw his arm into the water to right it again and kept on, water dripping from his sleeve.

Edgar was waiting for me at the museum. Weeks ago, we'd patched up our differences. He came round with a small basket of apples and an apology, and I invited him to see how his suggestions had improved my painting. He seemed genuinely pleased with the changes and urged me to show it at our next exhibit.

I hurried over the cobblestone plaza to the entry. We had met in the afternoons, walking the halls dotted with young copyists and their easels. Sometimes their eyes would lift from their canvases to stare. Edgar's presence garnered excitement.

He was a public figure then, the avant-garde artist who was refused by, and refused to take part in the Salon. I imagined they saw Edgar as the embodiment of rebellion youth naturally carry. The young painters revered him. He was breaking ground, discovering new ways of capturing life through paint. Only a few of the copyists knew me.

Edgar's painting *In a Café* had attracted considerable attention in the press. Critics reviled his subject, two downtrodden figures—the actress Ellen Andrée with a glass of absinthe before her, and the bohemian artist Marcellin Desboutin by her side. Both look weary and filled with too much drink. "Immoral!" cried the critics.

Though the painting appeared to reveal an unguarded moment, Edgar had asked his friends to sit for him. Inclined toward reality over romanticism, he wanted to depict the shadowy side of Parisian cafés. Apart from his controversial subject, a few critics mentioned the brilliance of his off-center composition, which strengthened the painting's feeling of social decay and loneliness.

We turned a corner and entered a new hallway while two copyists leaned away from their canvases to watch us walk past.

"They're wondering if we've been at Café Guerbois, sipping absinthe and staring vacantly at other patrons," I whispered, leaning into him.

He smiled, extending his arm for my gloved hand as we continued down the corridor.

"Never the esteemed Mlle. Cassatt."

He was right, of course. I could never sit with the men at the café, but my studio was a minute's walk from Café de la Novelle Athenès, an afternoon gathering place for the Impressionists. I intentionally walked past when they were there. Edgar always called out to me if he sat outdoors or saw me from the window. The others watched for me too, stopping me to talk or ask my opinion—which I gave freely—on their latest arguments. But meeting at the Louvre was different. Men and women could mix without chaperones.

Carrying his sketchpad, Edgar waited for opportunities to draw me unaware. He listened to my opinions and laughed at my brash commentary. He told me I fascinated him. In the hallways of the museum, we felt unencumbered by the usual rules of social etiquette.

We stopped at a small grouping of Rembrandts.

"What are you working on now?" he asked.

"Portraits. Lydia mostly."

"Your sister has infinite patience. I'd like to paint her myself one day."

"She would not take kindly to sitting for another artist. I stretch her patience as it is."

"She was under the weather the last time we spoke. Has she recovered?"

"Yes. That reminds me—have you heard word from M. Monet?"

Claude Monet's wife Camille had been ill. Edgar turned away from the painting he'd been gazing at for the last few minutes to look at me.

"I'm afraid his wife has taken a turn. She's bedridden." He looked back at the painting. I waited for him to continue, to express alarm or sadness for his friend. Mme. Monet was a year younger than I was, and a mother of two children.

"Now Rembrandt was rebellious," he said instead, gesturing to *Philosopher in Meditation*.

I stared at him, bewildered by the swift change of subject, and wondered if I should inquire further or turn to the painting. Edgar's own mother had died when he was a boy. Was the discussion of Mme. Monet's failing health difficult for him?

In Rembrandt's small painting, a gray bearded man sits at his desk in front of a bright window—books and papers strewn around him. The rest of the painting is dark, except for a fireplace in the right bottom corner that an old woman, perhaps his wife, tends. My eyes drifted around the dark portions of the painting, the room where the philosopher works, before landing on a spiral staircase leading to a higher floor of the house. Behind the old man is a small arched door. Warm light in the painting draws me into the philosopher's physical space, and the absence of light leads me to perceive the old man's interior life.

"How is he rebellious?"

"He doesn't line his subjects up to gaze at us. They're in motion. He captures an unguarded moment."

"Like you do."

"Are you flattering me, Mary?"

I never hid my admiration for his paintings and wondered then if I should. Edgar leaned toward me with a smile before turning back to the Rembrandt, his shoulder touching mine.

Time slips away in a museum, but standing next to him, it fell away faster. A kind of reverence came over me while standing before master paintings, the awe one feels in a cathedral or forest. Sounds dimmed. Even the scent of the Louvre's old hallways faded. Colors, shapes, and light rushed toward me, along with the emotion of a long-ago artist, transmitted through paint. Standing next to Edgar made the experience more intense—a deeper descent into Rembrandt's world. In Edgar's presence, I felt profound understanding. A new way of looking at the world had claimed me. Old ways were crumbling. The art world was ripe for change. Then there was, underneath it all, the attraction between us.

"My family has been talking about hosting a dinner party. I'd like to extend you an invitation," I said, breaking the silence.

"*Moi?*"

"If you accept, I must tell you my father will ask many questions. He'll inquire about your family and professional aspirations. He'll be polite, but he's curious since we spend time together. This is your warning."

"I'd like nothing more than to answer your father's questions. I know who you take after. We'll get along fine."

I don't know how much time passed as we stood before the wall of paintings, before one of us grew thirsty or sighed.

"I almost forgot," Edgar whispered. "I have something for you." He handed me a long, slim box, bidding me *au revoir*, before I could open it or say *merci*.

"Tomorrow at two, yes?" he called, hurrying down the hallway.

I watched him walk away before lifting the lid. Inside the package was a hand-painted silk fan of ballerinas. The gift, his brush strokes in my hands, took my breath away.

XI.

When I was fifteen, a circle of girls and I sat in the dining room of Mrs. Emma Carter's finishing school. Laid before each of us was a setting of china, crystal, silver, and a linen napkin pinched into a sterling ring monogrammed with a scrolling C. At the table's center was a vase of white lilacs, fragrant and spilling onto the ecru lace tablecloth. No food was served. This was an imaginary meal with proper etiquette. I imagined trays of asparagus with hollandaise, Cornish hens with wild rice and spring onions, strawberries with cream and chocolate pudding.

When I felt Mrs. Carter's gaze, I looked at each of the pieces of silverware as if in deep concentration. "Don't pull the soup spoon toward you in the tureen. Pull it away to fill the spoon before lifting it to your lips."

I nodded with the others. Mrs. Carter walked around the circumference of the table, hands clasped at her waist as she spoke, her composure matching her sharp tone.

"Now please select the piece of silver you will use for your second course of cabbage and potatoes."

I hated cabbage. Mrs. Carter now stood behind me. She'd notice if I looked to see which piece the others had selected. I puzzled over the four forks in the place setting and reached for the smallest to the right of my plate. Before I lifted the fork into the air, she slapped my hand. The sudden humiliation brought tears to my eyes. I replaced the fork and willed them not to spill onto my cheeks.

"That, Miss Cassatt, is the dessert fork."

"I beg your pardon," I responded, evenly as possible. When Mrs. Carter moved to stand in front of the sideboard, I longed to trip her.

"You, Mary Cassatt, are always daydreaming. If you don't take seriously these lessons of deportment and etiquette, I fear you will never find a husband."

I exhaled, looking down at my lap, gripping my hands until my knuckles turned white. How antiquated the notion that a girl's only purpose was to be chosen for marriage, as if a mere ornament.

Of five siblings, four of whom were still living, only my brother Aleck had married. Lydia and I, and our youngest brother Gard, remained single. Father worried often about me, despite my new community, good spirits, and vigor in the studio. He wished I wouldn't completely eschew traditional life.

"Marriage isn't useless, Mary," he said, pacing the floors of the apartment we shared. "People do it all the time. Educated women, even artists."

"Why would I want to be married when I have you, Mother, and Lydia?"

"We're here to maintain your respectability. And you begged us to come."

"I thought you came because you loved me."

My father sighed and sat down heavily in the sable leather armchair, glasses dangling from one hand as he rubbed his eyes with his other. He was right about my pleading. And about Parisian society requiring chaperones, like governesses for women. When would I be able to walk around freely like a man? I could work and hang my paintings in the same galleries. God forbid I sit with my peers at a café or walk alone beyond a respectable hour of the day. Despite my thirty-three years and professional success, Father's exasperated expression made me feel like a girl again. I was sorry to disappoint him. Both daughters had failed to marry and produce grandchildren. I signaled the maid to bring tea.

"I can't help it. You know domestic life would be the death of me. When would I paint? I'd be a terrible wife and mother. And anyway, you have Lois."

My brother Alexander's wife embodied domesticity. Lois placed my brother and their children at the center of her life. She ran her home as efficiently as Alexander ran Father's investment and banking firm. She was simply everything I was not.

"What does your sister-in-law have to do with this? It's not as though you don't have feelings for men, Mary."

Lydia looked up from her crocheting. She sat in the sunlight by an open window, a new kitten asleep in her lap. I had almost forgotten she was there. She hadn't felt well that day. Mother sat next to her reading the newspaper, trying to ignore our conversation.

"Which men are you referring to, Father?" I asked.

"Really, Mary, why do you wish to argue this morning?" Mother interjected, breaking her silence though never looking up from her paper. Anna set down the silver tea service for us. I poured Darjeeling for Father and stirred in his milk, listening to the spoon ting against the edges of the teacup until I could think of something to say.

"M. Degas is a colleague."

Lydia's eyes met mine as she put her needlework into the basket on the floor. The kitten jumped down from her lap and batted at the yarn. I poured a cup for my sister, Mother, and myself.

"You spend more time with him than the rest," Mother said, folding her newspaper.

"I'm not sure that's true, but even if it were, we understand each other. He's as dedicated to his work as I am."

"Is he dedicated to you?" Father asked, readjusting his glasses and taking his tea from the table.

His voice bounced back and forth in my thoughts. Placing my teacup in its saucer, I spoke directly. "I do not work with M. Degas because I'm looking for a marriage proposal."

I'd spent time with him and hadn't hidden it from my family. His talent enchanted me. His influence on my work was inestimable. I could no more extract him from my life than burn my paintings. He was that important, but Father disproved of my meeting with him socially. For his daughters, artists didn't fulfill his expectation of respectability, but I didn't care. I refused to let Father's feelings interfere with my friendship with Edgar.

"Would it be so different to be a married artist?"

"Why is it so important I marry?"

His words had been the same since I was sixteen, when I was a girl less interested in balls than setting sail for Europe. I had quickly become bored with the art school in Philadelphia. I didn't care about the gowns Mother had purchased for me, filling a dance card, or making small talk with suitable young men.

I offered Father more tea, ignoring his question. "Is it more grandchildren you want, Father?"

"No, it's not, May. I think you know very well how I'd like to see you settled, secure in a home of your own."

"Tired of me living in yours?"

Father turned in his chair to speak to Mother.

"Why does she answer me so impertinently?"

Mother shook her head, abdicating responsibility for either of us.

"You see I am working," my voice grew louder. "You know my aim is to support myself through my art. I pay for my studio. For my supplies. M. Monet's paintings are selling quickly now. And M. Degas—"

"Edgar Degas. I hardly know the man. Why don't you bring him around?"

The thought of Edgar in our home caused my hands to tremble. I clasped them together and tried to breathe evenly. "I'll invite him to our dinner party."

"What will you do when we're gone, May?" he asked. "It's not only the money. Who will be your family?"

"Lydia. Alexander's family. I have three siblings."

"None of whom, except Lydia, live in Paris," he retorted.

I'd grown tired of the exchange.

"But you and Mother are here now, Papa." I set down my teacup and walked to the arm of his chair. I draped myself over his shoulders. "And aren't you glad we're together?"

He sighed loudly, letting his body soften at my touch.

Mother stood up to hand the newspaper to Father, waving at the air with her free hand, as if to brush aside any lingering bad feelings.

"He only wants you to be happy," Lydia said later that night at her dressing table. I sat on my sister's bed while she brushed her hair. Lydia gazed at me from the oval mirror. Candlelight bounced from the cut crystal box on her table.

"When I think he's finally accepted my art, he announces again I should marry."

"He's a banker, not an artist. He wants collateral."

How many years had I worked and struggled? My professional life was finally opening, and Father had become more resolved than ever I should marry. Perhaps my advancing years gave him reason to think he should push again, a desperate last attempt. I knew what Father was thinking. *What would be my value to a man if I were beyond my child-bearing years? Who would marry me then?* Most of my friends had children. They relied on their husbands and were devoted to their families.

If I could support myself as an artist, I would be free to love or not to love. And free to paint any hour of the day. A woman who marries cannot know such freedom. How often do women give themselves to marriage before knowing their own hearts? Could there be a greater privilege than to choose one's life?

Lydia put down her brush and stared at me from the mirror.

"Is there no part of you that wants to marry, May?" she asked. "Not for Father, but for yourself?"

My thoughts turned to the gift of the painted fan in its box on the bureau near my bed. I'd admired it secretly for more than a week. When I painted, I kept him in my mind, as though he could see my canvas as I worked. I'd never desired so strongly to please anyone. I'd never desired to be so near someone. Lydia waited for my answer.

"No."

My sister turned to face me. "Will you really invite Edgar to our next dinner party?"

XII.

The apartment was quiet. Lydia was visiting a new seamstress while Mother and Father scoured the countryside to secure a summer house. They'd had no trouble with the transition from Pennsylvania to Paris, and now they looked forward to a summer in the French countryside.

The front door opened quietly and shut.

"Have you had success?"

"Yes!" Lydia answered. In my sister's arms were heavy papered packages she opened and laid on the table. "Mme. Blanche sews most beautifully. On my way home, I purchased fabric to take to her tomorrow."

I touched the soft green, blue, and orange linen and silks. Our income didn't allow for many purchases from couturiers like Le Bon Marché and House of Worth. Lydia's knack for fashion allowed us to remain stylish despite our clothing budget. She glanced at my easel.

Instead of working at the studio that morning, I blocked out a new painting at home from a study of Lydia I'd sketched the night before.

"You seem lively today," I said, noticing the pink in her cheeks.

"I am. Give me a minute and I'll sit for you." She hurried off and came back with such energy I almost forgot how she lay in bed with headaches and fatigue for days during the winter.

She smoothed her hair and picked up her needlepoint, a small tapestry of flowers and vines. After pulling a crimson skein of yarn from her basket, she threaded her needle quickly. Her hands were capable and in no time, she had finished a row of tiny, neat stitches. On my palette, I mixed the color of Lydia's complexion, which grew brighter with the late morning sun. The comfort between us found its way to my canvas.

People responded to Lydia's presence in my paintings the same way they responded to her in person. She carried herself with soft dignity and paid close attention to details. She seemed content to live without chasing ambitions. I often measured myself by what I hadn't done. I longed for greater productivity or to match the creativity of other artists.

Lydia found herself in the summer air, in the plot of a good book, in the tending of her window boxes. Every morning, she plucked away the wilted blooms. "How are your children this morning, Lydia?" Mother asked routinely from her newspaper. Red and pink geraniums and variegated ivy spilled from our windows like waterfalls. My sister's flower boxes were the most admired in the neighborhood. Strangers commented as they walked past. Everything she touched drew compliments from people.

Lydia reached into her sewing basket, grasped a small pair of scissors, and snipped loose threads from the backside of her needlepoint. I mixed a color to match the light reflecting from the floor onto her pale blue skirt. Some sisters grow up with a sense of competition, but we had very little. Our age gap prevented it, and we were different people. Lydia was content to live in Paris with me while I chased a career in art. Perhaps I painted her so often because I admired her tranquility. Was this the same quality that attracted Thomas to my sister years ago? I could still see them together. She was twenty-three, a year before the war started.

"June is a perfect month to be engaged," said Mother while she and Lydia addressed the invitations for her celebration.

Thomas held her chair when she sat at the table. He wore a tan linen summer suit, and my sister wore an ivory lace collared blouse and cotton skirt. Lydia had placed a pale pink rose behind her ear for the occasion. They were a color-coordinated picture of love, staring at each other, even in a roomful of people celebrating their future wedding.

Father and Mother had hired a violinist to play Mozart concertos through the meal. The dining room was lit by candlelight and the setting sun, and open windows cooled the house. A white cake with buttercream frosting and raspberries sat on a pedestal under a glass cloche on the sideboard.

Friends brought gifts for the couple, and after opening them, Lydia created a bouquet of ribbons from the packages and gave it to me. On the round table in the foyer, she displayed her new tea towels, crystal sugar bowl and creamer, silver platter and serving utensils, candlesticks, a carved wooden jewelry box, and a handmade quilt from our grandmother. I inspected each of them.

"Treasures," she called them.

Nearly twenty years later, I wondered where they were.

"Do you think it's possible you would marry again?" I asked, dabbing shadows into the folds of her gown.

"If *grand amour* could visit a person twice." She didn't look up from her needlepoint. I knew Lydia would have welcomed new love, but she devoted herself instead to us—to me. Even when she was ill, she sat for me. She said it was important to her that we created the paintings together.

As the sun moved across the floor, it fell behind Lydia's shoulders. Light danced on loose strands of her hair. I stopped painting and stared. Many friends had come and gone since I'd lived in Paris. Work endured. Friendships shifted.

"You look lovely." I paused, holding my brush, and Lydia smiled.

"How's Edgar?"

"He asked me to work with him in creating a new art magazine."

"What kind?"

"It'll showcase printmaking. We'll work together in his studio. With Berthe Morisot and Camille Pissarro," I added quickly.

"Won't it take away from your painting?"

I considered her question. My interest in printmaking returned when Japanese woodblock prints started trickling into French galleries. I felt drawn to their simplicity of form. I hadn't made prints since studying in Italy years before. Adding another medium to my repertoire, alongside my new friends, was an adventure I couldn't pass up.

"Edgar etches on copper," I said. "I'd like to try my hand at it."

To learn something new with him compelled me more than I'd admit to Lydia or even myself. Would working with him take away from my painting?

"I think printmaking will improve my painting." I brushed the yellow light into my sister's hair.

Lydia dropped her sewing into her lap and looked up, trying to read my expression, looking for a hint of truth in my face. I rarely kept anything from her. Lydia was my closest confidant. Unable to discern my thoughts, she picked up her needlepoint and resumed stitching. I shivered inwardly, my secret affection for Edgar slipping between us like a schoolgirl crush.

"Have you given anymore thought to the menu for Friday?" she asked.

Our dinner party was four days away. Besides Edgar, I'd invited Paul Durand-Ruel, the gallery owner who showcased Impressionist paintings, and Camille Pissarro.

"Pheasant *en croûte*?"

Lydia nodded, smiling. She loved to host friends. Mother and Lydia would draw up a list of ingredients for Mathilde, our cook, to buy from the market in town. Lydia preferred to work in the kitchen alongside Mathilde, harvesting the fresh herbs she grew on our sunny kitchen windowsills. Forgetting my silence about Edgar and caught up in the enthusiasm of entertaining new friends, she mused of white asparagus and petite potatoes baked in butter, thyme, and sage. By Lydia's and Mathilde's hands, we would be fed a spring feast. I moved my brush quickly to capture the joy in her eyes.

XIII.

The guests arrived almost at once. Father and Mother welcomed them, making introductions. I walked into the foyer to help them greet people when Edgar stepped through the door. He shook Father's hand and exchanged greetings with Mother, commenting on the warm evening.

I was happier to see him standing in the entryway than I'd imagined, my mother beside him, Lydia at my side. Anna took his hat and umbrella.

"Why Edgar," I said, "Are you expecting rain?"

"Always," he answered, taking in the atmosphere of our apartment, "But I believe I've changed my mind tonight." He smiled. The fragrance of good food and the glow of evening light flooded our apartment from the kitchen to the parlor. Mathilde brought in a large tray of tall, stemmed glasses bubbling with champagne and set it on the sideboard.

"*S'il vous plaît*," Lydia said to each guest, handing drinks around the room. When she finished, Father stood on the stone hearth, head and shoulders above our dinner guests, raising his glass into the air. He spoke in French.

"Welcome to our home. We will try to entertain you in a way you're accustomed in Paris. And if we fall short," he said slyly, "I hope you'll give the Americans another chance."

They laughed. Father's good humor always warmed a room.

To his left stood Durand-Ruel and Pissarro. They were discussing my painting on an adjacent wall — a portrait for the upcoming exhibit of Mother reading the newspaper. Father noticed the discussion and stepped down to join them. I walked over too.

"Mlle. Cassatt," Durand-Ruel said, acknowledging me formally in the presence of my father. "M. Pissarro and I were admiring your skill."

"As usual," Pissarro added with a smile. The oldest of our group, Pissarro was known for being the most cheerful.

"*Merci.* Is this one you'd like for your gallery?" I asked Durand-Ruel.

Coughing on his last swallow of champagne, my father shook his head at my eagerness to discuss business. "You must forgive my daughter. She's offering to sell her mother at our dinner party."

"I look forward to displaying your daughter's paintings in my store," Durand-Ruel said, smiling. "I predict her work will catch the attention of many collectors."

Paul Durand-Ruel, who had inherited his father's gallery, had an instinct for buying paintings from artists on the brink of public acclaim. He championed the work of Impressionist paintings before art critics and customers valued them. His gallery was the first to showcase their paintings and many Impressionists relied upon his patronage until their artwork sold well enough to support themselves.

"I was thinking of buying one of Mary's paintings myself," said Edgar over my shoulder, stepping into the conversation.

"I'm glad to make your acquaintance, M. Degas," Father said. Durand-Ruel and Pissarro backed away politely. "Mary thinks highly of your work and appreciates the opportunity you've extended to include her in your group."

"She fits right in—"

"Thank you," I said.

"But a woman like Mary cannot exactly fit into every environment you find yourself in, M. Degas. Can she?"

What was he talking about?

"I meant to say your daughter's work is as fine as any of my peers," said Edgar, ignoring his innuendo.

"Indeed. She spends a great deal of time with you."

"With all of us," Edgar added. "I have, in fact, recently invited her to join us in a new venture—a magazine called *Le Jour et la Nuit*. Did she tell you about it?"

"Day and night," Father said, glancing at me.

Edgar elaborated on the printmaking process. He explained how prints rely on the stark contrast of dark ink to light drawings—hence the title. He described the copper-to-paper process that allows reproduction of many proofs from the same drawing. Father listened carefully and when Edgar finished, he spoke as if negotiating my future.

"Mary is a painter. She doesn't even much like to draw."

It made no difference he was talking with one of the finest artists in Paris, with whom I felt honored to work. My cheeks flushed with embarrassment.

"Father—"

"I know my daughter's value as an artist. Believe me; I watched her fly like a bird from our home at a young age to pursue art against my will, I might add. I only have her best interest at heart."

I noticed a smile forming on Edgar's lips. He seemed to enjoy my father's questions.

"Indeed. I assure you of the legitimacy of this medium, M. Cassatt. You may inquire with M. Durand-Ruel about the demand he's seeing in his own gallery for prints."

"It is my decision, Father."

"Of course," he answered, before turning back to Edgar. "My daughter has been independent for many years. I simply don't wish to see her squander her time and talent in unproductive ways."

His tone was stern and paternal, a warning against more than a diversion from painting. Still, Edgar appeared unruffled. I looked around the room for Lydia, so she might rescue me. Thankfully, Anna appeared in the doorway, ringing a bell to invite guests to dinner. Edgar excused himself politely.

"Well," said Father, "Seems you two will work more closely together."

"Don't worry so much." I kissed my father's cheek, took his arm, and followed our guests into the dining room.

The large round table was dressed in butter yellow linens, white Limoges, and crystal. Lydia sat me directly across from Edgar. I watched him eye the floral arrangement and imagined him admiring the red and pink roses, their petals opening in the warm evening air. Was he sketching the flowers in his mind? Lydia had arranged them that morning before the kitchen filled with scents of bread and herbs. Guests chatted as Anna ladled mushroom *consommé* into small, fluted bowls. Lydia talked and laughed with Pissarro and his wife, Julie. Mother was in deep conversation with a longtime friend visiting from America. Father straightened his tie before dipping his spoon into the first course.

Edgar also straightened his tie, lifted his spoon, and stared across the table at me. I met his gaze. What was it about him? I looked down and smoothed my napkin.

"Do you think I will waste your time, Mary?" he asked in a voice barely above a whisper. I glanced at Father to see if he'd heard. Edgar smiled and pulled his spoon through his soup, waiting for my answer.

I shook my head slightly, so only he could see, and glanced up at him again. "No."

His smile broadened as he lifted the spoon of steaming *consommé* to his mouth.

Lydia looked over. She pushed a strand of hair behind her ear to get a better view of us.

When I could no longer take Edgar in my direct field of vision and Lydia in my periphery, Claudette, the family friend seated next to me, asked if I'd ever regretted becoming an artist and not a mother. I'd never been so happy to answer this dreadful question. My voice was not prickly, as if I'd never been asked the same thing a hundred times before.

"I simply don't have the time or inclination," I said.

Claudette's eyes grew wide before she resumed talking at length about the blessings of children. Edgar appeared bored, staring again at the flowers as she droned on, pushing away his half-eaten soup.

I hated that the conversation had turned banal and wished for more at our dining room table. I didn't dislike children — or more to the point, Claudette's decision to have them. Why did women have so little tolerance for lifestyles that exclude marriage and motherhood? Claudette sipped her soup now silently, trying to think of a polite response to my disinterest in the very thing that gave her life meaning.

"I sometimes paint children," I offered, forcing a smile. "I'm not sure I'd have time to do so if I were a mother as well."

"Mlle. Cassatt is a wonderful portrait artist," Edgar added. "You might hire her to paint your children."

I brought my napkin to my mouth, stifling a smile. How he stirred the pot — defending my life choices and art with utmost sincerity while also trying to secure a commission for me. I struggled to gather myself.

"Indeed, I might," Claudette said, putting an end to the conversation.

"I find it quite difficult myself to compose music with children around, and I am only a tutor."

Startled, I turned around. A young man with dark hair and eyes, a slight build, twenty years at most, stood behind me, a stack of musical scores in his arms.

Though he'd interrupted our conversation rudely, and thank God for it, Lydia rose from her chair and walked around the table to greet him.

"Monsieur Debussy?" she asked. He nodded. Lydia turned back to the table, which had become quiet when she stood to greet him. "M. Debussy has agreed to play for us tonight. He's leaving Paris in the next few days to live and work with a family in Russia."

I extended my hand. "I'm Mlle. Cassatt's sister. Would you like to dine with us before you play?"

"*Merci*, no," he said. "I should not have interrupted your conversation, Mlle. Cassatt. I'm an admirer of your work."

"Mlle. Cassatt has many admirers," said Edgar. I scoffed at the comment, but loved his attention.

"Do you know M. Degas' work then too?" I asked.

Debussy looked stunned. "*Bien sûr*. It's a pleasure to meet you."

Edgar nodded at the young man.

"Please, continue your dinner," he said, color rising in his cheeks. Edgar seemed to affect the musician in the same way he affected me. "I look forward to playing for you this evening." Debussy bowed to the table before Lydia showed him to the piano in the parlor.

After the dinner course was served and cleared, but before Lydia's favorite dessert—almond torte with hand-churned vanilla ice-cream, the kind Mother made in Pennsylvania—Anna served coffee and cognac. Edgar passed on the coffee but gratefully accepted the cognac, swirling the snifter. He stared again at the floral arrangement. After dessert, Father invited the men to the library to enjoy their tobacco and drinks in private. Edgar felt the insides of his jacket for his pipe.

He turned to Lydia before standing. "Mlle. Cassatt, you've outdone yourself with dinner. My compliments to you, your mother, and sister on this fine meal."

Everyone at the table echoed his sentiment, nodding and thanking Lydia, Mother, and me. Lydia waved off the attention bashfully, but my mother smiled with pride. I admitted I'd had little to do with it.

After the men left, the women sauntered into the parlor and took seats around the room. Lydia sat next to me on the settee and whispered how charming Edgar had been, and how flirtatious he seemed.

"Has he redeemed himself since his tantrum in my studio?"

"Has he to you?" Lydia teased. I smiled, clasped her hand, and looked away.

Quietly, Debussy played his first piece of music. The opening notes of Beethoven's *Moonlight Sonata* filled the room. Conversation died away. The notes rose and fell around the melody, each successive iteration becoming more urgent than the time before and falling again into diminuendo. I imagined the furor Beethoven's music elicited generations ago. "Too passionate," they said. "Inappropriate for young women!" Another artist who dared to break with tradition. And there we were, fifty years after his death—women and, by the third movement, men—gathered in the parlor, transfixed.

Father took a seat by Mother while Edgar and Pissarro listened from the side of the room. Edgar fixed himself in my periphery and stared at me frequently. When Debussy played the rousing notes of the last movement, the room burst into applause. Grateful and smiling, the musician stood and took a bow.

"It's hard to imagine he's only eighteen," said Lydia.

I called to him from the settee. "M. Debussy, you mentioned you were a composer. Will you grace us with one of your pieces?"

"Yes, please," Father agreed.

"I rarely play my own compositions in public," he said.

I clasped my hands to my chest, pretending to plead. Edgar clapped along to encourage him.

"But for you, Mlle. Cassatt, I will. I call this piece *Beau Soir*."

He sat down to play. A lush sonata sprung from the keys of the grand piano, notes conjuring airy images of fields, trees, and water. The music lasted less than three minutes, a layered melody that sounded like a dream or a poem.

"His song could be a painting, May," Lydia said.

What was this wave of change? Art and music transforming at once.

The room stood to give him a stirring ovation.

"Bravo!" I shouted. The others clapped and nodded their approval.

After the guests left, Lydia and I sat in the dining room recounting the highlights of the evening. I mentioned how frequently Edgar had stared at Lydia's flower arrangement.

"I noticed how often he stared at you," she replied, but Lydia was pleased to think Edgar might admire something she'd created.

Pissarro told me later it took every ounce of Edgar's self-control not to toss Lydia's spring bouquet out an open window. I laughed when he told me how much Edgar detested flowers during a good meal. He didn't like the scent to mix with the aroma of his food. Pissarro had taken pleasure watching him avert his nose from the glorious centerpiece Lydia had created.

"Truly, Mary," he said, "If it had been anyone else's dinner party, he would have thrown them off the balcony when your back was turned."

XIV.

When spring 1878 finally arrived, the flurry of celebration surrounding Paris' third Exposition Universelle, the World Fair, threatened to overshadow every other event in town, including my first exhibition with the Impressionists. Worried about a meager reception, the group delayed for another year. This news, which I learned from Edgar, left me morose for weeks. I'd stacked my finished paintings, side by side, against the long wall in my studio.

Lydia listened patiently to my complaining at first, but finally she'd had enough.

"May, no amount of pining over your art show will make it come any faster. Get your sketchpad and let's walk around the culprit Exposition."

The fair, largest in its history, stretched an area of sixty-six acres in the middle of Paris. Starting with the newly constructed Palais du Trocadéro, a meeting place for international organizations, it spanned from the right bank, across the Seine, and far along the left bank of the river.

We walked the length of it under our best parasols. The days were rarely hot, not like the blistering Pennsylvania days we'd known as girls. Parisian summers disarmed me when I first arrived. The pleasant temperatures made me forget the sun's strength. Without my parasol, my complexion reddened like it did when I was a girl. "Not fitting for a young lady," my grandmother used to scold.

The accoutrements of womanhood—parasols, fringed pocketbooks, feathered hats—were often an afterthought to me. I accepted them like I did most rules for women. The other Impressionists, the men anyway, did and wore whatever they wanted, just as they met anywhere they wanted. How I still wished to join every discussion. I settled for rare dinner parties.

"Where are your thoughts? How could you be anywhere else but here?" asked Lydia, stopping to gaze at the Seine. The sun shimmered on the river, wavering with wakes of passing boats. I took my sister's arm and smiled apologetically. "As if I need to ask," she added.

"I was wondering if Berthe Morisot stays in better touch with the men in our circle than I do."

"Perhaps she stays in touch with them through her husband?" Berthe was married to Eugène Manet, Édouard's brother, who was a good friend to Edgar and the others. Her brother-in-law liked to feature Berthe in his paintings.

"Have you heard about the human zoo?" Lydia asked, bringing me back to the fair before us. She described an exhibit featuring African people placed in scenes representing their way of life. Visitors observed them in make-believe habitat.

"Like animals? The name alone is offensive."

Thoughts of the war came back to us, slavery, the subjugation of Africans for profit and a deeply divided America. So many Pennsylvania men had died for the cause, like Lydia's fiancé. Crushing stories of cruelty had filled northern newspapers and stoked the fires of the Union and public support for the war. When the war ended, "information wanted" ads began appearing in newspapers. Slave mothers who had been freed searched for their children. Husbands and wives who had been split up through sale or trade hoped to find each other again. Reconstruction was underway at home, an ocean away from the World's Fair in Paris, and the "educational exhibit" turned our stomachs. Lydia and I walked past the line forming at the entrance.

From outside another exhibit hall, we heard the cries of a crowd. We wandered in to see two American inventors introducing their latest creations. Mr. Thomas Edison of New Jersey presented a talking machine he called a phonograph. He asked a man from the crowd to sing a line from a song into a large funnel, and after turning a crank on the device, Edison played a replica of the man's voice for the audience. The stunned crowd roared with approval.

"Now imagine another technology that allows two people to have a conversation from long distances—say France to America," Edison called to the crowd, gesturing for another man standing in the background to come forward. "I'd like to introduce Mr. Alexander Graham Bell."

Mr. Bell pulled two volunteers from the audience, giving each a handheld machine. He told one volunteer to walk outside and hold a piece of the machine to his ear. A long wire stretched between them. The man inside the exhibit was told to ask a question while speaking into the machine in a normal tone of voice. Soon enough, the man outside answered his question and the two men, though far from hearing distance, carried on a conversation. The crowd erupted in loud applause again. Bell waved and bowed shyly, while Edison threw an arm over his shoulder.

"You, my friends, are staring straight into the future," Edison shouted. "What was once impossible has become possible. Distance and time are collapsing. You will never need to wait weeks to correspond with someone far away again. The telephone, a tool of the modern world!"

Lydia placed her arm in mine as we stood in the frenzied crowd, tingling with the excitement of progress. The world moved at a speed no one had felt before. The limits of possibility shifted daily. Edison's electric lights continued their march, replacing more gas lamps along the avenue de l'Opéra and the Place de l'Opéra. If this was the Modern Age, Paris was its center.

"Let's go," Lydia whispered, pulling me outside to walk along the gravel pathway that ran the perimeter of the grounds. The breezes and quiet felt welcome after the excitement of the exhibition hall.

"Does it seem odd I feel scared by all this change?" Lydia asked. "Sometimes I feel the world will outgrow me, as if I'll be left behind."

"Wouldn't you like to talk to friends in Philadelphia from our parlor in Paris?"

"I prefer to visit with them. But if I can't, what's wrong with a handwritten letter?" She stopped and stared straight ahead. "May, look—"

At the farthest end of the garden of Trocadéro Palace stood a statue of a woman from mid-chest to head, wearing a pointed crown, twice as high as the tallest trees, and equally wide.

"Bartholdi."

I stood still, stunned by the sculptor's ambition. France had commissioned Frédéric Auguste Bartholdi to build a monument for America—to commemorate the friendship between the two countries. "Edgar says he's intent to build a monument larger than the pyramids in Egypt. Bartholdi calls it 'Liberty.'"

We walked to the mammoth structure, ascended the stairs to the platform, and stared up at Lady Liberty's broad face.

"Fifty people work on her daily. I'd like to visit his workshop."

"I'd like to come along," she said, smiling.

Lydia came to Paris when I needed her most. No one was a better companion. Standing on the platform brought back the feeling I'd known holding her hand as a child — diminutive, but stronger as a pair.

"Before long, people will come to see your artwork, May. Don't get discouraged. Think how many years you've waited already. Next spring isn't so far away."

After all the complaining, the Exposition Universelle that delayed the exhibit bolstered my resolve to work again. I knew the art world was swept up in its own wave of innovation and the Impressionists had plunged into the current. I needed to be patient. And to distract myself with something new. None of us had begun work on the magazine. Learning alongside Edgar would surely cure my impatience. He'd disappeared after our dinner party, leaving me to wonder again if I'd imagined his interest in me. But there was my art to consider, gratefully, always the art.

XV.

On an early morning, as sunlight streamed into the windows of the library, Anna brought a large square envelope to me, sealed with a bottle green wax stamp initial "M." The front of the envelope was addressed to Mlles. Cassatt. Lydia lowered her embroidery hoop as I reached for Father's ivory-handled *ouvre-lettre* to slice it open. On the white linen invitation, Berthe Morisot had sketched tiny drinking glasses filled with green-gray liquid and written fragments of French poetry. Across the top of the page were the words *L'heure Verte,* the Green Hour.

Berthe was the first woman to exhibit with the Impressionists, and I'd known her work long before we'd met through Edgar. I was glad for the invitation to one of her *jour fixe* dinner parties, which she always hosted with her husband Eugène Manet. Her flair for entertaining was unmatched and usually well attended by a variety of artists, writers, and musicians. Edgar must have asked her to invite Lydia as well.

"I believe we've been invited to an absinthe poetry party next Thursday. She's invited Stéphane Mallarmé to read for us."

"This will be the only green hour I attend," said Lydia, laughing. The five o'clock hour in Parisian bars, bistros, cabarets, and cafés signified the time of day when people began drinking absinthe. The milky green spirit, distilled in France and Switzerland, was popular with people of every class, not only artists, though artists certainly drank their share. Edgar's painting *In a Café* was the closest I'd ever come to the drink myself.

"I don't know that I'll take more than a sip. The last thing I need is to aggravate my headaches with drink. But I would love to hear Mallarmé read his poetry. Poems are always better spoken."

"The green fairy may take away your headaches, Lydia."

"Ha!" Lydia took up her embroidery again.

Artists and writers swore by the drink's knack for granting creative lucidity other alcoholic drinks, including wine, didn't provide. But there were also tales of obsession with the spirit. Seduced by the lure of green fairy stories, newspapers wrote sensational articles about people becoming crazy and committing violent crimes after imbibing the drink. Headlines like *"Méfiez-vous de la fée verte!"* —"Beware the green fairy!" — seemed to push the peculiar reputation of absinthe to greater heights. Who could have imagined a remedy for malaria, once given to French soldiers, would become a drink that rivaled French wine in popularity?

Lydia was especially excited to meet Mallarmé since she'd read one of his poetry collections. She wanted him to sign her book.

On the evening of the party, Lydia stepped out of her bedroom in a lilac silk dress with long sleeves edged in lace. She carried a small, beaded handbag over her arm and wrapped her shoulders in a generous lambswool shawl, the color of pearls, which she had crocheted over the winter. Her cheeks were pink and she was a picture of health. Father commented on it as well.

"I'm thrilled to see both of my girls in such good spirits."

I hugged him while Mother fussed with the bow at my waist—an olive silk dress with black detailing and appliqué along the neckline and bustle. "It will be fine," I assured her, kissing her cheek on the way out.

I carried the fan Edgar had given me. Its gold tassel fell from the palm of my gloved hand. Climbing into the carriage, Lydia noticed it.

"I don't remember that fan."

I opened it for her as we made our way across town, past the lovely park Jardin de Monceau, to rue Villejust, to the home of Berthe and her husband Eugène Manet. Edgar's ballerinas glowed in metallic and watercolor paint on silk.

"He gave it to you?" Lydia asked, captivated.

I smiled.

"May."

This was not a typical gift from a friend, and she knew it. That I hadn't shown it to her earlier meant I'd kept it a secret. Even in the dim light, I could see her hurt expression. And she could see my hopeful one.

I did not answer.

Berthe greeted us at the door, complimenting our dresses. She wore a gold silk gown with jade embroidery, striking as ever. The epitome of Parisian chic with her large brown eyes and dark hair, our hostess had tucked a white rose behind her left ear, which brushed my cheek as she hugged me and whispered how happy she was to see us. She welcomed Lydia, who, never having met Berthe, puzzled over her décor. Berthe read her expression and laughed.

"I think I've finally topped my previous efforts. Lydia, forgive me, I couldn't help turning my home into an absinthe-inspired trance. In there somewhere, you'll find the others."

Berthe had draped the parlor of her home in gauzy panels that hung from ceiling to floor, turning the room into a labyrinth. To walk from one side of the room to the other, we could either follow a path through the maze or sweep the translucent fabric out of the way to travel more directly. Light from lamps along the perimeter of the room filtered through the fabric. Berthe had also hung small lanterns from the ceiling at various heights and they flickered with candlelight. The effect was a dreamy space, with nooks created for conversation. She placed a couple of chairs here and there, places to sit and talk, in the bends and turns of the maze. Lydia and I could hear people's voices, but unless standing in front of them, couldn't see them clearly.

The novelty of the décor soon irritated Lydia, who remarked within minutes, "Only the Impressionists would appreciate being lost in a room swathed in curtains!"

I loved the novelty. Berthe had created a magical atmosphere.

Two servers walked through the labyrinth with silver platters of baguette slices topped with smoked salmon and tapenade. In the center of the maze, a large circle created with fabric, stood a small bar and a bartender preparing glasses of absinthe. As Lydia and I approached, we saw Edgar, Renoir, and Pissarro sitting on three of the five stools.

"Mlles. Cassatt," said Auguste Renoir while standing to greet us. Renoir kissed my cheeks, then my sister's. Edgar stood awkwardly, and Pissarro followed his lead. Finally, Edgar also leaned over to kiss my cheeks. The fragrance of his skin caught me off guard, bergamot and sandalwood, and a flash of desire pierced me. He held my gaze before kissing Lydia's cheeks.

"*S'il vous plaît*," said the bartender, gesturing to the empty stools, and we sat down. In a far corner, someone played an accordion, the Italian instrument *tout* Paris had embraced.

"We were discussing Raphael," said Edgar, sipping the milky drink. A few candles on the bar cast everyone's faces in flickering shadows.

"Renoir wants to return to the Renaissance."

"Have you visited Rome lately?" Renoir asked the group.

Renoir painted subjects he considered pleasurable—primarily women and nature. He was neither interested nor inclined to use his art for social commentary. I wasn't sure which he disagreed with more when it came to the Impressionists—political or aesthetic convictions.

"Not lately," answered Edgar. The bartender asked if my sister and I would like him to prepare drinks for us. We nodded.

"The Renaissance is always with us," said Edgar.

"When you see the quality of Raphael's drawings, you'll think twice about the so-called Impressionist style," said Renoir.

"How I hate that dreadful name," said Edgar.

"Like it or not, it's how people view you," said Lydia.

"Why must art be an either-or proposition—classical or modern?" I asked.

We watched the bartender prepare our drinks. Onto a small, stemmed glass filled with pale green absinthe, he placed a silver slotted spoon. In the spoon, he placed a sugar cube. Over the sugar cube, he poured a thin stream of water until it dissolved completely into the glass. When the sugar and the water combined with the spirit, the drink turned cloudy. He handed Lydia the drink before preparing mine in the same way.

"Everything modern appears cheap after my last visit to Rome," said Renoir. "The style we've achieved, while breaking with tradition, doesn't compare to the masters."

Lydia cautiously sipped her drink as the bartender slid mine over.

"We do not live in the time of the Renaissance," said Edgar. "Our art reflects that."

"I've grown bored," said Renoir. "My paintings have been placed in an exhibition that serves as entertainment. I'm suffocating, trying to paint what patrons wish to buy."

Lydia leaned toward the others, her chin resting in her hands. Thirsty, I swallowed the drink and asked the bartender for a glass of water.

"Evolve," Pissarro urged Renoir, "Artists must change. But there's no need to throw everything away."

Their words snapped around us. The notes of the accordion floated through layers of fabric and landed on the bar. I felt like dancing and the thought made me laugh.

The men turned to see what I found amusing. I waved their attention away. Edgar studied me longer than the rest. Lydia leaned toward me.

"Are you feeling odd?" she whispered.

I nodded and flapped my hands, like wings, which made us giggle. The men turned to face us again.

"Unfair to keep such mirth to yourselves," Pissarro said, stroking his beard and smiling.

"I believe the Cassatt sisters have met the green fairy," said Edgar. The bartender took my glass to prepare another.

"She's lovely." Then, to show I hadn't completely lost myself, I turned to Renoir. "None of us paint in the same style. We've simply declared our independence from the Salon."

"If I follow my artistic inclinations, my work will likely turn back to paintings exhibited by the Salon," said Renoir.

Edgar slapped his hand on the counter, which made the bartender and the rest of us jump. "Why would you give the Salon the privilege of judging your work when you've found an audience of your own?"

Renoir's cheeks reddened.

"What Degas is trying to say — save the theatrics — is our group needs you. *Bien sûr*, follow whatever path you choose, but if you leave our group and return to the Salon, your decision might be seen as a fracture," Pissarro said.

"I don't paint for the Impressionists, Pissarro, I paint for myself." Renoir stood to leave.

"All of us do," Edgar said, holding up his glass of absinthe. "But there's strength in numbers."

Renoir shook his head and left, tossing the fabric to make his way somewhere else. I sipped my drink and noticed how the sheer material rippled with movement. The gauzy room fluttered like large white moths encircling us.

Lydia stood. "I think I'll walk around."

"Come sit with me at dinner," Pissarro said. "I would like to catch up with you, hear what you've been reading." Lydia agreed before ambling through the maze.

"You won't catch many flies with that approach, Edgar," Pissarro said.

Edgar looked nearly forlorn. "Pour me another."

"What captures our interest can eventually imprison us," I said, trying to put the fluttering insects out of my mind. Did I bring my sketchbook? Such a drawing would surely confound people, even the Impressionists. I caught the sight of Edgar's fingers wrapped tightly around the stem of his glass. Candlelight softened his brooding expression. He appeared younger, like the self-portrait I'd seen in Durand-Ruel's gallery years ago. The startling stare. His dark eyes.

"I will see you at dinner." Pissarro stood to leave us in the undulating room.

"Save us a seat," I said.

"You're very attractive this evening," Edgar said. His voice was low, husky with drink. He noticed his fan, once clasped in my hand, now placed between us on the bar. The painted dancers, folded carefully, felt like an agreement.

I stared at him, feeling caution slip away with the drink, attraction roaring back. I took another sip.

"I fear our group will disband before its time," he said.

"People cannot be kept against their will."

"And you?"

His quick change of subject left me temporarily speechless.

"Do you remember dancing with me?" I asked. The absinth made me bold.

Edgar moved his hand over mine and smiled, ignoring the bartender in front of us. I let it rest there for a moment before taking a last sip. I slid off the stool, found my feet, and clasped his fan again. His dark eyes stayed on me as I thanked the bartender and turned to find the dining room through the fabric path. Diffused light glowed all around me as though I were in a cloud. Would he follow me?

"Where have you been?" asked Lydia as I took a seat at the table.

"In the absinthe labyrinth." I smiled.

"You found your way out?" Pissarro asked. "Seems there was another bar at the back of the room. Everyone there was lively."

Edgar entered the dining room and walked to the far end of the table. He glanced at me before taking his seat.

Renoir was still fuming while Berthe's waitstaff served. Berthe's husband Eugène and his artist brother, the debonair Édouard Manet sat next to each other, deep in discussion. Though not officially a part of the group, Manet pushed against academic traditions and socialized often with the Impressionists. Stéphane Mallarmé, the poet, sat opposite Berthe. He had a thick mustache and wavy, dark hair that fell to his shoulders. After everyone had been served, Berthe stood to introduce her guest, ringing her crystal water glass with a spoon. She said how much she'd enjoyed reading his poetry, how the pictures he shaped with words encouraged her when she had trouble with a painting. At her urging, Mallarmé stood.

"Poets, like painters, take something away when they name or show an object in its entirety. They take away the delicious joy of discovering a picture through suggestion. Your work," the poet said, gesturing to Berthe and all of us, "Inspires me to write poetry that reflects more than image. I hope to reveal a state of the soul."

"*Vraiment!*" called Édouard Manet, soliciting applause from the table. Lydia smiled and clapped.

After dinner dishes were cleared and a dessert of poached pears with chocolate was eaten, Berthe invited everyone into the parlor. Her waitstaff had climbed ladders while we dined, braiding panels together around the room, opening the space for poetry. They had rearranged her furniture—sofas and chairs—to create a sitting place for her guests to face a small stage for the poet. Two bartenders, on both sides of the room, dispensed after-dinner absinthe. Lydia and I sat together on a sofa next to Pissarro, chatting about poetry.

I scanned the room for Edgar. He strolled in, glass in hand, talking with Mallarmé. Edgar's interest in the arts spanned more than painting. He would find some element of poetry to inquire about, learn some bit of information to take back to the easel, to incorporate the idea into his own work. I wished to hear their conversation.

"Will everyone please sit?" called Berthe from the front of the room. "I give you Stéphane Mallarmé."

The poet nodded at Edgar and proceeded to the front. On a podium were two books of poetry. His long hair suited him— curling at his shoulders and bouncing with his confident stride. He reached for a book with slips of paper threaded between pages. Facing us, he turned to a poem, exhaled, and looked up with the ease of someone who performed often.

"I wrote this poem when I was twenty, and since it has found a wide audience, I will start with it tonight." He lifted the book higher. "The title is *Apparition*." Lydia reached for my hand and squeezed it.

The poem opens with a young man walking alone on an empty city street, longing for a girl he once kissed. How quickly the words elicited somber, wistful expressions among us. An atmosphere of loneliness reverberated through the room. Another girl appeared in the poem, like an apparition, in the young man's path. Mallarmé paused his recitation, as if to search for her in the audience, and his eyes fell on Lydia. He continued to recite his words by memory, speaking to my sister as if he'd written the verse for her.

When, with light in your hair, in the street and in the evening, you appeared to me smiling and I thought I had seen the fairy with a hat of light who passed in my dreams as a spoiled child, always dropping from her carelessly closed hand snow-white bouquets of perfumed stars.

The poet could not have chosen a more appreciative or adoring member of the audience. After the poem, during the applause, she glowed with delight and a touch of self-consciousness. I looked for Edgar who, I soon found, staring back at me.

After that night, Edgar took to calling my sister "the fairy with a hat of light." The endearment made Lydia blush, which pleased him. He liked to flatter her. Her tenderhearted presence charmed him.

"Edgar. Mallarmé. Who else will you enchant?" I teased, when my sister and I were back home.

Mallarmé signed Lydia's book with the inscription, "May you grow bouquets of perfumed stars."

XVI.

As the 1879 exhibit drew near, Edgar brought me a promotional poster announcing each of the artists. I read them silently, one at a time, mouthing my name alongside his and the others. His conviction my paintings were worthy of the Impressionists carried me during a time when nervousness and self-doubt nearly wriggled between the canvas and me. The poster featured my name. Women rarely had that privilege, but Edgar wasn't defying convention. He sought and recognized talent, whether men or women.

From a window of 28 avenue de l'Opéra, I glimpsed the street outside and wondered when my family's carriage would arrive. The Impressionists had converted the first floor of an apartment building into a gallery.

"Mlle. Cassatt, *êtes-vous prête?*"

"We're ready!" I answered the young man assigned to opening our doors. A sizeable crowd had gathered outside on a bright April day. Of the artwork exhibited, eleven pieces were mine. Twenty-five were Edgar's. The rest, about two hundred more, belonged to our friends.

Paintings covered the walls from ceiling to floor. A few sculptures flanked the rooms, like exhibits in the Salon, but that's where the likeness ceased. In our exhibit, on the morning of the Impressionist opening, we stared at the future, not the past. The spirits of the great masters were with us, of course.

All of us had modeled our work after theirs for years. As young copyists, we reproduced paintings by Rembrandt, Vermeer, Rubens, Poussin, and others. Our easels had stood in multiple rooms of the Louvre. In this makeshift gallery, paintings emitted a natural light that bathed landscapes and city scenes. Other paintings captured people in everyday life. Fleeting glimpses. Impressions. Moments. Lydia liked to say we captured what the heart could see, not only the eyes. People can perceive unseen details. Lessening form sometimes extends it. I imagined the old masters standing with us, cheering on the works of Monet, Pissarro, Gauguin, Bracquemond, Caillebotte, Degas, and Cassatt.

I walked hurriedly through the fare gate, toward the third room with my paintings. On the way, Edgar's sleeve brushed mine. Our eyes met. Edgar still had not hung paintings listed in the catalogue. Everyone knew his mania for adding final touches to his work, no matter how finished they seemed. His lack of preparedness angered some of the others. But I couldn't be angry. I felt honored to show my work alongside his. Turning to the sound of the crowd, we waited. Footsteps grew louder as they approached the gallery rooms from the hallway.

When the first patron arrived, Camille Pissarro, normally the calmest of us, fidgeted in his jacket. *En plein air* suited him more than a gallery. I wanted to be nowhere else. I'd begged my father to send me to art school. After leaving art school and coming to Europe, I painted in most of the great cities. I remember standing in the halls of the Uffizi Gallery in Florence, staring at the work of Botticelli and other Renaissance painters, sensing the exhilaration of the time. I imagined the rebirth of art, the movement from one aesthetic tradition to another.

I'd travelled from museum to museum, studio to studio, tutor to tutor, with little more on my mind than color, form, and an ache to learn new ways of applying them. I didn't spend my time chasing mere curiosity. No. I gave my life to painting. I wanted to be an artist. This dream I'd nurtured for as long as I could remember, the force of which pulled me and my family across an ocean, was finally coming true.

Claude Monet, with his dark beard and curly hair, entered the gallery with our visitors. He waved to Pissarro and hurried to stand next to him. The public associated Monet as a founding Impressionist. Though his name was synonymous with our exhibit, he didn't enjoy the formality of gallery openings or the bourgeois clientele. The two outdoor painters suffered the opening day together, alongside Pissarro's student, Paul Gauguin, who had been invited to showcase a statuette.

Gustave Caillebotte, our exhibit's primary financier, stood at the top of the stairs, surveying the attendees. I'd admired his paintings at the first Impressionist exhibit, hosted in Durand-Ruel's gallery. He'd carved a place for himself in the group with his modern subjects and compositions. Caillebotte took up the cause of showcasing our work as stridently as he did his own. Son of a wealthy textile businessman, he didn't require the sale of paintings to support himself. An idealistic thirty-one-year-old, he embraced the new direction of art and used his resources to support it. When he seemed satisfied by the number of attendees gathered for the opening, Caillebotte hurried to stand with his own paintings.

The crowd filed in and fanned out, people walking here and there. Fashionable women. Men of means. Students. Art collectors and critics. They commented and stared.

Félix and Marie Braquemond stood before their paintings. Marie's large, three ceramic tile panel—*The Muses of the Arts*—had received such acclaim at the World Fair, Edgar invited her to display it. Her printmaker husband had shown his work with the Impressionists from the beginning, but this was Marie's first year. I didn't know Marie well, but as the only women exhibiting, we took comfort in each other's presence. Berthe hadn't had time to paint after the birth of a daughter.

"May!" Lydia called out from the crowd. Her gloved hand waved over the heads of people gathering around Edgar's paintings. Lydia and our parents worked their way across the hallway to stand next to me. I saw the pride in my father's eyes as he smiled, taking in the scene. Mother listened to the people gathered around us.

"Did you say hello to Edgar?" I asked.

"How could I?" Lydia said, linking her arm in mine. Hearing this, Father stopped smiling and shifted his weight. The room teemed with even more people.

I held my sister's hand and motioned for my parents to follow me to the room with my paintings. I'd never had such a prominent showing before. Here I'd displayed my best oils, pastels, and gouaches.

Standing with them, I felt outside myself. I had a strange sensation of gazing at my pictures as if someone else had painted them. The first painting that caught my attention was of Lydia, *Woman in a Loge*. Centrally arranged in a group of theater paintings, my sister's blush silk dress, pearl choker, peach complexion, and golden hair shimmered against the gilded candle-lit interior of the Opéra. The theater paintings seemed to garner the most attention. The thrill rippling through the audience—to see fine Parisian performances, and to be seen in fine Parisian fashions—radiated from the canvases.

The remainder of my portraits hung on the opposite wall of the room—including *Portrait of a Little Girl in a Blue Armchair*. I'd learned since working with Edgar on the painting that he often changed his own compositions to present subjects in startling ways. I was happy with the painting, but I'd become more careful about inviting his opinions.

An old woman shook her head disapprovingly while standing in the room with my artwork. I imagined her distaste for bright colors. Other people praised the paintings. *"Très modern!"* said a man in a blue striped suit, commenting on my suggestion of detail, the blurred edges of form. The crowd closed in more tightly and I noticed the enchanted expression of a young girl staring at the theater portraits. She held hands with her mother, walking from one painting to another.

For days afterward, Father delivered kind reviews to my studio as they were published. I had my detractors certainly, but I knew this would be the case in exhibiting with the Impressionists. Mostly I was glad to have my work discussed, to have my name in the papers. Paintbrush in hand, I would open the door and he'd hand the reviews to me, smiling. One morning, he brought a review from *L'Artiste*.

There isn't a painting, nor a pastel by Mlle. Mary Cassatt that isn't an exquisite symphony of color. Mlle. Mary Cassatt is fond of pure colors and possesses the secret of blending them in a composition that is bold, mysterious, and fresh. The Woman Reading, seen in profile, is a miracle of simplicity and elegance. There is nothing more graciously honest and aristocratic than her portraits of young women, except perhaps her Woman in a Loge, with the mirror placed behind her reflecting her shoulders and auburn hair.

The French liked me! The sole American Impressionist.

XVII.

The exhibit, the reviews, and my new friends invigorated me. I rededicated myself to the work, to present more paintings the following year. I woke and slept in a world of new ideas, including printmaking, which took more time than I imagined. Finally, Edgar was ready to begin the magazine he'd talked about for more than a year.

During the summer months in Louveciennes, a countryside escape north of Paris, I sketched studies I'd eventually transfer to copper. I missed the city, and especially the proximity to Edgar, but I threw myself into the work. Garden scenes with Lydia. Morning scenes of my parents reading the newspaper or taking their tea. I monitored my progress as I worked, tallying the plates I'd finished. The urgency to finish the magazine's first issue propelled me to work faster than I would have otherwise. We aspired to produce and distribute the magazine's inaugural edition by spring, to coordinate timing with the next Impressionist exhibit, to garner a wider audience.

I still wanted financial independence from my family. I'd sold several paintings after the exhibit, but the magazine would introduce my work to a circle wider than Paris.

When fall came, Camille Pissarro and I delved into the work in Edgar's studio. Berthe Morisot joined when she could. Each of us had stepped away from other interests to devote ourselves to the project. We planned to launch the publication while showcasing our etchings collectively at the next exhibit. Side by side, we experimented with the printing process, trading ideas and tools for etching.

Edgar breezed in and out during the day between gallery business and meetings with other artists. He did most of his creative work late at night. I worked at my studio in the mornings before joining the group after lunch. Camille came to Edgar's studio in the late afternoon, after a day *en plein air*. Though he and his family lived in Pontoise, he took an apartment in Paris when he worked in the city. With a bulging portfolio under one arm and a wooden box of supplies under the other, he'd rattle into the studio whistling Bach or Beethoven. He brought the sunlight with him.

"How spare can a drawing be before it's no longer recognizable?" he asked me one day.

"*Bonjour*, Camille," I said, smiling.

"*Bonjour, bonjour.* Well?" He thumbed through his portfolio for a plate.

Once he found the etching he was looking for, he inked it and rubbed the image onto paper with the binding of a book, rather than sending it through the press. I set down my work and walked over. With ink-stained fingers, he pulled the paper gingerly from the plate and placed the image under a bright lamp. A stout woman raking hay in a dark dress and white apron appeared before us. Mere suggestion of clouds floated above her. A simple cross-hatched form, a pile of hay, lay at her feet.

"You're getting closer to the answer," I said, admiring the work.

He pulled at his long graying beard, staring at the print. "If detail doesn't render the spirit of a subject, what does?"

This was the sort of question he liked to ask, a philosopher's musing rather than a painter's. I could no more answer it than he could.

"Imagination?" I asked.

"Yes, but whose? The artist's? The observer's? Or both?"

"It is rather mysterious, how so few lines can render the feeling of her, Camille."

"How does an artist's intention come through the work if not through form? Even photographs don't always capture the spirit of something. I may change my calling card from Camille Pissarro, *peintre* to Camille Pissarro, *capteur d'esprit*."

"It may widen your audience. You could join ranks with the spiritualists."

"Instead of using crystal balls, we conjure spirits with ink and paper."

"But how will we get them to pose for us?"

"Ah *oui*, this could be difficult," he agreed, still smiling. "I may not be skilled enough to conjure the dead."

"Are you planning to visit the gypsies, Camille?" Edgar called from the doorway, a newly acquired painting in his hands. He never held back his disdain for spiritualists. The visible world was enough for him.

"Yes. They want to know when you're coming again."

"Never," muttered Edgar. "Let the rest of Paris flock to their black velvet covered tables to have their cards read."

"What are you afraid of?" I asked.

"Don't tell me the esteemed Cassatt family visits fortunetellers?"

"No, no."

"Well, that makes one family in Paris not seeking supernatural help for everyday decisions." Edgar said, unwrapping the brown paper from his purchase.

"What treasure are you adding to your collection?" I asked.

Edgar propped it onto an easel and turned it to face us. He walked to where we stood.

"His name is Utamaro Kitagawa, eighteenth-century Japanese printmaker."

"Stunning," I said.

The colored print was of a semi-nude Japanese woman combing her newly washed hair over a basin. How exotic it seemed, otherworldly. I admired the simplicity of the artist's lines, the portrayal of the woman in a private moment. The intimacy of the painting pulled at me as the viewer. An artist on the other side of the world, living a hundred years ago, followed an aesthetic we were exploring.

"I aspire to capture the farmworkers in Pontoise with the same tenderness," said Camille, his eyes fixed on the painting.

"You are an anarchist revolutionary with a paintbrush," said Edgar.

Camille smiled. His childhood and early school years in the Caribbean taught him to see beyond skin color and class. He'd married a woman who had been a maid in his mother's house. Although he'd come from a wealthy merchant family that supported him as a young artist, he eventually declined their patronage to live by the ability of his own hands. This was difficult with a large family to support. He believed in, and talked about, the egalitarian world-to-come — when colonialism and capitalism would collapse. When labor and wealth would be shared, regardless of family, race, gender, or age. He chose not to see divisions among people, and this quality endeared him to me. He considered me, and all women, his equal.

"I see something of your work in this print, Mary," Camille said.

He was right that my inspiration had come from the intimacy of my family's parlor, at a dressing table, in the library, or taking tea. But I sometimes felt alone with these themes. Ballerinas, laundresses, and other laborers — public by nature—seemed more important or laudable to critics. I struggled sometimes with not knowing what to paint. Still, Kitagawa's lean composition strengthened my confidence in our work at the printing press.

One evening, after Camille had left the studio and I was nearly finished for the day, Edgar stood behind me, watching. Working from three different sketches, I'd begun etching a copper plate of a woman in an opera box. She sits with an open fan. Her smile serves as an invitation for those around to gaze at her. She is passively flirtatious, dressed in her finest gown.

"Your light and shadow are in good proportion," he said over my shoulder.

I heard his breathing, the shifting of his weight from one foot to the other. My etching was spare, natural. He watched me carve the metal. Was my point of view original? Was the composition balanced? While Edgar watched me, I sensed him seeing beyond my strokes, past the plate, straight into my heart.

"One could not teach your kind of talent, Mary."

Such words. I felt euphoric.

Edgar handed me a rag, and holding it with me, moved the thick oily color to build shapes on the copper.

"Ludovic Lepic first taught me how to ink a plate," he said. A well-known printmaker, Lepic had guided Edgar's interest in printing years ago.

His hand clasped mine.

To transfer the image, he placed paper over the ink and ran both the plate and paper through the press. Again, he stood close behind me as I examined the first run, which did not pick up my etched lines, but shapes from which I could build the picture. Only the second and third states showed detail. We examined them again, heads close together under lamplight. Each run produced a distinct atmosphere. Darker registrations felt moody. Lighter registrations lifted the spirit of the composition. I didn't want to layer color like traditional printmakers, by running the plate and paper through more than once. Edgar and I sometimes worked overtop our images once the ink was dry, in pastel or watercolor, to emphasize aspects of a print. Edgar might tint the tulle of a ballerina's tutu with pale blue, as if she were cast in limelight. I might highlight the gold of a woman's earrings. The excitement was seeing how an etching would reproduce off the press. That was the mystery, the intrigue.

But I'd lost track of time. It was night, well past the acceptable hour to walk home alone.

"Would you like to see a new painting?" Edgar asked, glancing with me at the clock. I followed him through a narrow hallway into a larger room. Two easels stood open, with canvases propped against them. I tried to make out the paintings in the dim light. On the left wall was a row of open windows. At the room's far end was a rumpled bed. A small table sat next to it, covered in books.

His bedroom, I realized, feeling the blood rise in my cheeks as he talked about one of the half-finished paintings before us. My breath grew shallow. The air became charged. I watched his fingers run along the edge of the canvas as he spoke. He turned to look at me, but unable to hold his gaze calmly, I walked to a window to look outside. I could leave, I told myself, breathing fresh air. I could turn around and—

"Do you think I should alter the painting in this way?" he asked.

"I'm not sure." I turned to face him.

He stared at me and the silence between us amplified every ambient sound—the pop of a log in the fireplace, the clop of hooves pulling a carriage outside, the hush of the lamp next to his bed. I felt lightheaded.

Edgar moved toward me and stopped. We stared at each other, not speaking. He took another step toward me and, standing close, kissed me. He pulled away to look into my eyes. I felt weak, an aching heat rising in me, and he leaned forward to kiss me again until the passion burned hot between us. His fingertips felt the back of my head, unpinning my hair until it unraveled into his hands. He moved to stand behind me, and I could feel his chest rise and fall. Edgar placed his palms on my shoulders. He drew my hair to one side, unbuttoned my dress, and pushed it gently down my arms. I felt the sweep of a dry brush along my back. Trembling, I turned to face him. He stared at me, concentrating, as if imprinting my form to memory. Edgar lifted the paintbrush, ran its bristles over the contours of my clavicle and followed the curve of my neck to my chin. He touched the tip to my lips, and slowly, he kissed me. Something vital awoke in me. Tangled with him, turning, and stumbling toward his bed, I heard the brush clatter to the floor. I felt the warmth of his skin. The sweetness of his words. Underneath the artist's sharp façade lived a soft-spoken lover. The moonlight moved over our bodies with the hours, pastel in the night.

My eyes grew accustomed to the dark. On the left bank of the Seine, along a tree-lined quay, he caught my hand. In the night, we walked together, the river rippling with light from distant electric streetlamps. The government had commissioned the *lumières,* more plentiful than ever, to cast Paris in eternal light. Edgar snickered at the vanity of the lamps, the way they obscured the light of the moon and stars. "The government should concern itself with its own enlightenment," he scoffed. But there were still shadows where lovers could meet, pockets of safe cover. Benches. The quays. Under leafy branches in the Tuileries.

In that garden, bathed in soft light, the trees cast shadows of thin branches on the ground. Leaves cushioned our footsteps, falling even as we walked along the sandy path. Sweet autumn clematis climbed along a garden trellis, filling the cool night air with its perfume. I took long breaths, delighted by the fragrance.

"I could paint this," I said, stopping. "I'd set up my easel under this tree and paint until dawn. Think of the natural scenes left unpainted by women, simply because it's dark outside."

He laughed.

"Truly, imagine someone gazing at Pissarro's cityscapes, judging his sense of decency in painting buildings cast in twilight — or worse, moonlight."

"I'm trying to imagine that, Mary."

I frowned at him.

He laughed again. "No really, I am."

"You're not constricted. You can't imagine."

Edgar grasped my hand and led me to a cluster of metal chairs. He pulled two aside, and we sat in the open air, under the stars.

"Other than painting the night sky, Mary, what else are you missing? You're as educated as any artist in Paris. Critics esteem your work."

He sounded like my father, but worse, listening to him confused me. I felt embarrassed and ungrateful. Hadn't I attained a pinnacle of professionalism with the Impressionists? I had an audience. What was this yearning I'd felt as long as I could remember?

"I want what you have. I want full freedom." The truth of my words surprised me.

Edgar listened. A breeze blew leaves in lazy circles at our feet.

"Would it be easier for you in America?"

"I could paint the night sky in Pennsylvania, but I am too alone there. I long for Paris when I'm away, for the people, museums, history. And I'd miss you."

Edgar's mouth formed a half smile, and I immediately questioned myself. I didn't know how to talk about my feelings for him. Neither of us was inclined toward marriage. Work came before everything.

"Anyway," I added, with a tone of nonchalance, "We have a magazine to create."

"Indeed," he agreed, standing. "Shall we walk on?"

I gathered my skirt, and Edgar offered his arm. Within a few steps, clematis infused the air again. A full moon emerged from a cloud, luminous over the trees. The light spilled from branches and puddled at our feet. Wings flapped above, a startled bird. Night can be strange, seductive. The darkness conspires to reveal things too mysterious for daylight.

I walked on, heart beating, desire rising. I'd admired men before. None affected me like Edgar.

"How should I think of us?" I whispered.

"We are friends, Mary," Edgar answered, pulling me close. "Dear friends." He encircled my waist with one arm, drew the tips of his fingers across my face, and buried them in my hair. I grew weak in his grasp, breath shortening.

When his lips found mine, my body leaned instinctively toward him. The night enchanted me. Edgar possessed me.

The front door closed quietly enough. I took off my shoes and tiptoed over the floors in my stocking feet, making my way to my bedroom without waking even the cat. I lit the candle on a nightstand by the window and watched the flame flicker to life. My books appeared, and a cold cup of tea Lydia must have left for me. How strange the walls of my room seemed then, as though they had changed instead of me. Was this love? The thin floral stripes of the wallpaper, and the deep red drapery suspended over the window, the faint streetlight outside. The night sky seemed different as well—more familiar. I pulled the curtains closed.

Exhausted and turning toward my bed, the small flame revealed someone under the quilt. I didn't expect to see Lydia's head on my pillow. My sister might have woken and looked for me during the night. I imagined her worry. Our parents were visiting friends in Louveciennes. How long had she been here?

Taking the nightgown from the foot of my bed, undressing and dressing quickly, I slid under the covers next to Lydia and touched her long hair. She woke with a start.

"I'm sorry—"

"Why didn't you tell me you were leaving? Where were you?"

I stared into her eyes, guilt-ridden, searching for words. A knowing expression came over her face.

"Edgar."

Relieved of the confession, I sighed.

"Do you love him?" she asked.

"He's so talented, Lydia."

"Yes, but do you love him?"

I pulled the soft velvet quilt under my chin and thought about the way hours slid past unnoticed in Edgar's studio. I shook away the memory of his hands unbuttoning my dress.

"Edgar differs from other men. He sees me as an artist first, then a woman."

"You love him."

"I don't know. Maybe."

My sister rolled onto her side, her back facing me.

"I'm sorry I didn't tell you. I want you to know."

Lydia rolled back over, eyes moist.

"You've been lying to yourself and to me. How will this work, May? Father will want a proposal."

"Father always wants a proposal. To him, I must be Edgar's colleague. Nothing more."

I was asking my sister to keep a secret. Father's fretfulness about his un-betrothed daughters rippled regularly through the household.

"I need to know you support me, Lydia. Please."

"Is he worthy of you, May?"

"I wonder sometimes if I'm worthy of him."

My sister sighed. "Someone needs to be your chaperone."

"I'm too old for a chaperone."

Lydia knew this. I wasn't in need of someone to keep me on the straight and narrow path, guarding against a suitor's untoward advances. She wanted to stave off romantic rumors that would follow from my association with Edgar. She wanted to protect me, so she offered to accompany us whenever we were in public. In my shadowy bedroom, Lydia agreed to keep my secret.

My parent's expectations, Lydia's worry, the dictates of society, the confines of womanhood could not contain a fire ignited in me. I didn't want Edgar to be a secret. I wanted to go to him and burn to ash again in his arms. I never cared so little about what anyone thought.

XVIII.

Dancers. Frequently he painted dancers. He preferred to paint them offstage, as if peering at them through a keyhole—young girls stretching at the barre or tying satin ribbons of ballet shoes. Their movement and their commonness transfixed him. Young girls of ordinary upbringing pinned their aspirations to performing at the Palais Garnier. Years of rigorous practice took place behind the glittering grandeur of the ballet, where simple girls transformed into royalty. Girls strived to be the most graceful in examination classrooms, where principles were chosen, where prima ballerinas were born. Mothers often accompanied their daughters to rehearsals, fending off or accepting advances of *les abonnés*—wealthy male subscription holders who lurked in foyers, classrooms, and dressing rooms. Edgar captured them all.

Lying in a corner of his studio were worn and discarded ballet shoes. On that dusty floor, they lay pale pink, frayed, and torn. Some stained with blood. He said the shoes reminded him to paint the whole truth of a subject, not only its shiny exterior.

"You know, Mary," he said early one evening, running a print through the press, "In the ballet, queens are made of distance and greasepaint."

Hearing him from across the room, Camille couldn't let Edgar's comment go unanswered. "You like to take the magic away from us, don't you?"

"We see the world differently, Camille," he called back.

"But we agree it's the same world?" he teased.

Nearly two weeks had passed since I'd been alone with Edgar. I questioned if the night had even happened. Camille walked over while I tied an apron around my waist to protect my clothing from ink.

I'd finished drawing Lydia at her dressing table. Using an etching needle on copper, I sketched her figure in three quarters profile, head down, in front of an oval mirror. I placed a lamp at the edge of the composition to illuminate crystal boxes and bottles on the surface. One works in reverse in printmaking, darkening areas that would normally be lightened. When ink coats a plate, the etchings or indentations are the lightest areas to register on the page.

"What are you printing today, Camille?" I asked, looking up from my work.

"Let me guess," answered Edgar. "A landscape?"

"Each of us has our subjects." Camille handed me two of his most recent plates. "You have your dancers. Mary has her sister. And I have my landscapes."

Edgar did not look up from the print he was examining. "Don't forget the laborers and the peasants," he said.

"Aren't we all laborers and peasants?" Camille asked, chuckling. "Except for you, *bien sûr*, Mlle. Cassatt."

"He may have a point, Edgar." I said, admiring his farm scenes. "We've been laboring over this press all day, without the benefit of sunlight and breezes."

"I didn't know *en plein air* suited you. No one's keeping you here, Mary."

Edgar's words stung. I looked up from my plates and stared at him, face flush with embarrassment. He stood up from his stool, left his work, and walked out of the room. Camille shook his head, pulled a chair to the table next to me, and applied ink to an etching.

"I'm not sure what just happened," I breathed.

"He's insufferable sometimes, Mary. It isn't you."

Fatigued from the day's work and taken back by the exchange with Edgar, I wanted to go home. Fetching my things from around the studio—overcoat, umbrella, satchel of art supplies—I saw it. Next to the press was Edgar's newest print, entitled, in his handwriting, *Mary Cassatt au Louvre: Musée des Antiques.*

Still gripping my things in both arms, I sat down in a nearby chair.

"Are you all right?" Camille asked.

Edgar had sketched me at the museum a few days earlier, standing next to Lydia, stylishly leaning against my umbrella. I'd heard him—charcoal scratching paper—but paid little attention. He was always sketching.

After painting dancers for months, he'd chosen my sister and me for his subjects. I was an image he'd held in his mind and brought to life on the page.

Camille stood up and walked over. His eyes fell to the print. A knowing look crossed his face, and suddenly I felt exposed.

"Be careful."

"Pardon?"

"Ancient fisherman would not cast their nets in unknown waters for fear of sea monsters," he answered.

"Is that where I am? An unchartered ocean?"

"Edgar admires women deeply," he answered, holding my gaze. Camille picked up the print from the table to study it. "His perspective and technique are brilliant."

Together, we stared at the etched image.

"You realize he's utterly devoted to his art, Mary."

"As I am," I answered.

He smiled. "Edgar must love that about you."

Does he love me at all? I put one arm, then the other, into my overcoat and stood, tying the belt around my waist.

"It's close to dusk. Would you like me to find you a carriage?"

"Thank you, Camille. I think I'll walk."

XIX.

On Saturday before sunrise, I set a new canvas on my easel. I had slept little the night before and walked early to my studio. I turned up the lamps and sat in the Bergère staring at the blank board. Much as I'd appreciated printing, I missed painting. I looked forward to a day by myself. I'd grown tired of wondering when or if Edgar and I could be alone. Waiting for a man's attention, as if a lovelorn adolescent girl, troubled me deeply. I hated how he consumed my thoughts and took away my will to work.

I gathered my recent sketches, looking for something to pique my interest in the new painting. The lamps cast shadows on the white canvas, my tabula rasa, and I imagined form in their shapes as one does staring at clouds. In the largest shadow, I saw the silhouette of a man's head and sharp shoulders, as if he wore a suit coat. I rarely painted men, apart from my brothers and father, but I felt pierced with a sudden desire to paint Edgar's portrait. He would never have time to sit for me. The only way Edgar, like most artists, would be remembered would be through his self-portraits. I could try to capture his likeness while he worked —

A loud rap startled me. It was too early for a delivery. Carrying a lamp to illuminate the front step, I opened the door and there he was, standing before me.

"I saw the light from your windows," he said.

Did I conjure him? The timing was uncanny.

"Edgar, good morning. Come inside."

The wrinkles in his brown striped suit were unusual, as if he'd stayed up all night at the café before coming to my studio. He eyed the empty canvas.

"I've missed you, Mary."

My legs felt weak, but I held my voice and gaze steady. "I wonder if you feel anything at all for me. I've worked in your studio every day this week, and the week prior. You've said nothing to make me believe this is true."

His expression fell and his eyes grew wearier as I spoke. He rubbed them. "How can I prove I've missed you? Please come walk with me."

I extinguished the lamps and glanced back at my empty canvas before locking the door. The stars were fading with the dawn.

"Are you hungry?" he asked as we walked past a *boulangerie*. The bakers were already three hours into their workday, the aroma of fresh bread wafting onto the street. A woman wearing a tan dress and white apron placed large baskets of tall baguettes in the store's window.

"Yes," I said.

Edgar stepped inside and purchased two sweet brioches. He handed one to me, still warm, wrapped in brown paper. We walked on.

"I've finished a painting," Edgar said. "A commission I need."

"And so, the late hour?" I asked.

"There are no ends of the candle left to burn," he said.

Most artists endured financial pressures, but the mention of Edgar's need for money surprised me. His father had been a banker like mine.

"When my brother died, he left my father with more debt than he could repay. My inheritance. The sale of property and father's art collection took care of most of it, but now I'm a working artist like the rest."

"I'm sorry—"

Edgar stopped mid-stride and turned to me. "But why? I'm sorry for not explaining my situation sooner. I have left you wondering about my intentions, my whereabouts. And after our night together."

What were his intentions? I didn't want to ask. The sunrise bathed the street and buildings in a rose-gold light. I forgot about my empty canvas, the prints I'd worked on the previous week. We climbed the stairs to his studio and barely shut the door before he kissed me. The fire leapt inside me with the touch of his lips. I felt ravenous for him. He kissed me again before leading me to his bedroom.

Over Edgar's bed hung a small portrait of the Spanish tenor, Lorenzo Pagans, playing guitar. Right of Pagans sits Edgar's aging father—Auguste—listening intently to the singer. Edgar often gestured to the painting when he referred to his "dear Papa."

He mentioned him as the noon sun poured through his bedroom windows, white light bouncing through the room. We lay in bed, wrapped in sheets, my head on his chest.

"He died when I was forty." Edgar said, "When I was old enough to make my way."

I lifted my head to look in his eyes, which were focused not on me, but on the new paintings hanging on the far wall. Edgar's focus on printmaking was as practical as it was aesthetic. Printing produced more pieces to sell from one original plate. I understood the financial advantage of printmaking, namely the ability to reproduce and distribute our work widely. But he had not given up painting completely.

Edgar lived in Paris without parents or any nearby relatives. He was alone, working to pay off the debt of his father's estate. I knew his drive to sell more art had developed out of necessity. An artist, especially in the beginning, requires financial support from loved ones. Edgar's father served that role for years. Paying his father's debt was, in his words, "his responsibility." I could see it was an act of love.

"Why didn't you feature your father more prominently in the painting?" I asked, looking again at Pagan's portrait. The singer's emotional expression—as though mid-song— compelled me to gaze at him. Only a white score of music, placed behind Edgar's father, led my eyes to the right side of the painting. In the muted background sits Auguste, elbows on his knees, listening.

"He admired Pagans. I wanted to paint more than my father's likeness. I hoped to capture his love of music, and this is how I remembered him that night."

"Do you remember the song?"

Edgar grew quiet, thinking. In a soft voice, lower than a tenor, he sang.

El que quisiera amando
Vivir sin pena
Ha de tomar el tiempo
Conforme venga
Quiera querido
Y si te aborrecieren
Haga lo mismo.

"What does it mean?"

Whoever would dare to love
And live without regret
Should take the time
To be courteous
To the wants of their dearest
And even if you are hated
Do the same.

I settled back into his chest and pulled up the quilt. I don't know how long we lay in each other's arms. Edgar got up at times to paint. He told me he preferred low light because his eyesight was changing. In the center vision of his right eye, he could no longer see clearly. He believed the dim light of evening improved his compositions. I saw no evidence of decline—his work was meticulous—but he worried his sight would get worse, an unimaginable fate for any artist.

The sun slid quickly across the sky, and as it dipped below the rooflines, his bedroom turned cool. He hadn't apologized for his rudeness in the studio, nor commented on the print he'd made of Lydia and me. That his mood had shifted so curiously didn't deter me from wanting to be with him. Instead, I wanted to spend more time with him, thinking his presence and our lovemaking would steady me.

The next day, along the same quay we'd walked together at night, I passed booksellers. Their wares sparkled in the sun. I stopped to run my hands over worn leather covers of poetry, gold scrolling titles promising beauty. Keats glimmered on the table. I lifted the volume to my nose, the scent of old paper and sonnets mingling with the cool November air. Surely Keats wrote in gardens. I opened the book and the pages fell open to a love letter.

I cannot exist without you. I am forgetful of everything but seeing you again. My life seems to stop there, I see no further. You have absorb'd me. I have a sensation at the present moment as though I were dissolving.

Dissolving. Like paint melting in the rain. Nothing felt solid anymore. Not the ground, not my thoughts, not even my art. What would I paint? A wash of color? He touched everything I saw. The streets of Paris had become infused with him. With every breath, he lived in me.

I paid the bookseller. Clutching Keats to my chest, I walked on. That exquisite ache, to be close to him, returned. What human experience competes with love? How had it escaped me for thirty-five years?

XX.

Lydia and I packed a picnic for an outing to Jardin du Luxembourg. Fall leaves crunched beneath our feet as we walked, crimson and russet hues along the path. The air was warm for the time of year, summoning children outdoors. We sat on an iron bench watching them chase each other. The sun crested above as we unwrapped the small baguette sandwiches of brie, basil, and tomatoes with mustard.

"I haven't seen or talked with you lately," Lydia said, handing me a brown linen napkin from the basket. "You seem to have vanished into Edgar's studio."

"I'm learning a great deal about printing."

"And love?" she asked, nudging me with her elbow. "Are you in love with him, May?"

I watched a young boy kick a ball around a grove of pear trees. He wove in and out of the trunks with his ball, and when he got to the end of the grove, he proceeded back the same way he came.

"I've never felt this way about anyone. The thought of him keeps me up at night. I wake with the sound of his voice in my head."

Lydia studied my face. "Yes."

"Is that love? Is this how it feels? It's distracting."

Lydia kicked up her feet and laughed. "Welcome to the world, May. What about the others? You never felt love for them?"

"I thought I did."

"But not more than your art."

"Do you know I think as much about his art as I do my own?"

Lydia's eyebrows arched as she considered my words. I'd never put a man before my art. We watched as a young woman pushed a baby carriage along the path.

"Sounds serious," she said. She balled up the paper from her sandwich and pulled out her knitting. A pile of soft yellow yarn fell into her lap.

"Did you hear our sister-in-law is expecting again?" Lydia asked, wrapping the yarn skillfully around her index finger and moving the needles rhythmically. The start of a receiving blanket dangled from her hands.

Alexander's wife lived a life Lydia had once wished for, but if she envied Lois, she never showed it. She would have thrived as a wife and mother. I reached for the yarn to hold and unwind it for her.

"Do you ever wish—"

Lydia anticipated my question and put down her needles.

Her romance with Thomas began when my sister was old enough to marry. Before they'd met, she'd taken to embellishing the edges of pillowcases for a dowry chest. She also crocheted tablecloths and tea towels for her not-yet-standing, future home. I silently pledged against the old-fashioned ritual when it would become my turn, when I finished art school. Then when Thomas proposed marriage, after years of preparing for a future she once couldn't see, the objects she'd collected and embellished took on new meaning. The very act of stitching, moving needle and thread through fabric, seemed to pull him into her life. Once engaged, she embroidered his initials onto the carefully folded linens in her leather tooled trunk. Before he left for the war, she stitched his name inside the coat of his uniform so he would think of her each day he dressed.

"Really May, do you think as a child I dreamed of coming to Paris to follow you and your ambitions around instead of marrying and having children of my own?"

I stared at her.

"Sometimes you act as though you're the only person in our family who matters. I wasn't born with your talent. I'm not an Impressionist. But I loved a man. I know what it's like to wake up every morning longing for someone. Of course I wanted children. I'm here for you, for our parents, but I also had dreams."

"I didn't mean—"

"Sometimes love is enough. Sometimes a woman can be satisfied knowing she's found someone to share her life. If Edgar is that person, count yourself lucky." Shaking her head, she picked up her knitting again.

In Lydia's words, an image revealed itself like a photograph. I realized how selfish I was and how incapable I was of seeing beyond myself. Shame, amplified by my sister's admonitions, washed over me.

Twenty years had passed since Lydia's fiancé, Thomas Houghton, had died in the war. America had been under threat of true fracture. Thomas was one of many soldiers who gave his life to preserve the Union. He was a sad loss in a tragic war that touched everyone around us. Looking back from the garden bench in Paris—different time, different country—made his death more senseless.

I could still picture my sister and Thomas in the orchard behind our house. Our parents were gone. I'd come home early from school. I should have turned away instead of spying. His hands were insistent, kneading my sister's low back as he pulled her to him. Thomas tugged on the buttons of her dress, unfastening them one at a time. They kissed, and he pulled on her pink silk sleeves, opening her like a package. His lips trailed over her neck and shoulders. Their edges blurred under the afternoon sky, under branches of spring trees and birdsong, new grass tickling their skin. They pushed at each other's clothing, but this was too much. I turned and ran home.

My sister had lost the love of her life not long after she'd found him. I'd had no appreciation of the strength it took to survive his death. Only through my feelings for Edgar could I finally imagine my sister's pain.

"Forgive me, Lydia." I teared up at the loss. Her dreams of having a family of her own were dashed.

She put down her knitting and looked straight into my eyes. "If you love Edgar, don't walk away. Claim him. Your art will always be with you, but love can vanish."

The wind picked up with her words, scattering leaves. I pulled a shawl over my shoulders and looked for the boy with the ball, but the pear grove was empty.

XXI.

As Christmas approached, too many people mulled about Edgar's studio. Lydia often asked to come. Berthe Morisot worked there frequently too. Unable to be alone with Edgar, I wondered if he was bothered at all. He seemed lighthearted, laughing and working hurriedly. The urge to finish the magazine and get on with other projects encouraged everyone to work faster. Camille also stayed in town to work daily. The countryside had turned too cold for long bouts of bare-handed sketching on metal. He turned the wheels of the press over the many plates he'd completed in the fall.

Ballet dancers would come to the studio to model for Edgar. They'd ask for him at the front door and be led to the backroom by his housekeeper, Sabine. I tried not to care he spent more time alone with them than he did with me.

Producing etching after etching, I had no time to paint. Our next exhibit was four months away, and I had only three paintings finished. We'd agreed to hang our prints at the exhibit, but I wished for more time to work in pastel and oils. Printing had consumed me since summer.

The piece I worked on that day, *Waiting*, was a portrait of a woman in a three-quarter profile. Sitting in an upholstered chair, her eyes turn toward the floor but fix on nothing. She longs for something out of reach.

"Will the Cassatts have visitors for the holidays?" asked Berthe while she inked a plate.

"Not for Christmas, but Alexander has agreed to bring his family this summer," Lydia said, looking up from her knitting.

I hadn't heard the news. "Did you receive a letter?"

"I meant to read it to you last night, May, but we got home so late from the theater."

Alexander and Lois had never brought their family to Paris. Our parents would be thrilled to spend the summer with their four grandchildren.

"I'd like to meet more of the Cassatts," Camille said, smiling at the thought.

"We'll have you and Mme. Pissarro for dinner at our summer house," said Lydia. "Our father has rented a villa in Marly-le-Roi."

"You'll be country folks like me," he said.

"That will never happen," said Edgar. "The Cassatt family is as close to Parisian as Americans can be."

Lydia chuckled at the half-compliment.

"If it helps me to paint like you, Camille," I said, "I can't wait. And Paris can be so gray."

"Especially now," agreed Berthe. "That's why I've chosen a colorful theme for my next *jour fixe*. You'll come, won't you?"

Lydia agreed at once.

"I would never miss your soirées," added Edgar.

"I want to hear about the latest Zola novel, Lydia. I haven't had a minute to read since Julie was born," said Berthe.

"Or paint," Edgar said.

Berthe shot me a look and shook her head at his impatience with her to resume painting again.

"What's wrong, Degas?" asked Camille. "Can't imagine how a small, happy child might distract you from art?"

"I know you've missed me, Edgar," said Berthe, smiling. "You can't imagine how much time a baby absorbs in a day, but I'm here with you now."

"Camille comes often, and he has six children — at least."

"Eight, but mine are grown and heaven knows I didn't tend to them in their early days. I'd like to see you change a few diapers, Edgar."

We laughed at that, even Edgar, though he brushed the thought aside like a fly with his ink-stained hand.

"Haven't you kept that poor dancer waiting long enough?" asked Berthe.

"I'm paying her, aren't I?" Edgar answered, concentrating on his work.

"I imagine you're an excellent mother," Camille whispered to Berthe, who leaned into him and put her head on his shoulder.

Edgar put down the copper plate he'd been carving and walked over to where I was working.

"May I?" he asked, and I nodded. He lifted my latest print from the table to get a better look.

"Such longing," he whispered. I did not respond or move. I simply stared back at him. He placed the print back onto the table and traced his fingertips over my hand, lingering at my wrist.

"I shall now return to the ballet!" he announced quickly.

"*Merde!*" Camille called, meaning "break a leg" in English, but literally "shit" in French.

Lydia laughed again, entertained by a conversation she'd never normally hear. Berthe waved. I watched Edgar turn to walk out. I wanted our work to be finished for the day. Was I jealous he was painting the ballerina in the other room?

"*J'ai faim!*" said Berthe suddenly, looking up from her work. "Who wants to walk with me to buy some bread and cheese?"

Lydia joined at once, and after some persuading, they convinced me to go, too. We promised to bring back lunch for Camille. My feet fell upon the stones outside and the sunlight and crisp air enlivened me. Never underestimate a mid-day walk to awaken the mind. My usual way of working, Edgar's too, was to push against fatigue by working harder. I set aside those rigid ways and looped arms with my sister and friend. Berthe had a favorite *boulangerie*. She led us down one narrow street, and another. She refused to purchase loaves from any other baker. Finally, the scent of warm baguettes infused the air as we walked toward a storefront with a royal blue awning. The large window displayed round, rectangular, twisted, sugared, herbed, and salted loaves piled high in straw baskets. Berthe selected three thin baguettes and a loaf of brioche.

Three doors down, on the same side of the street, stood the *fromagerie*. Berthe and Lydia purchased rounds of Gruyère, herbed chèvre, and Camembert. I rarely shopped for food anymore since Mother and Lydia had taken over the household. The stores stirred my senses. The owner wrapped the cheeses, and I stared at his extensive selection. Opposite the case stood his daughter, a petite girl with sandy brown hair and dark eyes. She peered from behind the counter, wearing a navy and white striped dress with a crocheted raspberry flower at her waist. Parisian perfection, she smiled at me and I wished for my sketchbook as the child clutched her father's apron.

Bread and cheese in hand, Berthe led us to a wine shop, where she selected two bottles of Bordeaux. The shopkeeper asked about Berthe's daughter and inquired about the next Impressionist exhibition.

"Monsieur, you must remember the paintings of my friend?" she said, placing a hand on my arm. "Let me introduce Mlle. Mary Cassatt."

The storekeeper searched his memory a minute before realizing he did, in fact, know my work. "*Oui!*" he said excitedly, "My wife and I loved your Opéra pastels."

"*Merci,*" I said, surprised. "You must then meet *ma soeur*, Mlle. Lydia Cassatt, the subject of those paintings."

As if it were too much, as if he might fall over, the man threw his hand over his heart and turned bright red. "*Mon Dieu!*" he said. "*Ma femme* will be devastated to have missed you. How rare to have esteemed guests pass through our shop."

I smiled at the recognition, exactly the boost I needed.

"Today," Berthe said, "We are working at M. Degas' studio, along with M. Pissarro—do you know their work?" The shopkeeper quickly nodded. "And decided we must stop by your store to buy wine for our lunch."

Berthe had a gift for making people feel special, but she didn't expect he would refuse to take payment for our purchases.

"I insist," he said, shaking his head as she presented our francs.

"*S'il vous plaît,*" we pleaded.

"*Non.*" The storekeeper's expression grew serious, and he crossed his arms over his chest.

"*D'accord,*" Berthe said, with a tone of resignation. "Then you and your wife must attend our next exhibit in the spring free of charge. I'll deliver the tickets." He agreed as he walked us to the door, kissing our cheeks.

"*J'adore* Paris," said Lydia as we walked back to the studio. I nestled into her side, happy she'd grown to love France as much as I had.

Camille found wine glasses while Berthe looked for a corkscrew. Lydia cleared a table and pulled a clean cloth from her sewing basket for our meal. Berthe opened the cheeses and placed them before us. I poured the wine, looking up to see if Edgar might join.

"*À votre santé,*" Camille said, lifting a glass.

"*À la vôtre,*" we replied.

We tore pieces from the baguettes, which were still warm, and Camille sliced the cheeses with his pocketknife. A peasant's lunch, he said, laughing, "my favorite kind." Simple, perfect. Berthe's preference for the *boulangerie* became clear when we bit through the baguette's hard crust to taste the soft bread inside, delicious with the creamy Camembert. Not everyone achieves the combination exactly—the crunchy and soft textures in such a slender loaf. French bakers are artists too.

"Would you have a spare glass for a tired painter?"

Edgar slid next to me at the table while Sabine led his model out of the studio. He rubbed his eyes while Lydia poured his wine.

"That was fast," Camille said, noting the time on his pocket watch.

"I needed her for some last details," Edgar said, reaching for Camille's pocketknife to cut a slice of Gruyère.

"Are you saying you've finished a painting?" I asked.

"Of course not," Camille said. "Edgar's paintings are never finished."

"*Vraiment*," he agreed. "Who can look at a painting and not see something to be improved? I let them go."

"Begrudgingly," added Berthe.

"And sometimes I take them back!" Edgar said. He finished his glass of Bordeaux and poured himself another before passing the bottle around the table.

"Why don't we do this more often?" I asked.

"Your nose is always in your sketchbook," said Lydia. "And I can't prepare lunch when I'm modeling for you."

"I'd like you to sit for me, but I'm afraid you wouldn't have time for anything else since you sit for Mary," said Edgar, tearing a piece from the baguette.

Berthe stood, yawned, and apologized. Rather than using a wet nurse, she insisted Julie sleep in her bassinet beside her every night. She needed to get home. She rarely spent an entire day at Edgar's studio, and despite wanting a day alone with him, I realized how much I missed my friend.

Berthe gathered her artwork and belongings. Lydia picked up her knitting. Camille, Edgar, and I went back to our work. A silence settled upon the studio as the sunlight slid along the floor from midday to late afternoon. Eventually, Lydia packed her things and went home. I walked her to the next block and promised to be home before dinner. Camille left soon after, placing a handful of fresh copperplates in his leather portfolio.

"Might be a couple weeks before I'm back," he said. He planned to return home for the holidays and come back to his apartment in January.

"*Bonsoir, mon ami,*" I said, kissing his cheeks. "Say hello to your wife for me."

When the door closed and I was finally alone with Edgar, I relaxed. How I'd missed him. He sat across the room from me, next to the printer, staring.

"I could barely keep my hands to myself at the table, Mary."

He stood, walked to where I was sitting, and pulled me to standing. I felt my knees falter when his hands moved to the small of my back. His lips touched mine and lingered. A ravenous appetite rose between us. He pulled me in with one arm while his other hand clasped my hair. He kissed the nape of my neck repeatedly, then inhaled, as if to bring my essence inside him. As cool as he could be on the outside, Edgar had a deep sensuality that enticed me. We made our way to his bedroom.

"You are irresistible, Mary," he whispered, unbuttoning my dress.

XXII.

I arrived for Berthe's Thursday night dinner party at the same time as Edgar. Lydia was unwell so I went alone. Edgar was dressed in a black silk hat and a crisp three-piece suit. His gloved hand reached for mine as I stepped down from the carriage to the gravel road. His eyes steadied on my face, taking in the details as if to paint my portrait. I held his gaze as Berthe and her husband, Eugène Manet, came to the doorway to greet us.

The artist Édouard Manet followed his brother and sister-in-law outside. In his left hand, he carried a letter with a telltale red wax stamp and handed it to Edgar. To make out the words, Edgar held the paper at arm's length and angled toward a streetlamp.

"Doesn't that dinner suit come with a monocle?" Manet asked Edgar.

"Haven't you changed your mind about exhibiting with the Salon this year?" he replied, handing back the acceptance letter.

Though Manet continued to exhibit with the Salon, he was ever-present in our circle. He'd painted Berthe's portrait so often, the public identified the dark-haired beauty as his muse before coming to know her as an artist in her own right.

"I'm waiting for you to change the art world for all of us, Degas," Manet said, slapping him on the shoulder. He turned to me and held my hand to his lips. "Mlle. Cassatt, what a pleasure to see you here tonight. You're beguiling."

Edgar shot him a scornful look before taking my arm.

"Welcome to Morocco," Berthe's husband said, leading us through the front door. A maid came for our coats. Exotic spices swirled in the air, along with the notes of a single flute.

"Yes, welcome," echoed Berthe.

Colorful fabrics hung in folds from the ceiling of the parlor. Sheer silks draped the windows. Candlelight glittered from intricately carved brass lamps. A servant passed through the room with a tray of silver teacups steaming with mint tea. I sipped the beverage, listening to the flutist who played in the corner. I spotted Camille, staring at the décor and pulling at his beard. Edgar scanned the walls, filled with paintings by Manet and Morisot. I watched him examine the artwork in silence, his eyes stopping here and there. Manet leaned into his ebony cane with the ivory handle. His eyes followed his sister-in-law, Berthe, as she summoned the musician to lead us to dinner like the Pied Piper of Hamelin.

On the large dining table were platters of Moroccan chicken, cinnamon dusted oranges, sweet potatoes with chickpeas and almonds, and a pile of bright green beans with red peppers. Servers brought in wine, baskets of flat round bread, and bowls of dates. A beautiful arrangement of pink and white peonies spilled from a pale blue Limoges vase sitting directly in front of Edgar.

"You've outdone yourself," Auguste Renoir said to Berthe as she invited us to take our seats. His beautiful companion, Aline, sat beside him. Renoir's eyes fixed on her as she adjusted the clasp of her pearl necklace, moving it to the back of her neck. Manet watched her as well.

"You can't imagine how one's imagination blossoms within the constraints of domesticity," Berthe said, raising a glass and waiting for her husband to toast their guests.

"To motherhood," he said.

"To Julie," she agreed, smiling. "That child has me pining to paint more than ever. I have less time but more ideas every day."

"I'd like to see your recent work," said Edgar.

We nodded in agreement while the servers carved the chickens and placed the spicy sweet dishes before us. Camille pushed the vase of peonies closer to Edgar when he bent down to retrieve his napkin that had fallen to the floor.

"Mary, I understand you are passing your days with these fellows, trying to resurrect the art of printmaking?" Renoir asked, his hand flapping toward Camille and Edgar.

"I didn't realize it had died," I answered. Edgar pushed around his sweet potatoes, eyeing the flowers.

"I assume you're still painting in your spare hours, after receiving such reviews on your oils and pastels at the exhibition?"

"*Merci*, Auguste, I haven't given up painting altogether, but I'm learning a great deal while printing."

Renoir continued. "And this magazine you aspire to publish, Edgar, do you really believe you can reproduce your work at a high enough quality to distribute it *en masse*? Doesn't the commercial aspect of such a project conflict with your sensibilities?"

Since Edgar found it nearly impossible to finish anything until it met his uncompromising standards, Renoir's comment irritated him.

"Don't the masses deserve to see artwork confined to a few galleries in Paris?" I asked, hoping not to sound defensive. "Auguste, a man of your talent would surely prefer more people to see your work."

"He's jealous," interrupted Berthe.

"Well, it isn't possible to reproduce color paintings, so perhaps you're right," Renoir demurred, out of politeness to our host.

"Could you imagine that?" Manet asked suddenly, "Our paintings printed at will? I understand the allure, Edgar."

"But won't copies cheapen the work?" Renoir asked, grateful to Manet for allowing him to continue.

"It seems rather snobbish to make our art only available to those who can afford it," said Edgar. "What does it mean if Camille routinely paints laborers in the fields, but laborers themselves have no access to images depicting their lives?"

"Do you plan to sell our magazine to laborers, Degas?" asked Camille, smiling.

"No!" Edgar said, slapping the table with his palm. "I plan to sell it to the bourgeois outside of Paris." The table erupted with laughter. "But my point—prints are like photographs. They extend the reach of our work."

Under the table, Edgar touched my knee and drew his hand up my thigh. Weakened with desire and moved by his vision of our future, I held my expression steady. His eyes fixed on me.

"Imagine a world with innumerable, full-size Impressionist reproductions," Manet said, still laughing. "Your dancers, Edgar, in every parlor. Monet's water lilies in bedrooms everywhere."

I hated those water lilies, like glorified wallpaper, but kept my mouth shut.

"And *Le Déjeuner sur l'herbe* hanging over dining room tables," Edgar said to Manet.

"Well, that will never happen," Berthe said. "Which of your paintings would you want printed, Mary?"

I could only think of myself at the Louvre as a copyist all those years ago, attempting the excruciating task of duplicating the iridescent light in Vermeer's paintings. I couldn't imagine capturing such detail or color in print, and shook my head at the thought.

"Well, anything with Lydia, *bien sûr*," said Berthe.

Was Lydia the subject people would most connect with my art?

Servers brought in dessert—rice pudding in crystal stems, and small plates of pastry layered with honey and toasted almonds. They served strong coffee too. Edgar moved the vase of peonies away when Berthe's head was turned. Camille's eyes caught mine, and I stifled a laugh.

A trio of musicians, the flutist and two guitarists, played after dinner in the parlor. In the back of the room, under a sheer red canopy, sat a Moroccan fortune teller. She wore a long black gandora with floral embroidery along the placket, and saffron pointed slippers. A sheer scarf edged in tiny gold beads covered her black hair. A candle floated in a crystal bowl filled with water and rose petals, which sat on the red and blue striped table. Her fingertips kept rhythm with the music, tapping a small deck of cards, and she seemed to rest easily among us.

"Berthe has succumbed like everyone else in Paris," whispered Edgar, gesturing to the fortuneteller. I felt his breath on my neck.

"Why don't you experience it for yourself, then judge?" I asked, intent on talking with her. I was as curious as anyone. Edgar sighed loudly before walking over to Renoir to strike up another argument. Berthe, seeing him leave my side, took my arm to lead me to the woman's table.

"May I present Mlle. Cassatt," she said, pulling out a chair. The music and conversation dimmed, and my attention fell upon the woman.

"Mix the cards," she said, eyes bright. The deck looked small in my hands as I shuffled them. When I finished, the fortuneteller asked me to spread them across the table, face down, and to select five.

As I flipped over cards, the woman arranged them in a cross and studied the symbols on each.

"I see you painting at your easel. The future of your art is very bright. Do you have children?" she asked.

"No."

"I see motherhood in your cards," she said, her voice too low for anyone else to hear.

"Which card suggests it?" I asked, shocked and scanning the cross of cards before me. She pointed to a woman in a gown with a single flower in her hand. She was neither pregnant nor holding a child. The fortuneteller saw the doubt in my face.

"The information comes to me through the language of symbols. I look at the cards, which point in certain directions. In my mind I see pictures, like the images that come in dreams, only I'm awake. Clearly, I see a mother and child."

She fell silent, her eyes losing focus, as though she were listening. I waited for her to speak again.

"You will undergo a period of unrest and trial before motherhood will enter fully into your life. You'll pass from one way of life to another. I see another woman next to you. Her soul is beautiful, and she helps you. Do you know who I'm talking about? I see her knitting."

My skin prickled.

"You're very close to her, like sisters. She teaches you about love."

The fortuneteller's eyes narrowed. Then she gathered the cards into her hands and laid them again in a stack beside the bowl. She looked at me kindly and I thanked her.

"Camille," I said, seeing him walk past. "Would you like to sit down?"

"I'm afraid I might have little future ahead of me. And the days I have left, I prefer to keep a mystery."

The music and conversations around me returned at full volume. I smiled and carried on as though I'd never sat at her table, as though the woman's words had not unsettled me. I'd disregarded the possibility of marriage and children and left them in Philadelphia years ago.

"Have you been duly briefed on your future, Mlle. Cassatt?" Edgar asked when I sat with the group again.

"I won't know the answer to that question for some time," I said, "But she seemed to describe Lydia." I looked at him with more curiosity than usual, trying to imagine him as a husband and father.

"Perhaps she's read about you and your sister in the newspapers," said Edgar skeptically.

"She didn't know us when I hired her," said Berthe. "But I told her this was a dinner party for painters."

Edgar sighed.

"Where did you find a magical Moroccan woman to fit your theme?" asked Manet.

"Last week at the market, she was sitting at a table near the barrels of cayenne and cumin."

"No detail too small for Berthe's entertaining," said her husband.

"There seems to be a fortuneteller on every corner lately," said Manet, "More people are consulting gypsies than priests."

"And when exactly was the last time you went to confession, Manet?" asked Edgar.

"Ah, my dear friend. When you feel compelled to go, I will join you."

Imagining Manet and Edgar in an old church, heels clicking on tiles, looking for two open confessionals, made us all laugh.

"They'd have their sketchpads in hand," I said to more laughter.

Manet smiled with characteristic grace. Edgar crossed and uncrossed his legs until we were finished. Why couldn't he laugh at himself?

"The last thing the world needs is more religious art, even from the Impressionists," Edgar said, standing. He complimented Berthe on another fine *soirée*. She signaled her maid to bring his coat, and he left without looking back. I longed for him to whisper goodbye, to look into my eyes. Manet stood to see him out, hobbling with his cane to keep up.

"Has he injured himself?" I asked after Manet had left the room.

"Yes, but that's not a story for mixed company," said Eugène.

Berthe raised her eyebrows at her husband and asked if he'd refill her wineglass. When he was gone, she turned to me.

"You'll hear the truth eventually," she said. "I'm sure you've noticed Manet charms many women. He hasn't exactly been selective."

I stared at her, waiting for her to finish. I'd heard rumors about her and Manet, but she'd married his brother. Berthe was a beautiful woman. Surely she'd only agreed to pose for Manet's paintings.

Berthe looked down at her hands, shoulders slumped. "Complications from syphilis," she said quietly. "Prostitutes."

They were legal in France. Twenty thousand worked in Paris alone.

"And his wife?" I asked.

She shook her head and shrugged her shoulders. "Lucky, I suppose."

Eugène walked back into the room, handed us two fresh stems of merlot, and the conversation shifted. Berthe's husband was less charismatic than his brother but devoted to Berthe.

I curled up on the sofa next to her and listened to stories about Julie. A fire roared in the old stone fireplace, our cheeks glowing from its warmth and light. Berthe's eyes shined when she spoke of her daughter. With the fortuneteller's words still in my ears, I tried to imagine myself in her place, with Edgar beside me, musing about motherhood. But I could never summon a proper picture of Edgar as a father. In my mind's eye, he shifted in his seat, sighing, waiting for the discussion to end so he could rush back to his studio to revise a painting. Hadn't I always done the same?

But Berthe's love for her daughter moved me. Here was a determined artist, giving herself to a daughter *and* her canvas. Father's voice came back. "Would it be so different to be a married artist?"

Perhaps it was the fortuneteller, or seeing the contentment in Berthe's eyes, but on that night, I considered a possibility I'd long ago set aside.

XXIII.

"Oh Mary, you're home," called Mother from the parlor.

On the carriage ride, still under a Moroccan spell, I replayed the events of Berthe's party. I shook a few snowflakes from my coat and hung it over the armoire, wondering why Anna hadn't helped me at the door. Inside the armoire sat my satchel, bulging with new prints. The handles were stained with ink. I fought the urge to open the bag and thumb through the pages. Mother called out again.

My parents sat in the parlor waiting, neither looking well. Mother sat on the edge of the settee with an open book, while Father sat in his chair by the fire.

"Dr. Doucet is here. Lydia has a terrible fever. Her arms and face have been swelling all day and her vision is blurred."

"Why didn't you send for me?"

"Lydia didn't want us to bother you," said Father, picking up his pipe.

"She's my sister. You should send for me." I heard my voice rise with anger, or guilt, I wasn't sure which. "How long has the doctor been here?"

"A half hour," Mother said. "Will you get us some tea, Mary? Anna had to leave early."

In the kitchen, Mathilde was tidying up. On the counter was a tray with Lydia's uneaten dinner. I filled the water kettle and set it on the stove. Mathilde hurried over.

"*Voulez-vous du thé, Mlle. Cassatt?*" she asked.

She retrieved the silver service and arranged a small plate of china with tiny cakes. I lingered in the kitchen until she was finished, watching the doorway from the corner of my eye should Dr. Doucet walk past.

When she had finished, I took the tray from her hands to deliver it myself. Surprised but grateful to get back to her cleaning, Mathilde smiled at the gesture, then asked about Lydia. My sister ran the household and managed the staff with the same kindness she showed everyone. Mathilde and Anna loved her.

"We haven't heard from the doctor yet."

"I shall pray for her at mass tomorrow," Mathilde said, patting my hand before getting back to work.

I'd never imagined Mathilde attending mass, or any activity outside our home because I knew little about her. I hadn't stood in the kitchen in more than a year. This was the world of Lydia. She planned for meals and cared for all of us without complaint. Lydia's daily life was more foreign to me than mine was to her. A knot tightened in my chest. How could I have not known how much Lydia's headaches were affecting her lately?

I poured Father's tea, then Mother's. When we heard Dr. Doucet's heavy footsteps, Mother stood to retrieve his overcoat and hat.

"I can't say what she has yet. But it looks like her fever has broken. I've given her something to relieve her swelling and I'll check back in the morning to make sure the medicine's working properly. I'm worried about her vision."

"Could it be the fever?" asked Father.

"It's possible. Has she had these symptoms before?"

"Not that I'm aware of," said Mother.

The doctor nodded, taking his coat and hat. "Well, keep a close watch on her. She should sleep better now that her temperature is stabilizing. I'll stop by in the morning."

My parents saw him to the door while I hurried to Lydia's bedside and climbed in beside her. Her eyes were swollen shut, and her cheeks were red with fever. The room smelled sour.

"I love you, sister," I whispered, feeling her warm forehead. She slept, breathing shallowly. I lay next to her, gazing at the ceiling. Despite my worry, I felt relieved to think about someone other than myself and Edgar, or the magazine. The prints in my satchel were no longer urgent. The events of Berthe's party vanished like a fog. Even Edgar took his rightful place outside the circle of our family.

Why is it we rarely consider our loved ones' health until it falters? I couldn't imagine a life in Paris without Lydia. I devoted most of my waking hours to art, but that night, I realized how the comfort of Lydia's presence gave me the courage to work. How little I supported people the way my sister supported me. Next to Lydia I finally slept, but fitfully.

"May?"

I heard her voice as dawn light edged the curtains. Lydia ran her fingers through my hair. Remembering, I opened my eyes. Lydia was sitting up, gazing at me. Her face was still swollen, but less so. She stared at my rumpled dress, the one I'd worn to the party the night before. I hadn't bothered to change for bed.

"Are you all right?" I asked.

"Just a little thirsty." She forced a smile. "Seems I'll do anything to spend more time with you."

I felt her forehead and looked into her eyes. "You had us scared. Do you see me clearly?"

Lydia settled on her pillow and sighed. "Yes, I feel much better."

"Let me take care of you today, Lydia," I said, climbing out of bed. I lit the lamp and went to the kitchen to ask Mathilde to brew some tea. While the tea brewed, I helped her by gathering bread and fruit, arranging a small vase of flowers, and placing them with the teapot on the silver tray. Mathilde carried the tray to the foot of Lydia's bed before drawing her curtains. Lydia, who had fallen back asleep, awoke to the light. I climbed under the covers again, pulled the tray into my lap, and poured a cup for her.

"Let's have a day of games, reading, and knitting," I suggested, watching Lydia take her first sip.

"Won't they miss you at the studio?"

"I'd miss you more than they'll miss me. If you're feeling up to it, I want to see what you're working on." I glanced at her knitting basket, spilling onto the floor by the window.

My sister studied my face. She took another sip of tea, then set her cup and saucer back onto the tray, reclined on her pillow, and closed her eyes.

"When you feel up to it."

Lydia nodded. I crawled out of bed and left her to sleep, closing the door quietly. Tired and desperate to take off my dress and corset, I turned toward my bedroom and heard Mother's footsteps.

"Is she better this morning?" she asked.

"She seems fine, but tired. Her vision has returned."

"Thank you for staying close to her, May. I checked on you both a few times during the night."

"Thank God," Father said, overhearing as he entered the hallway.

"May, I wonder if you could stay home today to help me with your sister?" asked Mother. "I have shopping lists to make for Anna and other household duties to manage."

"I was planning on it."

"Good girl," said my father as he passed. His tone gave me a sudden urge to run to Edgar's studio. From the way he'd dressed, in his navy wool suit, I knew he was on his way to the club to read *Galignani's Messenger*, the European newspaper published in English, drink coffee, and discuss world events with expats. Mother continued talking while gazing at her notebook.

"I'm sure there will be some time for you to sketch today. Dr. Doucet will be here shortly, and I need you to listen for his arrival. Your father has an engagement, and I'll be meeting with Anna and Mathilde in the kitchen."

"I still need to bathe and change this morning—"

Mother looked up from her list. "You won't have time to bathe, but I'll wait for you to change and fix your hair. I'll send Anna to help you."

I sighed. With only ten minutes to myself that day, I didn't want to spend it with Anna at my dressing table.

When Dr. Doucet arrived, he was pleased to see Lydia's progress—her swelling was gone and her vision had returned to normal, no fever at all. He shook his head at her recovery.

"Your sister is a different person than the woman I examined last night," he said before leaving. "I see nothing to suggest she won't be back on her feet in a couple days."

The news cheered me and I went to Lydia's bedside to tell her, but she had fallen back asleep. I hoped she would feel up to playing cards, knitting, or talking. I couldn't wait to tell her about Berthe's party and the fortuneteller. Instead, I checked on her hourly, brought her soup and bread that went uneaten, and stoked the fireplace in her bedroom.

With Mother busy managing the household and Father off socializing with friends, I wandered the apartment thinking about Edgar. Could we have a future together apart from art? I picked up a sketchpad and sat down to draw.

"Do you need a model?" Lydia asked in a quiet voice, standing in the doorway of the parlor, still in her nightclothes.

"I'm relieved to see you standing!" I said, jumping up to help her to the settee. "Are you hungry?"

"Famished."

"Hurrah!" I hurried to the kitchen to get her another lunch.

When I returned, Lydia was sitting on the bench by the window with a shawl over her shoulders and the cat in her lap, her cheek pressed against the glass. Thick snowflakes fell from the sky.

"The sidewalks are nearly covered, May. I'd like to plop down on that street and make a snow angel or two. Everything looks so clean in the winter. Where is everyone?"

"Father left for the club this morning and Mother is running errands."

Mathilde arranged Lydia's lunch on the side table.

"I'm so pleased you're well again, Mademoiselle," she said.

"Oh Mathilde, *merci*. I'm starved."

Lydia tucked into a large bowl of soup, her cheeks pinking with the steam.

"We should wrap up and go outside before Mother and Father return," said Lydia between mouthfuls.

"If I agreed to that, they'd kill me."

Lydia finished her soup, sat down again by the window, and pressed her forehead against the glass. The warmth of her skin and breath fogged the window, and she drew a snowflake with her fingertip in the condensation. I imagined how she felt. When illness fades and the body recovers, when one's attention expands again, the world comes rushing in anew. Afternoon light. Familiar voices. Baking bread. Steaming soup. Soft yarns. Lydia's fingers twined the open weave of the alpaca shawl Mother knitted years ago.

I wanted to give my sister snowflakes. I could summon the sleigh, so she didn't have to walk. Anna could find the fur blankets for us. What if Mathilde loaded our pockets with baked potatoes? I'd make sure Lydia's head was covered and her neck was wrapped in the warmest muffler we had. Would that be so dangerous, if only for thirty minutes?

I walked into the kitchen and asked Mathilde to load the oven with potatoes and Anna to let the driver know we'd need the sleigh in an hour.

"Mathilde, did Mme. Cassatt say when she would return?"

"*Non*, Mademoiselle."

"Could you ask Anna to gather the fur blankets for the sleigh?"

"Is Mademoiselle all right?"

"*Oui, oui*. She's wants some fresh air. I know my parents won't approve of this. We'll only be gone for a half hour."

Mathilde crossed her arms across her ample chest and stared at me like a mother whose naughtiest child had upended the household again.

"I know, Mathilde! I promise to have her back in no time. The snow will make her happy."

Mathilde muttered in French while she checked the oven's temperature and loaded the shelves with potatoes. "*Mon Dieu!*" I heard her proclaim more than once.

With every small sound I heard in the house, I expected Mother and Father to arrive and put an end to my plans. When the horses were ready and the sleigh was loaded with furs and hot potatoes, I told Lydia, who was still sitting by the window.

"Here is your coat."

"You're joking."

"If you want to feel the snow, you'd better hurry. I don't know when Mother and Father will return."

We weren't teenagers who piled into sleighs anymore, but the idea delighted my sister. Her face lit up more brightly than I'd seen in months. She laughed. "May! They're going to kill us!"

"If they find out." I wrapped her neck in the thickest lambswool scarf I could find and handed her a hat. "I can't help but think we're in a scene from *Little Women*."

We'd been friends with Louisa May Alcott's younger sister, Abigail May, who came from Massachusetts to study art in Paris. She'd married a Swiss man, but sadly died giving birth to a daughter, her first child. Lydia and I attended her funeral. We missed her lively personality and thought of her often.

"You're definitely Jo," Lydia said, "Even if she was a writer."

Mathilde met us in the foyer and put a potato in each of our coat pockets. Giddy, Lydia pulled on her gloves while Mathilde stood with her hands on her hips, glaring.

"Don't worry," Lydia whispered to her as I pulled the door closed.

The air bit our cheeks as we stepped into the sleigh. I tugged the furs under our chins. The warmth from the potatoes radiated under the blankets. Lydia tilted her head back to the gray sky, eyes closed, and felt snowflakes land, then melt on her face. When she opened her eyes, the small white flakes stuck to her lashes, and she sighed contentedly.

"Where to?" asked the driver.

"Around the city, please," I said, smiling. We were girls again, sisters on an adventure. Lydia reached for my hand under the blanket and we sat back to watch the white city glide by.

Snow spiraled from the sky. The sleigh turned soundlessly along the streets. Even the hooves were muted as if we'd slipped into a dream. I tried to peer into the fogged windows of Café de la Novelle Athenès, wondering if I'd glimpse Edgar and the others. I imagined patrons warming themselves over coffee and Edgar stomping snow from his shoes and tamping tobacco into his pipe. He would enjoy seeing the two of us in the open sleigh.

Over rooftops, smoke billowed from chimneys like dark ribbons in the sky. I mixed the colors in my mind, graduated values of black and white. A world absent of color refreshes the imagination.

"Does the city look peaceful because our minds are more peaceful, not having to assimilate all the normal details, colors, and textures?" I asked Lydia.

"The snow does feel restful." We watched a man hurry home with two little children. "I hadn't thought about it that way before, May."

"I've been dying to tell you about Berthe's party," I said, glad to confide in her finally.

"I forgot about it completely! I feel like I've been unconscious for days. Tell me. What did she serve for dinner?" She was almost as pleased to experience the party secondhand.

Lydia sat enchanted as I described how Berthe's home had been transformed—the musicians, the draped fabrics. I described each dish in flavorful detail. Lydia loved different cuisines, especially desserts. She collected exotic sweet recipes. She wondered if Berthe would share hers, and when I mentioned the fortuneteller, my sister squealed.

"How could I miss this party? Were you invited to sit with her? Did she tell you anything?"

When we were children, Lydia and I would scare ourselves witless by discussing supernatural tales. My sister had recently learned about a "talking board," a smooth wooden playing board with painted letters and numbers that sits on a card table. By placing one's fingertips lightly on a small carved triangle, spirits were said to move the triangle to spell out messages. Lydia couldn't wait to try one herself.

"The fortuneteller saw you actually," I said slowly, drawing out the suspense.

"Saw me?"

"She described you precisely. Said she saw you knitting. Called your soul beautiful."

Lydia's expression filled with wonder. "The world is more mysterious to me every day."

"I have something else to tell you. She saw motherhood in my cards."

Lydia's mouth opened and closed. "Edgar," she said. Her eyes searched my face for acknowledgment.

"For a split second, Lydia—"

Lydia squealed again. I didn't have to tell her I wondered what it would be like, if I could manage being both a mother and a painter.

"You love him then."

"Yes, I love him."

Lydia leaned her head against my shoulder and wept softly. The driver looked back to see if he should circle the city again. Mother and Father would be home soon if they hadn't arrived already. I couldn't imagine how angry they'd be, and I hardly cared. I'd told Lydia about my change of heart and my sister's happiness was palpable, as though my chance at love and happiness was hers too.

"Let's go home," I told the driver. He nodded and pulled the reins to turn the horses toward our apartment. We arrived ten minutes before Father, enough time to get Lydia back into bed and the evidence stowed out of sight. When Mathilde brought us steaming bowls of *café au lait,* her anger dissolved in relief to see Lydia under her quilt again.

XXIV.

"Which of these do you think would be best for the magazine, Camille?" I asked the next morning in Edgar's studio. He studied a stack of prints I'd selected, considering each of them carefully.

Even with the windows shut, we could hear the strains of a string trio playing Mozart on the street. The music seemed to announce the beginning of spring, still undetectable to anyone other than the sparrows. The blend of violin, viola, and cello mirrored our work together that winter—coming together for one project.

"*Ceux-ci sont magnifiques*, Mary," Camille said, pulling three of the prints from the stack.

"We're nearly there," I answered, threading my arm through his and giving him a hug.

"Are we?" Edgar's voice boomed from the doorway. He walked over to us slowly, sighing, as if we were his students and not his peers.

"I think you have at least a couple months before you produce something worthy of the magazine, Mary."

The strike of his words made my eyes blur. Camille winced but kept his arm in mine, a kind of protection.

"You cannot tell me this woman's art is not ready for your yet-unpublished magazine. Her prints are some of the finest in

Paris. Her work, along with mine, and yours—whenever you get around to finishing it—will comprise the pages of *Le Jour et la Nuit*. This is *our* magazine, Edgar. You invited us to work with you, not to be judged by you."

"I don't make it a practice of keeping my opinions to myself, especially when my name is at stake," said Edgar.

"Do you feel my prints sully your reputation?" I asked, shaking.

"Oh, for God's sake," Camille yelled, throwing his hands into the air. "You're doing it again, Edgar, sabotaging another project because the hinges of your heart have forgotten how to open. *Pathétique!*"

Red-faced and sputtering insults like "self-centered dandy-bastard," Camille crammed supplies into his satchel and walked out, slamming the door behind him.

Edgar seemed oddly satisfied with himself, a half-smile on his lips as I stood bewildered.

"How could you?" I asked, my voice still trembling.

"What? You think because we're lovers, I don't have to tell you the truth?"

His words cut me at the knees, and I fell into a chair.

"I never asked you for this. Forget the prints. How can you be so cruel? How dare you embarrass me in front of a peer, our friend?"

"You flatter yourself, Mary."

"Who are you?" I asked, choking on words through my tears.

His eyes stayed cold. The veins in his forehead throbbed as he banged his fist on the table closest to me. "You don't own me, Mary."

"What?"

"Berthe came to visit me yesterday. She asked about you. If you think I'm going to marry you and give you children, you're mistaken."

His words knocked the breath from my lungs. Had Berthe spoken to the fortuneteller? Horrified by the thought but relieved his anger was not directed at my art, I stood up and reached for him.

"Please, Edgar, give me your hands. Look at me. I've never expected that."

"I'm too old to entertain girlish fantasies of marriage and baby carriages." He pulled his hands away.

"Do you love me at all?" I asked, tears flowing, my heart tearing at his indifference.

Seeing my vulnerability and fear, he cowered and stepped back, shoulders caving into his chest. He crossed his arms, as if protecting himself from my words, from me. I'd revealed how utterly devoted I was to him. A look of terror flashed in his eyes, and I realized my need for his love and acceptance terrified even me.

"I don't think I own you, but you, Edgar, own me."

"I cannot afford to love anyone who would take one ounce of attention away from my work. Marriage is not in *my* cards, Mary," he said. "I thought you were first an artist, not just another woman."

I stepped closer and stared into his eyes, which darted around the room as if looking for escape. His desperation to run away instead of comforting me felt like a sword to the heart. "What have I done to deserve this? I've given my life to my art, including the last nine months in this studio. I stopped painting to take up printing at your invitation, ignoring warnings from family and friends. Even Camille tried to warn me. I've invested as much time into this magazine as you—if not more. How dare you call me just another woman, and not the artist that I am!"

"Maybe you should have taken their advice," he said, a trace of hurt in his voice. "I don't think we're ready to publish a magazine. It's not coming together the way I envisioned."

"What?"

"I'm simply not interested anymore."

"In me, or the magazine?"

He crossed his arms more tightly and refused to answer.

"Don't do this, Edgar. Don't throw away our work because you're not in love with me. I will leave. Put the magazine together without me, but don't abandon it after we've invested so much time." My desperation and anger turned into loud, uncontrollable sobs. I was crumbling, unable to contain the wreckage, crushed by the man I'd admired more than anyone. And now I'd have to figure out how to salvage my career too? I couldn't bear the weight of it.

I wanted to forget the last night we were together, the way he'd clung to me as he slept. He was pushing me away with the same desperation I'd felt in his embrace. Everything I'd worked on and hoped for was fracturing. I looked around frantically for my things, wondering how fast I could gather my prints and supplies and walk out, but Edgar walked out first. He didn't say goodbye.

The questions churned in my stomach as I looked around the empty studio. How quickly the day had turned. I picked up the three prints Camille had praised and placed them in my satchel. The rest, I'd clean up later with Lydia if possible. Thank God for Lydia.

As I walked out to the street, an icy wind blew straight through me and I was glad for the jolt, to feel something other than betrayal. It continued to blow against me, holding me upright. How lonely, cold, and gray Paris could be. My eyes did not lift from the stone street, but my thoughts spun to find a stronghold, a way out, a strand of hope. I could catch a train to Seville, the place I'd lived and painted years ago, before Paris. I could return to the sunny studio in Spain. I could revisit the portraits of Murillo and reconnect with Madrazo. But no. My parents and Lydia were here now to support me, and I was still part of the exhibit scheduled a few months away. I couldn't walk away from that. If I doubled my efforts, I could come up with two or three new paintings. I could display my best prints. I wouldn't have as many paintings—damn him—but I'd make a showing. I'd support myself, as I always had before, in art. I'd paint furiously, cling to the work like he once clung to me. I tried to push away thoughts of him—the tenderness of his eyes lit by candlelight, the warmth of his hands on my skin. He was two men in one, infuriating to know and love—gentle and caring at best, a cold-hearted genius at worst. But he was a genius. I sobbed into my hands on the street.

No matter how he treated me, I could never deny his talent. He was the most brilliant among us. Naturally, I wanted to be in his presence, in his studio, in his bed. Had he come back only to pick up his palette? Was he mixing fresh paint? Washing brushes? Imagining him doing even mundane tasks pained me. I pushed away thoughts of him by noticing what was around me. A carriage. Breath of horses hanging in the air like smoke. Clap of hooves on cobblestones. A young girl's red hood and sleeves edged with black fur.

"Are you warm enough, Aimée?" asked her mother with love and concern.

I missed my mother. Only three blocks away, my gaze fell back to the ground. The wind dried my tears.

XXV.

Walking through the front door of the apartment, relief rushed over me like a wave. I wept again, unbuttoning my coat, no energy left to hide. But I wouldn't tell Mother and Father about Edgar, not everything, anyway. I could only confide in Lydia. Pulling a handkerchief from my satchel, I patted my face, a precaution that proved pointless.

In the library, my parents sat together at the small reading table, sharing morning newspapers and drinking tea. An orange fire leapt in the fireplace while they whispered to each other. Father's face lit up when Mother laughed suddenly at one of his comments. He reached for her hand, which he clasped momentarily before she read him a few lines from another story. Their intimacy soothed me, then elicited longing.

"Good morning, May," called Mother. I waved, tried to smile, and walked purposefully toward Lydia's room before they could ask questions.

Lydia looked up when I walked into her room and closed the door. Sitting in the chair by her window, she had the cat in her lap and a novel in her hands. She was surprised to see me, then alarmed as I strode toward her and fell to my knees, dropping my head in her lap. The cat's fur brushed my cheek before he jumped to the floor. I burst into tears again, grasping her skirt.

"May, what's wrong?" she asked more than once.

I was unable to speak. Lydia stroked my hair while I cried. When my breathing finally slowed, I told her bits and pieces of what had happened in the studio. I felt my sister's back straighten when I told her how Edgar had questioned the value of my work at the same time as our relationship.

"But I thought—"

"That he loved me?"

Lydia sighed. "Yes."

"I love him. I can't get him or his work out of my head. He seemed to feel the same about me."

"Did he tell you he loves you, May? How can he be so cruel?"

"He never did."

"But you believed he did. He gave you every sign. I saw it myself."

"I thought so." I wasn't sure anymore. Had I imagined it?

"Oh May." Lydia's fingers still combed through my hair. My tears soaked a wide circle in her skirt. Under my cheek rose the scent of wet wool.

"I don't care how brilliant he is. His words were careless and unkind. He sounds scared."

I looked up at Lydia. "Of me?"

"I suspect any woman who might ruffle his composure. You've knocked him off his feet, and for that, he's punishing you."

I sat up and squinted in the daylight. "Camille tried to warn me."

Lydia's concerned expression hardened. "Edgar might be a coward in love, May, but don't allow his shortcomings to make you doubt yourself as an artist. He fell in love with your talent as much as he did you."

I lowered my head into her lap and cried more, my body weak with emotion. Eventually I crawled into my sister's bed and pulled up the covers to block out daylight, falling asleep an hour before lunchtime. Lydia stayed with me. When I finally opened my eyes, the light in the room had turned golden. Lydia put down her knitting and asked if I was hungry. The thought of food made me want to sleep again. The only experience or nourishment my body craved was to be with him. Thinking of that morning brought a sharp pain to my chest. I couldn't inhale deeply enough.

Someone knocked on the bedroom door. I opened my eyes and Mother walked in.

"Lydia told us you weren't feeling well." She seemed irritated as she placed her hand on my forehead.

"I'm tired of sick daughters," she said. "Should I have your father summon Dr. Doucet?"

"No, Mother." I felt sorry to worry her, but not enough to tell her the truth.

She nodded, pushing back the hair from my eyes. Her voice grew soft. "Not like you, May, to take to bed midday."

Mother held a small brown package tied with red string. When my eyes fixed on the parcel, she laid the package on the pillow.

"I almost forgot. This came for you."

I picked up the package and saw the familiar handwriting.

"It doesn't have a return address," Mother said. "Should I open it for you?"

"I'll help her with it," said Lydia.

"Okay then. I'll have Mathilde prepare you a tray for dinner."

Mother left the room before I sat up to inspect the package. Lydia sat next to me.

"It's from him, isn't it?"

"Yes."

"Could he do anything that would take away the terrible things he said to you, May?"

"A begging apology?"

"I'd prefer to hear it in person." Lydia fluffed one of the pillows, beating it repeatedly while I untied the string and unwrapped the paper.

I lifted the lid of the small box and unfurled the white tissue paper. Inside was a key tied with another red string threaded through a corner of a tiny, folded note. My heart quickened as I read it.

I'm sorry. If I give you this key, will you care for it tenderly? - E.

I exhaled deeply. The immediate change in my mood surprised even me. I pushed aside the irrationality of relief hanging on Edgar's change of heart. I lifted the key and note from the box and held it out to Lydia. She looked at them both and gave them back.

"I don't understand, May. How can he be sensitive enough to send you something like this, and so frightful in the way he's treated you?"

"It took a lot for him to send me this." I traced my fingertip over the key.

How quickly I wanted to forgive him, to erase my hurt feelings with his gesture. This was how desperately I loved him.

"So that's it?"

"I don't know." My affection for him roared back as if nothing had happened. I thought again of Berthe's party, the fortuneteller's prediction, of rekindled hope my life might be large enough for art and love. The enormity of my desire for him, to have him as my lover and partner in life, overwhelmed me. Tears stung my eyes again.

"He's the only man who understands me." The conviction in my voice startled me, but Lydia's expression softened. She sighed, sat beside me on the bed, brushed away my tears, and reached for my hand.

"If he truly loves you, he'll put you before himself, May. Don't forget it. I've never seen you like this."

"I've never felt like this."

"Maybe you'll make a life with Edgar. Maybe not. But you'll always be an artist, May. Don't let him tell you otherwise. I'll never forgive him for that."

"Please, don't say anything—"

"I'd rather keep your secret than see Father disappointed." Lydia gathered her knitting and tossed the yarn and needles into the straw basket hanging over her arm. "I'll check on you after dinner."

Sunlight faded from the room. I reached over to Lydia's nightstand for matches to light the lamp. Inside the drawer was a stack of letters tied with a blue hair ribbon. Letters from Thomas. The pain in my chest returned. I lifted them from the drawer—eight, perhaps ten letters. How would it be to never hear from him again?

I replaced the letters carefully, closed the drawer, and lit the lamp. The lamp's flame threw a pool of light onto the nightstand and the top corner of her bed. The household sounds settled me, including the whispered *wha* of kerosene. Down the hall, beyond the closed door, came clangs of meal preparation in the kitchen, and further, in the library, Father's muffled voice. The tension in my neck relaxed and my head sunk deeper into the pillow.

I'd received Edgar's package. All was well.

That's what I told myself when thoughts of the magazine came back, months spent in a new medium that had yielded my most spare drawings. My art had been changing from the inside out. I'd taken risks with form like never before. The thought of abandoning the effort brought forth another wave of anxiety. How could he possibly walk away? His name alone assures the magazine's success in France and abroad. He couldn't disappoint Camille like that. Or Berthe. Or me.

I reached for the key and held it to my chest. All is well, I said to myself again. I wanted to think about something other than the last time I was in his arms. He fell asleep with his fingers curled in my hair, my back against his chest, which rose and fell against me. Sometimes, sweetly, he kissed the nape of my neck and pulled me closer as he slept, inhaling deeply. He liked my perfume, the way it mixed with the scent of my skin. Closing my eyes, I almost willed myself into his presence. If only I could spirit myself into his arms, curl up in his bed, and warm myself against him. I remembered how, last time we were together, the air had grown chilly as the fire burned low. Neither of us could bring ourselves to add another log, to poke the embers, to stoke the flames. We were drowsy with lovemaking, contented by our own warmth under the quilts.

I knew, of course, Edgar could not lie still for long. Soon enough, a lamp would be lit and carried to an easel. The fire would roar again. He did not sleep long stretches, not even at night. Charcoal, pastels, paints, and brushes were always at arm's length. He lived alone and did not need to keep his art separate from his living areas.

How could he possibly invite a wife or child into his space? His demand for productivity and perfection was so great he barely fit within his own life. Instead of this impossibility dissuading me from loving him, I loved him more. His dedication to art enthralled me. I knew, even then, I'd fallen for a man who would change art forever. Knowing this and being close to him felt intoxicating. My love for him was a kind of devotion. I wanted to be near, to watch him, to learn from him, to feel the assurance of his approval. The possibility he might someday cast me aside was too horrible to bear. Forgiveness was easy.

Would we be alone tomorrow?

"May, are you awake?" Lydia asked through the closed door. Dinner. I almost answered but wasn't ready to push aside my reverie. I pretended to sleep. Lydia didn't open the door. I heard her carry the tray back to the kitchen, my sister's footsteps falling faint in the hallway.

XXVI.

Sunday morning was not a time he'd expect me, and Edgar's studio was cold and dark when I arrived. I wanted to get back to work, to rescue the magazine, to fall into his arms. I brought breakfast for us—brioche, oranges, coffee. I cleared a space at the table and set down the basket of food.

I opened curtains and lit a lamp. I walked the length of one table, then another, looking at the prints scattered around. Camille's farm scenes. And my print—*Warming His Hands*—a profile of a man with his hands over a fire. I'd experimented with crosshatched marks over his body, hat, face, and hands. I teased Camille that the drawing paid homage to his haystacks, which were also crosshatched. When I'd finished printing from the plate, Edgar took my original etching and boasted he could turn it into a different painting, which he did. He turned it sideways and etched laundresses into the existing drawing. My etching of a man in profile faded into his composition. We experimented, learning from each other's discoveries. My time in his studio had been an education.

Had Edgar sent Camille an apology? It might be more than a week before we saw Camille again, if he believed there was any possibility we'd resume the magazine.

The tables around the press were dark and strewn with prints, plates, and rags stiff with dried ink. Edgar must have worked late. I couldn't make out his images in the dim light. Drawing a match, I lit the stove and shoved a few sticks of wood through the door, then the rags to ignite the fire faster. I tried to light lamps but, finding them empty, searched for kerosene. In a supply cupboard, I found a bottle. The iron stove began to creak and groan with heat I couldn't yet feel.

Shivering, I filled the lamps and turned them to their brightest hue. Pools of light fell onto the tables. As my eyes adjusted, prints of women appeared. Rooms full of nude women sitting open legged and taunting fully clothed men. Prostitutes. No lurid detail spared. I stared at the prints without feeling at first, shocked at their vulgarity, trying to piece together their meaning. I knew whose hand had carved them. I couldn't catch my breath. His renderings were characteristically realistic, and sadder in the shadowy medium. Almost cruel. His talent for capturing unguarded moments extended even to this. My corset felt tight. I wanted to tear the bodice of my dress, to free myself. I was staring into a brothel through the eyes of the man I loved. How many plates had he made? I counted ten. These women were not models. What else had he done? Gripping the table with both hands, I forced shallow breaths. While Camille and I worked daily to make prints worthy of the magazine, Edgar made prints no reputable gallery in Paris would touch. Had he slept with them? Had he exposed me to disease? The image of Manet limping away from Berthe's party came to me. And the thought of twenty thousand prostitutes in Paris. I sipped at the air until a flame surged in me, white hot, enervating my limbs.

I stormed out of the studio into his living quarters, past the sitting room cluttered with newspapers, down the hallway toward his bedroom. I could hear movement and continued until, gasping for breath, I stood before his bedroom door, his muffled voice on the other side. A woman's laughter. Out of my mind, as if standing inside the brothel he'd skillfully etched, I pulled on the latch, which gave easily under my hand. The door opened and hit the wall with a thud.

He stood behind a ballerina, his chest to her bare back, and in his hand was a paintbrush. Edgar and the dancer whipped around.

"Mary."

My stomach lurched.

How could this man have become so tantalizing to me? I could never admit to myself, let alone Lydia, how my desire to paint diminished when I fell into his arms. And I would be silent about this too, catching him seduce a model half his age.

I can't remember how long I stood there, my breath arrested, hand over my mouth. The dancer disappeared behind Edgar. She was too young, her hair still pulled tight from an early-morning rehearsal. Her leotard was only half on, and her pink satin shoes hung on the chair by his bed. His expression turned dark. I wiped away my tears with the edge of my sleeve, and saying nothing, turned to leave.

Edgar pulled on his shirt and followed me downstairs.

"Mary," he called authoritatively, like a parent might demand the attention of a child, no trace of guilt.

I said nothing and grabbing my coat and satchel, tried to escape. Edgar rounded the corner, entered the studio, squinting in the light, and hurried to stand in the way of the front door. His eyes fell upon his prints by the press.

"Mary."

"Don't repeat my name like you have something to say. You've destroyed every ounce of trust I had in you."

Slumped, Edgar shifted his weight.

"You couldn't disappoint me more." My voice caught as I dug through my satchel, feeling for my final goodbye. My fingers caught on the red-threaded key and I threw it to the floor. He blinked twice before looking up again.

"How dare you betray me! Did you think these prints would suit our magazine? When did you become a patron of brothels? Or an *abonné*? Or is she giving herself away for free?"

"I'm not your husband, Mary," he said calmly.

"You pompous bastard. I'd never marry you!" I moved to leave.

Edgar flinched, stepped aside, but kept his hand on the door.

"I will not risk my reputation by spending one more moment alone with you. You've undermined me professionally. You won't destroy me personally. Get out of my way."

Edgar removed his hand from the latch as I reached for it.

"Aren't you being dramatic, Mary?"

I turned toward him then, his face six inches from my own, and slapped him. I imagined my handprint on his cheek as I walked out. Across the street a young woman with a red umbrella walked past, her eyes averting my gaze. Could she feel my rage from twenty feet away? Not much older than the ballerina in his studio, I watched her disappear. A feeling of desperation overcame me. My chest tightened with each step.

I could only think about getting to my studio. I couldn't go home. Couldn't hide my heartbreak from my parents. Couldn't tell them Edgar had burned the magazine to the ground. They'd be furious to know how he'd wasted my time. He'd wasted their time, too. And the brothel. How did I make such a mistake?

"I hate him," I said aloud, but as I spoke, I tasted tears. Sadness impaled me.

In my studio, I lit a fire and fell into a chair by the stove. I couldn't recall when I'd last worked there. Dusty, empty, it had become a place to pick up or drop off supplies and finished prints. I'd move in again. I didn't have long before the next exhibit. I could fit in a few more paintings. I'd exhibit the prints

I'd completed too. Camille and I could display an arrangement of our prints together. Planning the rescue of my career distracted me momentarily from the shards of his betrayal.

How could he? I would never again know the comfort of his arms. If I pushed myself, I might produce a new painting every two weeks. Would he never again whisper my name? I opened the wooden box with my paints, taking inventory.

His etching of spread-legged prostitutes roared back—taunting me. Then the dancer's flushed face. Was she merely a model, or was he supporting her? What difference did it make? And the brothels. Did he not consider his own reputation? Or my health?

Lydia's worry had been justifiable. How fast my reputation might have gone up in flames. And I still desired his arms around me. I tried to forget about the key, his eyes, his voice. I wanted to hold onto the anger, but it slipped away into doubt. Had I imagined our love? It seemed more real than anything I'd known.

Art was all I had left, my sole refuge and purpose in life. I would replace thoughts of him with new compositions.

Had Camille known? If he had, he would have warned me more vociferously.

Unbidden, I thought of the Opéra, the Louvre, and the gift of his painted fan. From the beginning, I'd sought his company. I ached to be close to his immense talent. To learn from him. To be seen and loved by him. He made it easy. He presented himself as a gentleman. I believed him.

XXVII.

"Wake up, May."

I heard my sister but couldn't bear the light filtering through the curtains. It came earlier and earlier. The lengthening days felt cruel. I didn't stir. Lydia sighed and left.

She'd return. This is how it was then. Lydia would pull me to my feet and push me into the day. I hadn't heard a word from Edgar. Two months. I declined Berthe Morisot's invitations. I avoided being seen near the café and refused to attend the Opéra. When I left the apartment, Lydia accompanied me.

Mother and Father accepted my explanation. Edgar had walked away at the last minute from the magazine. He claimed he wasn't ready—*we* weren't ready. My parents were angry, knowing how much time I'd invested. What surprised me was their joy at having me home again and to see Lydia with me when I did walk outside.

The plans I'd made—to paint steadily until the next exhibit—withered. Admonishing myself and my lack of productivity had no effect at all. Whenever I touched a brush to a canvas, I lost interest. I could no more paint a still life than a decent portrait. Lydia offered to sit for me daily. She suggested locations and poses, but I couldn't.

When I woke, the wine-colored fabrics in my bedroom came rushing toward me. How heavy was the color! I longed to burn the textiles and replace them with no color at all. *Give me an all-white room so I don't have to bear this heaviness, so I won't mix the wretched colors in my mind anymore!* I wanted the world to dim itself. I wanted the outside to match my insides. Color was painful.

Lydia arrived again, this time with a tray of tea and toast. She didn't ask but poured me a cup. The milk splashed on the tea's surface after a clink of the tiny pitcher. Then, the ding of a small spoon. The scrape of a butter knife. The ring of the crystal marmalade jar, opening and closing.

"May, sit up."

I opened my eyes enough to show my sister I wasn't ignoring her.

"Have some tea."

I rolled to my side and followed my sister's instructions. Lydia gave me the pink floral Spode teacup and saucer from the set we'd purchased together in London. I sipped the tea and chewed the toast.

"Well?" she asked. "Aren't you going to say anything about the tea?"

I took another sip, trying to taste it this time.

"Rosebuds?"

Lydia smiled. She'd found our favorite English tea somehow in Paris—the Queen's blend of black tea with pink rosebuds.

"Thank you, Lydia." My eyes welled up. Lydia was the only reason I got out of bed in the mornings. Who roused her in the weeks following Thomas' death? I was too young, still in school.

"How did you do it?"

"I noticed a little English shop the other day while I was out buying bread."

"No, I mean, how did you recover from Thomas' death?"

Lydia placed her cup and saucer on the tray and her hands fell to her lap as she considered my question. She stood, opened the curtains to let in more light, and sat back down again.

"I haven't fully, May. I think about him still."

I remembered the months after Lydia had received the last letter from him. For a while, her hands flew with colorful yarn and all kinds of needles. She stitched an intricate tapestry of vines and flowers for her future home, pieced together an ivory wedding quilt she would spread on their marital bed. She knitted Thomas warm socks and sweaters to fill up his dresser drawers. When she completed a new project, Lydia folded it carefully and lay it in the large cedar trunk at the foot of her bed.

One day, her hands became still. She sat all afternoon in the parlor, waiting. Pennsylvania had lost many men. The Union had no routine way of reporting deaths. Sometimes a telegraph. The news would occasionally travel with a wounded soldier who returned home. Local pastors visited families with the news. Letters of condolence sometimes came by mail on horseback from the regiments.

Lydia continued to send letters to Thomas daily. Mother and Father worried about her. She hardly spoke. Before Thomas left, on the inside coat pocket of his uniform, my sister embroidered his name, our county, city, and state. She reminded us of this often when we heard about unknown soldiers who lay dead in the fields, unidentifiable to all but the families they'd left behind.

"But how did you go on, Lydia?"

"Minute by minute, at first. I didn't have a choice."

"It hurts to breathe."

Lydia picked up the teapot to refresh my cup. Then she lifted her own teacup, steam curling upward, and inhaled.

"You must decide, May."

"To breathe?"

She nodded. "You didn't come to France to meet Edgar. Your life is not dependent on his."

"But it intersects his. As long as I live in Paris, my life and work will overlap with his."

"And what if it does? Could you be grateful for the way he brought you into the collective without despairing over love he can't give you?"

"What can I do with these feelings, Lydia? Lock them away, go back to the way I was?"

"You could be grateful."

I wasn't that noble. But I knew I couldn't continue to live like this. The exhibit was a month away. I'd have to gather myself, hang the paintings I'd finished, the prints I'd worked on during winter. And I'd have to see him again. The thought of carrying on a conversation with Edgar and the others, as though nothing had happened, troubled me enough that I woke at night dreading it. Could I hold my expression steady? Would I have anything to say? What could he possibly say to me?

He hadn't sent a note. No apology. I couldn't bring myself to return to his studio to retrieve my things.

He'd talked with me at length while planning and organizing the last exhibit. I knew so little about the new one. Berthe sent word the apartment he'd chosen was not centrally located. She worried about its location, along with his delay in printing posters. If she wondered why I wasn't more involved, she didn't ask. She closed her letter simply. *I've missed you. B.*

I looked at Lydia over my teacup. My sister had pushed a chair next to my bed. She sipped her tea and placed it gently back on its saucer. Such grace. I saw my sister with fresh eyes. She had overcome worse—

I felt myself throw off the covers then. "Perhaps it's about time I paid Durand-Ruel a visit. I'd like him to sell more of my paintings."

Lydia exhaled. "I'll go with you." She took the tray and carried it to the door.

"I still don't know how you did it, Lydia."

"People do it every day, May. You're just catching up."

The morning warmed our cheeks as we climbed into the carriage. I closed my eyes while we made our way to the gallery over the narrow stone streets. When I opened them again, I saw the tight green buds on the trees. Crocuses would soon peek from the tops of window boxes. My sister would shop for plants for the balcony. Summer would arrive, along with Aleck and Lois and their children. I struggled inwardly to catch up with all that was happening on the outside. The horses slowed, approaching rue Laffitte.

I stood before the picture window, adjusting my hat in the reflection, feeling something, a hint of the old excitement visiting the gallery. How long had it been?

"Mlle. Cassatt!" Durand-Ruel called, breaking from his conversation with a customer. He stood at the far wall, gesturing to a painting by Monet—a winter sunset along the Seine titled *Soleil Couchant sur la Seine, Effet d'Hiver*.

"I'll be with you shortly."

Orange and blue hues. The feeling of winter sky and fading sunlight on water.

"It's stunning," said Lydia. It was. I felt the stir of something sweet staring at the painting. Yearning.

Nearly ten minutes passed before I pulled myself away to look elsewhere around the room. My eyes caught a few Japanese prints, and as usual, I admired their simplicity of line. Then I noticed Berthe's painting—*Jeune Femme à sa Toilette*. The back of a woman fixing her hair while gazing in a mirror. A black ribbon choker around her neck. I promised myself to write and congratulate her immediately.

Lydia saw the wall of dancers and motioned to me. Ballet dancers in bright costumes of blue, green, pink, and yellow covered the wall—floor to ceiling. One of the more subtle pictures, a seated dancer tying her slipper, drawn in charcoal, and accented with royal blue pastel, stopped me cold. I stared at it, stunned by its straightforward beauty—was this her? Edgar's talent washed over me as if I'd never seen his paintings before. I couldn't take my eyes off the drawing—that enigmatic perspective and composition. My admiration for his work had not waned.

"May," said Lydia softly. She gestured to another painting a few feet away. I stared at it before the image became clear. A woman sitting in a chair, leaning forward in a most undistinguished way, holding playing cards.

The woman in the portrait was me.

"You've seen your painting," said Durand-Ruel, walking over as we stood gaping in disbelief. "Edgar brought it in last month."

"*Bonjour*, M. Durand-Ruel," said Lydia quickly, "We didn't know about the portrait, so of course my sister and I are surprised to see it."

"*Oui*," I said, not bothering to mask my distaste. He'd portrayed me as a common fortuneteller. Nothing about the painting showed I was his peer, an artist, or a woman who would never carry herself in public so brashly.

"I think it's well executed."

"*Bien sûr*, technically —"

"I think what my sister is trying to say," interrupted Lydia, "Is it's a surprise. She didn't pose for it."

Nor agree to it. He'd painted it out of anger. I could feel a wave of retaliation rush toward me from the canvas. I looked at the wall of dancers, then back at the painting. He'd brought no grace at all to the portrait. He elongated my face, accentuated my angles. There was nothing soft about me in the painting at all, not to mention I'd been stripped of class. This looked nothing like his past paintings of me — at the milliner's, in the Louvre.

"*Mais*, to be Degas' subject —" Paul argued, hoping to flatter me.

I forced a smile, wishing to end the conversation and talk instead about my paintings.

"I wonder if you would be interested in some prints I made at M. Degas' studio last fall?"

"Your work sold well after last year's exhibit. Bring them, but I'm especially interested in paintings."

The front door of the gallery opened, sounding the bell and sending a gust of air against my neck. Lydia froze as Paul looked up to say *bonjour*, or *un moment*, when we heard his voice.

"Imagine my surprise."

We turned to see Edgar standing behind us in a charcoal suit and hat, the tip of his black umbrella planted firmly on the Turkish carpet.

"Mlle. Cassatt! Are you okay?" cried Durand-Ruel. I turned around again to see my sister teeter into his arms. Edgar lunged to Lydia's other side and together, they led her to a nearby chair. Durand-Ruel called for an assistant to bring water. I kneeled at Lydia's feet. Edgar stood awkwardly to the side, any smugness replaced with genuine concern.

"*Merci*," said Lydia, embarrassed. "I promise I'm fine now."

"Well, stay put," I said, handing her the glass of water. I stared at her, as if to say, *I'm okay.*

"I'll get you a carriage so you can take your sister home directly," said Edgar. His eyes were soft and sad.

"I'm fine now," she assured. "Really."

Edgar placed a hand on her shoulder before leaving the store. In a matter of minutes, he'd found our driver. Durand-Ruel held out his hand for Lydia to stand. She tried to convince him she was well.

"Please come again soon. Bring those prints, Mary."

Edgar looked at me, even sadder, as I waved and nodded.

He helped Lydia into the carriage, then offered his hand to me, which lingered after I'd climbed the steps and sat down. I pulled my hand away and looked at him squarely. His eyes brimmed with sadness and concern.

"Did Berthe let you know about the time and place for our next exhibit?" he asked.

"Yes. I will need to come by your studio to retrieve my prints. If my sister feels better tomorrow, I'd like to stop by in the morning."

"I'll make sure Sabine knows you're coming." He would not make it more difficult by being there.

"*Merci,*" I said as the carriage pulled away from the store.

We didn't speak for blocks. "Why did he have to stop by the gallery today?" Lydia eyed the buildings and storefronts as we passed. "And that miserable portrait!"

Hot, angry tears slid down my cheeks. "How could he portray me like that? He knows everyone will see the painting!"

Lydia, the beautiful subject of my paintings, reached for my hand. Her eyes were tender in the day's soft light. How would it be, to be the muse who inspires, instead of the artist? Would he have loved me more if I hadn't been an artist? If I hadn't been me? Banish the thought.

I'd been sad for too long. I thought if I'd turned events around enough in my mind, I might find another perspective, some facet I hadn't considered, a way to keep him, to mend the break. The time I'd spent in bed and Lydia's efforts to drag me back to life each morning couldn't continue. Before he appeared, I'd felt an inkling of the woman I once was. I grasped for that spark, the one I felt staring at new paintings in the gallery.

Riding home in the carriage, sitting next to my sister, I knew I would never love him the way I'd hoped. Even anger and sadness surrender eventually. I forced myself to breathe deeply and imagined releasing myself like a bird from a cage, door opening, wings flapping.

XXVIII.

"Is there a month more languid than June with its long days?" asked Lydia. We'd been at our summer home in Marly-le-Roi for two weeks. She, along with Mother and Father, were overjoyed to see Aleck, his wife, Lois, and their four children. I was getting to know my nieces and nephews. I'd lived in France when they were born. I asked my brother to tell me stories and news from home.

I tried to keep the promise I'd made to myself to be kind to Lois, whose puritanical, ill-informed opinions bored me. She would eventually inherit my father's property alongside Aleck. If only she were easier to like. Daughters—like Lydia and me— were naturally supposed to marry into other families' fortunes. Because we hadn't, I sometimes imagined how Lois might involve herself in my affairs. The prospect of her opining in our future finances incensed me. I had to make a living for myself, and if I could support Lydia too, I would. Lydia didn't seem to be bothered by the prospect of Lois' future influence on the family's purse strings. She did an excellent job of taking our sister-in-law under her wing, listening patiently, and uniting her with our seamstress in Paris.

Lydia posed in the garden for me, so I could paint again. "Is it difficult to crochet in your gloves?" I asked. She sat in a wood chair in three-quarter profile, eyes on her stitches, the yarn trailing onto her lap. She wore a new dress she'd had sewn in Paris before our trip, royal blue linen with colorful embroidery at the sleeves, shoulders, lapels, and skirt. A crimson silk sash fell from her waist in a bow. Her sleeves were edged in Normandy lace, and she tied her hat with a length of the same lace.

"I would peel them off instantly if you weren't painting me. Obviously, ladies who vacation in Marly must wear gloves in the afternoon sun. Aren't you painting in gloves, May?"

I dabbed sunlight onto the canvas and glanced at the dried paint on my hands. My white smock was smeared with color. I hardly thought about the way I looked. What did it matter? My sole focus, apart from being in the company of my family, was to paint. Edgar's portrait of me flew into my mind—no-frills, practical me.

I accentuated the purple-leaved hedge with touches of red, to draw the eye back to Lydia by way of her sash. I planned my work with more fervor than I had before Edgar crushed the magazine and my trust, before the last show where I exhibited only eight pictures, fewer than the year before and less prominently, too. The press took notice of course, calling my work and the show overall "darker," less interesting. Printing as a medium was by nature less colorful, relying on dark and light values to create images. The work was smaller too, not showy like large pastels or oil paintings. It didn't help I wasn't on hand to help choose a venue or contribute to the organization of the exhibit. I couldn't be in Edgar's presence more than necessary. It also didn't help Monet defected, along with Renoir, Sisley, and Cézanne. Our group continued to diverge stylistically. The press pounced on the defections, calling the Impressionist style a short-lived experiment that could never compete with artistic traditions. Edgar's preference for the name independents seemed more appropriate than ever—a declaration of autonomy rather than a categorization of our art.

I didn't care what we called ourselves. Edgar had given me the opportunity to show my work to a larger audience, and by wasting my time in the year that followed, he nearly dashed it. I was determined to win the press and public over again.

Lydia kept my secret. To our parents, my sadness could be explained easily enough as a professional conflict. Edgar might as well have betrayed my family, too.

Lydia yawned. I put down my brush. Clouds had changed the light.

"Why don't we resume this after tea?"

Lydia had accompanied me everywhere. I leaned on her strength. Life and art seemed possible again because of my sister. I took comfort in the dream of a shared future together.

"I'll tell Mathilde." Lydia stood and stretched.

I cleaned up and walked into the house to wash my hands. In the hallway, outside the library, I overheard Lois commenting on my work.

"I don't understand why Mary spent so much time on prints when the public loves her paintings."

My sister-in-law's opinions were as pompous as they were unconstructive. I'd come to the countryside to forget about winter, to shake off the feeling I'd wasted time in Edgar's studio. I'd come to mend my heart most of all. How dare Lois say anything? Mother folded her newspaper and set it aside, probably frustrated her daughter-in-law couldn't tolerate sitting in a room without talking.

"Mary," Mother answered finally, "knows an opportunity when she sees one. It wasn't her fault Degas wasn't ready. By allowing the magazine to fold, he has thrown away an excellent chance for all of them."

"Aleck told me she modeled for *his* paintings. Doesn't that make her seem less professional, even if her pictures hang next to his on the same wall?"

"I'm not in the business of telling Mary—"

"What to do?" I finished Mother's sentence from the doorway. Lois' normally pale complexion turned scarlet. "Yes, it's a good thing not to tell me what to do, Lois. I never listen." I spoke then to my mother. "Have you seen Lydia?"

"Mary. . . I . . ." Lois stammered, but before she could spit out an insincere apology, the hallway filled with sounds of her children who had finished their lessons.

Eddie, Katharine, and Rob ran screaming down the hallway while Elsie, the youngest, chased the older siblings with a stick. When she got close enough to swing, they ran screeching and taunting her more. Elsie didn't give up easily. She chased them still. Finally, Mother shooed them outside.

"Aunt May!" Elsie called before leaving, "Help me catch them!"

Since the children had arrived, I'd somehow become their favorite adult. And I sincerely hoped this perplexed their mother.

Outside, I grabbed the stick and chased the children, tapping each of them on the head. Elsie cheered from the garden.

"We win, Aunt May! We win!"

Smiling, I ran over to Elsie, picked her up and spun her around. "Want to paint with me later?"

She nodded, smiling. I didn't imagine how much having the children around would brighten my mood. Elsie threw her arms around my neck and hugged me before wriggling down to run to the others who had begun a new game. I'd almost forgotten about their dreadful mother.

After tea, Lydia and I sat with Aleck, who had come home from the stables. He was elated to learn two Arabians came with our summer property. Working as a bank president didn't allow him much time to ride. He spent many mornings at Marly in the stable helping the *entraîneur de chevaux* feed and care for the horses. It reminded him of his summer jobs as a teenager.

"One of you should ride with me tomorrow," he said. "There are places you should see."

Lydia agreed, if he promised not to ride faster than a trot. My equestrian skills did not match my brother's, but I agreed to ride if he'd sit for me.

"How long has it been since you've had a decent portrait?"

"Will I become famous like Lydia?"

My sister laughed and waved away his words with her knitting.

"You might. Will Lois mind?"

"I doubt she'll have an opinion," he said, taking a cookie from the tea tray. "She told me she'd like to spend more time in Paris. Mother and Father have offered her the apartment. She seems to be designing and buying our wardrobes for the next decade. Thanks for that, Lydia."

"Mme. Blanche is a very fine seamstress," said Lydia, smiling. Aleck had seemed stiff when he first arrived, but long days at Marly—the sun set at nearly ten o'clock in June—had softened him. Even he had time and space to recover and rest.

With so much daylight, I could paint *en plein air* in two different gardens, enjoy long meals with family, take winding walks through the countryside, play with my nieces and nephews, and still have a little daylight leftover. I filled the time with as much art as I could. A sense of possibility bubbled in me once more. I knew Edgar and I would never again be lovers, but I missed his talent. I missed our creative work together and tried to push away all that had been lost.

"It seems someone has found you here after all, May."

Father walked into the parlor and handed me a letter. Aleck looked up from the newspaper and Lydia from her knitting.

Someone had written my name in the middle of a tiny village sketched on the cover of the envelope. I'd know his artwork anywhere.

> *Ma chère Mary,*
>
> *I'll be traveling from Paris to Pontoise on Friday, but thought I'd detour through Marly to meet more of the Cassatts if the invitation still stands?*
>
> *Bien des choses à tous,*
> *Camille Pissarro*

"Well?" asked Father. "Which one of them has written?"

Lydia sat still. Aleck went back to reading his paper. I knew what Father was asking. Would we again be entertaining Edgar? Had his daughter's anger cooled enough to allow the man back into our lives? If he knew the entire story, he'd never allow Edgar or his artwork into our home again.

"Looks like Camille has accepted the invitation we extended last winter, Lydia. He's traveling home from Paris on Friday and would like to stop through Marly."

"I'll plan a lovely meal," Lydia said, relieved.

"I'll tell him in my letter."

"Should I take him riding?" Aleck asked.

"I'm not sure he could keep up with you. He's closer to Father's age. Plus, he lives in the country. Horses don't hold the same novelty for him as they do for you."

"I'll enjoy the company of another ancient equestrian," Father said, irritated, before leaving the room.

Lydia stood up and walked after him, frowning. Ever the peacekeeper.

"So," said Aleck, "One of your famous friends is coming to Marly. Lois will be sad to miss him. She leaves for Paris on Thursday."

"Camille is as humble as they come. I'm not sure he'd make much of an impression on her, anyway. His paintings, on the other hand—"

"Blessing in disguise. I can't afford to have my wife collecting art, too."

"If you decide otherwise, Aleck, now is the time to buy. I could advise you, of course." I'd given a lot of thought to collecting and traded my own paintings for the work of other Impressionists.

"May," Aleck said, laughing, "You could be a banker."

XXIX.

I didn't know how happy I'd be to see Camille arrive, driving a team of horses, towing a cart of goods he'd purchased in Paris. From under his straw hat, his hair stuck up in every direction. The children, who had been playing badminton, threw down their rackets and ran to greet him. He smiled at the attention, pulling on his beard, patting their heads as he stepped down.

"I'm glad to see you're keeping active, Aunt Mary," he said in English, nodding at the racket in my hand as we greeted, kissing cheeks.

"Welcome, Camille. Children, this is M. Pissarro."

"*Bonjour*," they said in unison. Each child shook his hand as I introduced them by name. Camille delighted in their curious and careful demeanors. Lois had instilled in them good manners, one quality I genuinely admired.

Aleck, Father, Mother, and Lydia walked out of the house to welcome Camille.

"I'll tell our stable hand to make sure your horses are watered and fed," said Aleck in French, shaking Camille's hand. "My wife Lois asks you to pardon her absence. She left for the city yesterday."

"Ah, well. My loss, but *mon plaisir* to meet you. I can't tell you how much Mary has strengthened our little group."

Aleck beamed. To have him in France, to have him meet Camille and show him I'd finally made something of art, meant a lot to me.

Lydia extended her hand. "Welcome." Camille held it and smiled.

"How I have missed the Cassatt sisters!"

Father clasped Camille's shoulder while Mother asked about his trip. Walking into the house, Camille handed mother a small package wrapped in brown paper—fine-milled, gardenia-scented soaps. He'd heard her comment once at a dinner party about her love of gardenias. For Father, he pulled a small package of tobacco from his suit pocket.

"Let's share this after our meal tonight," said Father. He stepped livelier.

"I have something for you too, Mary," Camille said, turning to find me. "Once we get settled, I'll retrieve it for you."

How I'd missed him! I couldn't wait to ask his opinion on my paintings, hear the latest news, and learn what he'd been working on that summer. I wondered what he'd have to say about Edgar. We hadn't spoken privately since working together last winter.

Camille pulled paper-wrapped sweets from his pockets and dropped them into the children's hands. My nieces and nephews jumped up and down and ran off to count and trade their candies.

In the house, the scent of fresh bread filled the living room. A conversation among friends began, peppered with questions about Camille's wife and family, his home in Pontoise. What I loved about Camille, what most people loved about him, was his *joie de vivre*. One could not help but feel better in his presence. He lifted the atmosphere of every room he entered.

"What is the news in our city?" asked Lydia, who preferred novels to reading the newspaper.

"A Romeo and Juliet occurrence has the gossip pages in a tizzy," said Camille.

"Oh, tell us more."

"A young shopman of the rue St. Denis found his parents would not permit marriage to his young dressmaker amour. Unable to imagine a life without the other, the shopman and the dressmaker asphyxiated themselves in her apartment on the rue Trudaine."

"*Quelle horreur!*" Lydia's fingertips flew to her neck.

"*Absolument.* Sometimes young men and women cannot see one minute past beyond their vanquished hearts."

"How could death be a more acceptable alternative?" asked Father, shaking his head. "They've punished their poor parents."

"Indeed! By intention, of course."

"Why not run away?" I asked.

"And abandon their home?" asked Lydia.

"But to throw it all away so easily, as though nothing more would come of their lives," said Mother.

"It takes many years before that sort of wisdom may seep through the cracks of a broken heart," offered Camille quietly. "I would guess their heartbreak felt lethal."

The room grew silent. Yes, I knew the feeling. Lydia stood and excused herself to check on preparations in the kitchen. Surely, a part of her had died with Thomas. Mother sighed and, as was her way, began fidgeting in a room marked by too much emotion. She slapped her knees to move audibly beyond the subject of suicidal lovers.

"Aleck," she announced, "Perhaps our guest would like to see the Arabians? Why don't you take him to the stables?"

Aleck, who had remained silent, jumped at the chance to share the horses with someone who might appreciate them.

"If you'd be interested, M. Pissarro—"

"Camille," he corrected. "Lead the way."

When Edgar abandoned the magazine, when he betrayed me, art returned as the ground beneath me. Without it, would I recover? Without it, would I have met him? Had art saved me?

I wondered about these things in the garden, cutting an arrangement of roses and lilacs for dinner. The deep purple blossoms fell onto my hands, leaving their perfume on my skin. I placed them in the burnished silver vase, cascading over and under white and butter-colored roses. The slight yellow hue complemented the purple blossoms and green leaves. Satisfied with the bouquet, I carried the arrangement into the dining room, set it on the table, and wandered back into the garden to stand in the usual place of my easel.

I imagined Lydia in her chair, the beautiful dress, and light reflecting from her hair. Maybe it was the newspaper story, but standing there, watching the sun move over everything, I cried. Love and grief. Life and death. Sunlight and shadow. One cannot exist without the other. My paintings, like life, were a study in contrast. Nothing would be recognizable without the appearance of its opposite. So now, a thirty-six-year-old woman, I could finally recognize love by its absence.

"Eying your next picture, my friend?" Camille walked up from behind me. I dabbed my eyes with the bottom of my sleeve, pretending to push the hair out of my eyes.

"Yes, it's underway. Another portrait of Lydia in profile. Sitting there, in a chair angled against the hedge."

He stood next to me for a few minutes silently. "The light is lovely. After seeing the Arabians and some of the property, I understand why your father chose this summer escape."

"I like it too, Camille. I'm glad to be out of the city."

"I worried about you when Edgar discarded the magazine."

"And months of work."

"He does this, Mary."

"Disappoint people? Break promises? Put careers at risk?" My anger surged again.

"He runs from love."

My breath caught in my throat. Camille turned toward me and held my hand. Tenderly, he watched my tears spill.

"It's not your fault," he said.

"If I hadn't—"

"He would've found another way to sabotage the magazine. It's not your fault, Mary."

Camille had tried to warn me. Lydia doubted him. Father never trusted him.

"If I'd only listened, maybe we'd have a magazine now. Maybe I'd still be working in his studio. Why wasn't that enough for me?"

"Trust me about this. He's not capable of loving you the way you love him."

"But why—" I stammered. "He pursued me."

"He's incapable of genuine love, Mary. He has trouble finishing things he starts. Have you noticed?"

"But he's brilliant."

"As an artist," he said, shrugging his shoulders.

Was I merely another painting? A subject who captured his fleeting attention?

"I found him with a dancer." I choked on the words. Camille didn't flinch. He gazed at me softly.

"Aren't you mad?" I sputtered. "He wasted your time, too. All those beautiful etchings."

"*Bien sûr*, but I'm angrier at him for mistreating you."

His words sat with me a moment before I threw my arms around him and sobbed. For his care. For Edgar's failings. Camille touched my back and spoke to me consolingly.

"You'll come through this, Mary. Whatever's happened, you have work to do. We need your talent. Edgar knows this. Use the summer to paint, my friend. I expect to see the walls of our next exhibit lined—floor to ceiling—with your fine portraits."

The press had been so cruel about the work I'd hung the previous spring. I cringed thinking of the reviews.

"Start fresh," he said.

"Have you forgiven him?" I asked.

"He hasn't asked for it. I read a speech one of your countrymen gave this spring. The author Mark Twain said, 'Forgiveness is the fragrance that the violet sheds on the heel that has crushed it.'"

"*Alors,*" I said. We stood together quietly, thinking about Twain's words. "Edgar is a heel." A slight smile formed on my lips.

"*Oui,*" agreed Camille, "I'd rather be the violet."

"Dinner is nearly ready, you two," called Mother from the doorway. I took Camille's arm, inhaled deeply, and walked with him into the house. Anna met us in the parlor with a tray of silver flutes, bubbling with champagne and fresh raspberries.

"*Magnifique,*" said Camille, plucking a flute from the tray after I had taken my own.

"To our new friend," toasted Aleck when everyone had assembled. Camille smiled and raised his glass shyly, thanking him.

Before he left in the evening, Camille pulled a few packages for me from his cart. The first, a heavy package wrapped in canvas and rope, contained fresh copper plates.

"I thought you might need a diversion from your oils and pastels. Make use of the skills you learned last winter, Mary."

I hadn't planned to make any prints that summer. I accepted them graciously, but knew I would not return to etching for some time. Then Camille handed me another, smaller package. A framed picture. I tore the brown paper and inside, found Camille's print of a woman raking hay.

"I've always loved this one," I said, holding it before us, admiring his skill. "I'll hang it in our parlor in Paris. *Merci.* For everything."

Camille nodded and kissed both of my cheeks.

The children came outside to say goodbye, little Elsie holding three red tulips in her hand. Camille made a big show of appreciation when she gave them to him, kissing her on top of the head and tucking them into the front of his coat. The blossoms bounced and curled out of his brown suit as he climbed back into his box seat—a splash of red under his chin. He waved as he drove off, his horses kicking up a trail of dust. We watched him drive away until the road curved and he was out of sight.

XXX.

Love renders everything else pale by comparison. What is there to do? For me, paint. But I wondered where I found my motivation before knowing him. The light had seemed to leave the world with his exit. I could only see my life in two chapters—before Edgar and after. Before knowing him, I was one person. After knowing him, I became another, a woman whose eyes were finally open, who painted light and colors that radiated from the canvas. When he left, he took my brightest colors with him. Some mornings, even in beautiful Marly, I woke sad and disbelieving he was gone. I wanted him to glance over my shoulder while I worked. To comment on the light, the line, or what he would do differently.

What would bring me relief from this desire? When I stopped pining for a moment, I'd hear a bird singing. Or catch a prism of light from the window. I'd think of a kindness to do for Father, to walk into town and buy him a newspaper, or to bring Mother some chocolates. Sometimes the feeling of my feet on the floor would bring me back.

One morning, before everyone was awake, I heard little Elsie's voice and walked barefoot through the house in my robe to find her. Maybe she'd had a bad dream, or woke up earlier than the rest, ready to play. I caught sight of her in the library, in her mother's arms. Lois quietly read her a book to avoid waking the other children. Elsie leaned back, utterly content, head against her mother's chest. I imagined her wispy hair under my chin, her soft body resting against mine. The work of motherhood, however tiring, seemed to turn sweet in a minute. I ached watching them, and it was not unlike the ache I felt missing Edgar. Nothing surprised me anymore.

I continued to paint what was around me—Lydia, as usual. I leaned into my sister's companionship. Sometimes, late at night, we'd imagine our future together—the dinners we'd host, the guests we'd entertain, the parties we'd attend. We planned to live our lives in France, to care for our parents and travel together as old women.

But thoughts of him were resilient. Even with my brother and his family to entertain and enjoy, some part of me felt out of place. The closest I came to finding myself again was in my work.

Autumn arrived faster than any of us preferred. Marly was too quiet after seeing Lois, Aleck, and the children off to the train station, the first leg of their trip back home. Hosting them for the summer gave us all a boost. After hearing how much Aleck had enjoyed France, my youngest brother, Gard, wrote to say he would visit the following summer. This was cheerful news, but we missed the children terribly. The quiet within that big country house depressed us. A year sounded like an eternity. With one week left until our return to Paris, I put the finishing touches on my two last paintings.

"I've felt so well here," Lydia said, sitting for me.

"How have your headaches been?"

"Mostly gone. Dr. Doucet may have been right about cutting back on cheese and milk. I feel better without them, though I miss brie dearly." Lydia shifted and stared at the garden, which had withered from frosty nights. The gardener had cut it back. I waited until she resumed her pose.

"Fifteen more minutes, May?" she asked. "I want to read the paper and have a cup of tea. Warm my hands."

I nodded, trying to paint quickly. Edgar once asked when I knew my paintings were finished. When I couldn't answer him, he quoted Leonardo da Vinci. "Art is never finished, only abandoned."

I realized then that a feeling comes to me when I'm done. I don't see perfection, just diminishing results. When I could no longer improve a painting, when I simply moved elements around instead of enhancing them, I knew. Certainly, I'd see something amiss in a few weeks or months. Sometimes years. But then my instincts as an artist were changing. I was not the same person I was five years ago, nor the same person I'd be five years in the future. And perfection isn't found in nature either. I wasn't afraid of declaring something finished. Like a seamstress who tires of the same fabric, I finally cannot wait to move on. Edgar could've sold a lot more work if he'd abandoned it like the rest of us, but I knew the other side of his madness was also his genius.

I declared *Lydia Crocheting in the Garden at Marly* finished. No one was happier than Lydia. She hurried over to see it on the easel. I wanted her to be pleased with it. She turned and smiled.

"Does this make your seventh new painting since we've been at Marly?"

"Eighth."

Even with the busyness, perhaps because of the busyness, I'd worked productively all summer. And I had many sketches of my nieces and nephews to develop into new paintings. I'd also completed the portrait of Mother reading to the children—one of my favorites. Mother had already begun imploring me not to sell it. This was the challenge of painting family members. Except for Lydia, how quickly they—especially

Mother—accused me of being opportunistic when I talked of exhibiting their portraits.

"Your work is better than ever," said Lydia. "M. Durand-Ruel will think so too." My productivity pleased Lydia. Though my enthusiasm was not what it was a year ago, I was glad for the discipline I'd summoned at Marly. The next exhibition had been on my mind, but also the need to earn money. Soon I would select which pieces to show and which to sell. The fees for my studio would come due again soon. I hated asking Father for a loan the last time I needed to cover rent. Edgar was to blame then, but I was done painting copies for tourists. I'd accept commissions for portraits, if need be, but that was it.

More leaves fell from the trees every day. The forest grew thinner, and I walked through it daily, the ground slick with yellow, red, and orange leaves. I had only a couple days left, packing to do, paintings to wrap in paper for protection on the carriage ride to Paris. I hadn't stepped foot in the city since June. October felt like a different country with its chilly mornings and shorter days, and I felt myself at a threshold.

Our time away had allowed me to recover my heart well enough. I wondered what would await me at home.

"I'm sure you're ready to get back to your studio and friends, May," said Father, as if reading my mind.

I stood at the table in the library, tying twine around a wrapped set of canvases. He watched as I double knotted and snipped the string with scissors.

"I'm ready to get back because Marly was so good for us." I picked up two more canvases to wrap.

"I think your mother would like to have the children year-round."

"Philadelphia must seem appealing again after having her grandchildren here."

"We hardly saw Lois, Paris so enchanted her. I do not know how they'll make it across the ocean with the furniture and clothing she purchased."

"If her love of Paris brings Aleck and the children back regularly, I'm happy. Her nosiness bothers me less now I know my nieces and nephews."

Father shook his head, but even he had a difficult time warming up to her when she and Aleck first married.

"I can always count on your honesty, May. She's an exemplary mother."

I finished wrapping my canvases and stacked them against the wall for packing before Anna called us to dinner. Pumpkin soup steamed in deep bowls on the dining table. Lydia had lit candles for the meal. Flickering light reflected from the wine goblets. She passed a heavy sliced bread around the table made from rye flour and pumpkin seeds—an American recipe. Still hot from the oven, butter slid across the bread easily.

"Thank you, Lydia, for planning a meal to quench our homesickness," said Mother.

Lydia looked satisfied.

I recalled that dinner often after we returned to Paris. Everyone was well then. By Christmas, Lydia's headaches and fevers had returned. Some days, she was fine and would sit hours for me. Other days, she took to her bed. Dr. Doucet continued to worry about her kidneys. He prescribed oil of poppy for extreme pain but offered no other treatment, other than altering her diet and making sure she got sufficient rest. When her headaches returned, Lydia retired to her room and drew the draperies. Mother and Father worried but I knew she would recover. I refused to believe there was no cure for her illness and told her so.

"You are in charge of your life, Lydia, not Dr. Doucet."

"May, I'm doing my best."

"You'll get well again. Remember how fine you felt at Marly?"

Determined to see her healthy, I watched for the color to come back into her cheeks. To make sure she felt a sense of purpose, I'd ask her to sit for another portrait. I'd invite her to go shopping for dresses, to take city walks. I'd ask her to accompany me to the Louvre. To attend the theater with me. My resolve seemed to keep Lydia out of bed.

By the end of November, I had enough work to select a handful of paintings to offer Durand-Ruel. I arrived at his gallery before he officially opened. He appeared, unlocked the glass doors, and invited me inside. His assistant brought two large cups of *café au lait*, still steaming, and placed them on a small table. Durand-Ruel placed my portfolio on his desk, then hurried to pull out my chair. Dressed in a black suit and bowtie, he was old-fashioned in his formality, but I appreciated his deportment. Mindful of his clientele, and respectful of his artists, he was a better fine art collector than anyone. After the coffee and small talk, Paul opened my portfolio and propped five of my new pictures against his bookshelves.

More than a year had passed since he'd sold any of my paintings. I didn't want to appear too desperate for his opinion. He appraised them silently.

"They're superb, Mary."

No matter how many years I'd painted, I always felt nervous waiting on the opinion of my peers. I held Durand Ruel's opinion in high regard.

"I'll take them all," he said, turning to me, smiling.

"They're yours. I'm happy to have more work in your gallery again. I wonder if the prints I left you with last spring have sold?"

"Only one, I'm afraid. Buyers don't seem to want your prints as much as they do your paintings. People fell in love with your pastels and oils at your first Impressionist exhibit. These will sell quickly."

I cursed Edgar again under my breath. "I wasted so much time on the magazine."

"It was a commendable project, Mary. We could have distributed the magazine to patrons in London. Your disappointment is justified. A high-quality publication would have done a lot for print sales—not only yours."

Durand-Ruel knew a magazine could educate art collectors and increase public interest in printmaking. I might have tried to revitalize the magazine with everyone but Edgar, but I worried about circulation. My work was somewhat unknown beyond Paris. Edgar had more influence.

"I'm sorry we won't be finishing it, Paul. I wasn't happy to walk away from that kind of opportunity."

"Let's sell your paintings, Mary. Your oils should fetch a good price."

He accepted Edgar's madness because he was a patient man whose passion for collecting art enabled him to endure all kinds of temperaments. I got along well with him because I was as interested in selling my art as I was making it.

Durand-Ruel had exquisite taste as a collector. He knew what people in London and Paris were buying. He also took great financial risk to support artists because he trusted his instincts, buying pieces he admired. His father had imparted a sense of responsibility in his son—to champion and collect worthy paintings that would not otherwise be seen. The Impressionists owed an enormous debt to Durand-Ruel. He was our exclusive dealer for many years, the only person who would dare to exhibit and support artists refused by the Salon. He talked to me often about his dream of selling Impressionist paintings throughout Europe, and eventually, America.

I left my paintings with him and pocketed the small check he'd written from the sale of my print. Looking forward to more sales, I walked to my studio. I missed making prints, especially the mystery of what a picture would look like before peeling paper from the plate. I'd tucked away the copper plates Camille had given me in a supply cupboard because I didn't have the tools to continue as I had in Edgar's studio, but I'd return to it eventually.

As for Edgar, I hadn't seen him. I didn't notice any new paintings from him in Durand-Ruel's gallery and was glad to see the awful portrait of me removed from the wall. I'd have to socialize with the group again sometime.

I opened my easel and looked through my satchel for sketches. A knock at the door pulled me from my thoughts. Lydia stood outside with a basket over her arm of flowers and fresh croissants. She looked well.

"I thought you could use a break," she said, stepping in and hanging her coat. She walked toward the little kitchen, put the flowers in water, and filled the teakettle. I told her the news immediately. She clasped her hands together and smiled.

"But my prints haven't sold well." I showed her the small check. Lydia waved aside my complaints.

"Do you truly feel you wasted your time, May?"

"I don't understand."

"Did working all of those months with Edgar, Berthe, and Camille fail to yield anything?"

"I'm hardly better off financially than I was before my first exhibit with them. After the poor reviews from the last exhibit, I see little progress."

Lydia passed me a croissant and a teacup. She sat thoughtfully while I nibbled on the buttery pastry.

"I know you long to support yourself, May, but if you tie your worth to the price of your paintings, your contentment will come and go like the weather."

"I only want what Aleck and Gard have—a profession that rewards them for their time and talent. For twenty years, I've paid my dues."

"You have, it's true. But not everyone can be a famous painter. Many people can run businesses or banks. Your talent sets you apart and Paris has embraced you! The money will come. Maybe the last year was an investment in your future, and anyway, you weren't working with Edgar to sell paintings."

I cringed. She was right. I hardly thought about money when I was with him. The work had not come first. His love came first. My work paled compared to being with him. I sighed and twirled a loose strand of hair around my finger, trying to understand it. How would I account for our time together? I didn't feel the same excitement I once had.

"Money's a cheap replacement for love," said Lydia.

"Is that what I'm doing?"

"What was it like working with him?"

"I would have given him anything. Watching him work made me want to put his art before mine."

"Now you know what it's like for Mother, Father, and me."

Her statement shocked me. I stared at her, feeling the depth of her devotion.

"Now, before you accuse me of being sentimental, let me temper it. Love makes you give yourself willingly. We're here by choice."

"Oh, Lydia." My career worries felt petty and selfish. I'd spent my whole life chasing art—education, the best tutors, exhibiting at the Salon, working with the Impressionists. Now I'd become focused on earning more money when what I truly wanted was to give myself away. That my sister named it so easily astounded me. I'd learned a lot working with Edgar, but I would have given that up for him too.

"All of this time, I've lived only for myself."

"I know," she said, putting down her teacup on the small table beside her. She didn't lighten our conversation or tell me I might find love again.

I gathered the dishes into the sink and washed them. When I finished drying and putting them away, I noticed Lydia had fallen asleep in her chair. The light had turned rosy with the setting sun. Strands of my sister's hair glowed pink against the dark fabric of the chair. I threw another log in the woodstove, fastened the latch, and pulled over a chair to sit next to her.

The warmth from the stove and light streaming from the windows comforted me. Lydia was well enough.

XXXI.

Melting snow dripped from the roof of my studio like a metronome that changed pace as the sun grew warmer. As the dripping increased, my brush quickened on the canvas. I'd been at the easel since early light, working from studies of the children I'd made during the summer. How I missed their laughter and noise. Holidays were lonely without them. I would have boarded a ship home to Pennsylvania that afternoon if someone had handed me a ticket. I stood back from the painting to observe it from across the room when I heard a knock.

Lydia, perhaps. Or Father stopping by to say hello after a morning in the club. I set the brush down and wiped my hands. Winter air seeped under the wood door. I braced myself for the cold.

In his hat and long black winter coat, Edgar stood outside holding a large package wrapped in cherry paper tied with a gold silk ribbon. Neither of us said a word at first. He stammered, "*Bonjour.*"

I opened the door a little wider to invite him inside. Speechless, I stood waiting for him to say why he'd come. His eyes moved to my painting, then back again.

"This is for your family," he said, handing me the package.

"*Merci.*" I put it on a nearby table.

"I saw your new paintings in Durand-Ruel's gallery."

"*Oui?*"

"My visit is overdue. I've come to extend an olive branch. I know I made a mess of things." He waited for a response. "The portraits you've painted of your family are some of your best, Mary. Our group needs your talent more than ever. There's so much infighting lately."

He didn't apologize about the dancer. Said nothing about the brothel or discontinuing the magazine. I stared at him again, not knowing what to say.

"You. . . mean a great deal to me, Mary."

"I've seen little evidence of that."

"I will never marry. Surely you knew."

"Don't blame me for your behavior. I never demanded you marry me. But this is old news. Why are you here?"

"To extend my friendship again. To honor you as my colleague and to ask you join us again socially. Everyone has missed you. They blame me, *bien sûr.*"

I weighed his words. I saw his sadness. His longing. His complexity — brilliant and human. "I exhibited last spring. I haven't left the group."

"Thank you. We couldn't survive without you. With Renoir and Monet saying they won't exhibit again with us — "

"The power of the group has diminished," I said, finishing his sentence. Here was the ease, the opening. The opportunity to fall back again danced between us.

"I don't understand why we must all paint in one style. I have never claimed one way over another, nor do I intend to start now. We disagree on why we formed. We announced our independence from the Salon. It isn't my fault a journalist renamed our group to symbolize a narrow view of what our paintings should look like," he said.

He was right about the limitations of style if we all stood under the Impressionist umbrella. Where would the group be tomorrow if anyone employed a drastically different way of painting? If we defined ourselves too narrowly, it was a matter of time before the group disbanded. Some artists could explore one style for a lifetime. Edgar could never be that dogmatic. Monet, on the other hand—

"The name doesn't bother me. It brings us a large audience that doesn't mind our diverse paintings under one label," I said automatically.

"We'll lose artists if we can't come to an agreement about who we are." He seemed pleased he'd drawn me into the discussion.

"It's a silly argument when all of us stand to make less money as people defect."

"Perhaps you could slip in to Café de la Novelle Athenès unnoticed one morning and join in the discussion."

"I'm sure you'll pass along my opinion."

It occurred to me then how rude it seemed not to ask him to stay, but doing so required more goodwill than I had. As if reading my mind, he rubbed his gloved hands together and bid me a *Joyeux Noël*.

"Please say hello to your sister and parents for me."

I closed the door behind him. Like that, Edgar Degas reentered my life. No longer my lover. Not much of a friend. A colleague, he'd said.

I went back to my easel and picked up a brush, glad he'd mentioned my paintings at Durand-Ruel's gallery. Would I ever get over my desire for his approval? I wanted it and felt irritated his opinions still mattered. But I'd survived his visit. I didn't crumble when I saw him, or cower when he made excuses for his behavior. I spoke the truth.

Maybe we were never meant to be lovers. I would never regret a minute with him, I knew, but had the man I loved even existed? Not in the way I imagined. I saw him as I'd wanted to see him. I'd rendered him in my heart like a painting, a man composed of impressions. Is it possible to truly know another without expectation? My attraction to Edgar happened before I'd even met him. How could he meet the ideals I'd placed on him before he stepped foot in my studio?

"Are you excusing him?" Lydia asked when I said as much that evening. "He betrayed you, May, personally and professionally."

"Yes, but what is it about love that makes us less forgiving of a person's faults?"

"You've forgiven him?"

"I've worked with other artists whose exploits were hardly different. I've apprenticed with them and learned from them."

"You weren't his apprentice—"

"Yes, but why shouldn't the same hold true for Edgar now? I am not his wife. I am free."

Lydia looked baffled by my turn of perspective. She rubbed her temples with her fingertips and closed her eyes.

"What is the alternative? Cutting him out of my life? I can't do that." I waited for my sister to answer. "Does your head hurt again?"

Lydia ignored the question, dropped her hands into her lap, and opened her eyes.

"You were heartbroken, May."

"I wanted more than he could give me. I'm not excusing his behavior. Why should I lug around a heavy satchel of sadness when I could make more room for paintings?" I smiled at my sister, feeling lighter.

"You're finished with him, then?"

"I hope so. I'm not finished with his artwork. I'm thinking about collecting a few of his pictures. They'll be worth more in a few years, and if I'm serious about supporting myself—"

"Oh, May." She hated talking about money.

I laughed. "I have you, Lydia. We have Mother and Father with us. Gard's coming this summer. Aleck wants to bring Lois and the children back soon. I'm surrounded by family. How many artists can claim such fortune?"

"I can count one," she said, standing up and walking over to the package I'd placed on the hallway table. She pointed to it and looked at me.

"Edgar."

"He likes to give gifts." Lydia ran her fingers over the smooth paper and soft ribbon. He'd tied a small twig of pine at the top of the package. She pulled on the ribbon, tore at the paper, and opened the box.

Inside were three bottles of spiced *gluhwein*, a German wine steeped during the winter holidays with orange rinds, cloves, and cinnamon sticks. The scent reminded us of Christmas markets in Heidelberg, when Robbie was still alive. Lydia, Aleck, Robbie, and I would walk from one market tent to another. There were wooden toys—knights with swords, castles, boats, trains, and puzzles. Colorful glass ornaments sparkled from baskets. "Smokers" of various designs—houses with chimneys, St. Nicolases, and elves with pipes—contained incense emitting tiny puffs of smoke. And the food—waffles with warm cherries and whipped cream. Potato pancakes with applesauce. Roasted chestnuts served in paper cones that warmed our hands. Bratwürste. Fat pretzels, salted and sweet.

Edgar had listened to our stories, how the Cassatts loved the holidays in Germany. His gift was thoughtful. Mother said so when she looked in the box and saw the bottles.

"Do you think it's time we invited him to dinner, May?" she asked.

I shrugged. Mother took my nonchalance as a yes.

With that, the family welcomed Edgar back into our home. I turned the page on my love affair like a chapter from a Zola novel. I did not know if Edgar had merely dabbled in disreputable curiosities, but I refused to riddle those questions any longer. His manners and outward decorum hid a secret life. Whoever he was, whatever his choices, his commitment to art superseded everything else. I knew this about him. That's how I could forgive him.

Mother sent an invitation to Edgar for tea a few days after Christmas. Then, a winter party in January. Feeling welcome, he began dropping by again unannounced. I was no longer the focus of his visits. He smoked with Father and talked about the news with Mother. He genuinely liked my parents and Lydia. He still showed interest in my paintings, asking to see them, but politely withheld criticism. Unless, of course, I asked for it.

XXXII.

The light entered my bedroom early, and I pulled back the curtains to scan the street below. Sun glistened on the rain-washed cobblestones, a sheen that would evaporate before breakfast. A beautiful spring morning for my third Impressionist exhibit.

I opened the doors of my armoire to find the right dress. For previous exhibits, I'd left nothing to chance, including having a dress sewn months in advance. With Lydia taking to her bed more often these days—healthy then sick—I hadn't the chance or energy to talk with Mme. Blanche, our seamstress. I selected a French blue linen dress. Its three-quarter sleeves would feel cooler and more practical in the gallery if I needed to arrange or move artwork. The skirt was manageable, no train, which would allow me to walk up and down stairs easily. I lay the dress on the bed and sat at the dressing table. My hair had grown longer in the last year. To make it presentable, Lydia often styled it, but given the early hour, I would have to ask Anna to assist.

The paintings and pastels I assembled in the apartment gallery on 35 Boulevard des Capucines were some of my best. Durand-Ruel and Edgar thought so too. Since I'd worked continuously through the year, I could select my favorite pieces from the lot of finished paintings. I'd joined Berthe the day prior to make sure everything was in order in the makeshift gallery. I stood before my new collection and couldn't help reliving the previous year's events. Edgar. The magazine. Poor reviews from the prior exhibit. The summer at Marly with Aleck, Lois, and the children. And painting Lydia in the garden.

How the family had helped me! I'd produced a worthy show during a year that might have been lost. My paintings showcased nearly every member of my family. The faces of my nieces and nephews shone from canvases as if I'd halted time. How I missed them.

"Quite a different year for us," said Berthe. She too had lost productive time because of the magazine. Though her daughter Julie kept her from working as actively as she had before, Berthe also hoped to change the minds of critics who frowned upon the last exhibit. We both worried about the departures of Renoir and Monet, who'd returned to the Salon, and for the first time, Caillebotte had walked away too. All three artists were linked closely to the Impressionist circle. Their popularity with critics and patrons made the departure hard on everyone. Our show was weaker without them.

But I couldn't dwell on such things on the morning of the exhibit's opening.

"Mlle. Cassatt?" called Anna from the hallway, knocking on the door. She set a breakfast tray on the dressing table. "Mlle. Lydia is ill again this morning. Your mother would like to know when you need the carriage to take you to the gallery."

"Nine-thirty. Is Lydia sleeping?"

"*Oui*, but she wants you to wake her before you leave."

Even ill, she thought of me. If I told Anna to let her sleep, Lydia would be angry. She knew how important this day was.

"Could you press the skirt for me, please?"

Anna gathered the linen dress in her arms, promising to return shortly. Mother stayed with Lydia. Father would accompany me.

At age forty-four, Lydia was too young to spend so much time in bed. Her health was a riddle I tried to solve repeatedly. She'd been well at Marly. With a warmer climate ahead, her health would brighten again. Mother and Father talked about visiting spas in the coming summer. How I wished to loan her my strength. No matter how badly I felt, I always came around quickly. Except for last spring. Lydia pulled me out of bed nearly every day. My determination doubled to find a cure for her.

"May?" Mother stood in the doorway with a basin of water and a washcloth over her arm. "I'm sorry I can't be there for your opening. Lydia and I will spirit our cheers and congratulations from home." She kissed my cheek.

"You will be with me, smiling from the gallery wall along with your beautiful grandchildren."

"Please tell me you don't plan to sell the grandchildren too, May."

"I'm an artist who paints portraits of domestic life. I do not set up my easel in cafés, bridges, or train stations. I would have nothing to sell."

"Not the grandchildren, May!"

I sighed and picked up my hairbrush. "How is Lydia?"

"Headache. Nausea. Same as yesterday. Is Anna helping you with your hair today?"

"Yes."

"Good."

I laughed. Skilled as I was with a paintbrush, my family knew my limits with my appearance. When Anna finished, I went to my sister, knocking lightly on her door. Not hearing her voice, I cracked it slightly to see if she was awake. She opened her eyes and forced a smile.

"I wish you could be with me, Lydia. This exhibit is as much yours as it is mine. I couldn't have done it without you."

She shook her head and tried to sit up, hand to her head. "You did it, May. Your work will thrill them. And I'll see your paintings without the crowds, when I can get a good look at them grouped together."

I felt her forehead. No fever. She looked tired. I offered her tea, but Mother had already tried. Lydia attempted to shoo me off, promising she'd be better soon.

Father was waiting in the library, sitting in his leather chair by the fire and reading the day's news. He stood and smiled when I entered.

"Big day for my girl," he said, folding the paper. No matter how old I was, Father would always see me this way. On that morning, with Lydia sick and Mother home, with critics and patrons about to judge another Impressionist show, I appreciated the paternal care.

He held my hand as I stepped into the carriage, then sat next to me. Dressed in a stone-colored linen overcoat, he looked fashionable and distinguished. I wished Lydia and Mother were with us but was grateful to be alone with him too.

"Your paintings will charm them, May." Father patted me on the knee, trying to quell my nervousness. "We know how hard you've worked this year." He normally bristled at sentimentality, and rarely gave compliments, so when he looked at me directly and said, "I'm proud of you, daughter," my eyes brimmed with tears. I'd struggled to gain his acceptance for so long. The Impressionists made it possible to prove myself to my father as much as the critics. Despite everything, I inwardly thanked Edgar for the chance.

The gray streets and buildings appeared cheerier in the morning sun. The crisp air smelled of spring. Knowing these would be my last few minutes to relax, I leaned against the carriage seat and watched Paris pass by. A *patisserie* and *boulangerie*. The side-by-side *parfumerie* and *millinery* with new *chapeaux* on display in the season's colors.

Men, women, children, small dogs on leashes. Cafés. *Les bouquinistes* with their tables of books along the Seine.

When we arrived, people had already gathered outside the door. They stood aside as Father and I walked toward the front. Some recognized me from previous exhibits and said hello.

"Mlle. Cassatt!" called a man, waving with his wife at the front of the crowd. I recognized him as we walked closer — the wine store owner we'd met with Berthe and Lydia more than a year ago.

"Mme. Morisot brought us tickets again to your exhibit this year."

"How thoughtful."

He introduced me to his wife, and I introduced them to Father before apologetically rushing away.

"*Bonne chance!*" he called.

Attending the front door was a seventeen-year-old art student Edgar had hired. I'd met him days before while arranging my pictures for the exhibit. An especially short man, he opened the door for us.

"*Bon matin*, Mlle. Cassatt," he said, tipping his hat.

"Father, this is one of M. Degas' shining students, M. Henri Toulouse-Lautrec."

"Mary!" called Berthe's voice from above. She leaned over the railing, waving. "Where have you been? Edgar is still not here. We have empty spaces on his walls, and a vitrine with no sculpture."

I looked at Father, then at Henri. "Your teacher, though talented, is exasperating." He nodded.

"Go," said Father, "Do what needs to be done. I'll stroll around before the crowd comes in."

I hurried upstairs. "Thanks for watching the door for us today, Henri!"

Berthe kissed my cheeks quickly and led me to Edgar's room. Our skirts swished past the empty glass case for his not-yet-present sculpture. Together, we looked at the empty walls. Where was he? Berthe searched my face, as if I might know, as if I could get him there faster. We should have been standing in our own rooms, anticipating the opening, feeling satisfied with the culmination of another year's work.

"Do we let it go?" asked Berthe. "The others are irritated." It would be a half hour before Henri would unlock the door.

"Let's move these paintings, slide them over, to cover the space."

"There's no time to patch holes," she said, looking around for a hammer. "We'll have to be careful."

Camille came to the doorway as we moved Edgar's few paintings to the center of the room. He offered to help carry the heavy frames. "Is he not here yet?"

"Not only is he not here—" started Berthe.

"He hasn't put up all of his art." I finished her sentence.

"Nor brought in the sculpture," Camille said, eyeing the case. "He doesn't deserve your kindness." Berthe and I agreed.

We rearranged the paintings to fill in the gaps on the walls, and when finished, with five minutes to spare, appraised the change. The case would remain empty.

"Merci," said Berthe, "*Bonne chance, mes amis.*"

Camille's paintings were in an adjoining room, and he stood to the side so we could hurry down the hallway. "I'll let him know how grateful he should be when he arrives."

The wood floors trembled with footsteps. I took a last look at my paintings. Soon, the rooms filled with people. I wondered if Henri had been told to keep count, to not let in too many people at once. We hadn't rented a fare gate like previous years. The crowds would surely tower over him.

The room with my paintings became so full of people Father and I stepped outside.

"Do you find it strange to have people gazing at our summer memories from Marly?" he asked.

"I paint knowing people will see them. Is it strange to you?"

From the doorway, we watched a group of three women gather before the portrait of Mother reading to the grandchildren. Each pointed to different parts of the painting, commenting on the sweet faces of the children.

"It's like inviting strangers to traipse through our home while we're drinking tea or reading the newspaper. I don't like the idea of our family portraits in someone else's parlor."

"You could buy them," I teased.

An old man stood for a long time in front of my painting of lilacs. It was a rare still life for me, and I wished to hear his thoughts. A man wearing a ginger silk scarf stepped close to the portrait of Lydia crocheting in the garden. He spoke to his companion, gesturing to the canvas.

"Your mother and I like our privacy. Now that our family is no longer anonymous—"

"I should hire models?"

An art student with a sketchpad studied my portrait of Aleck. She concentrated on his face, drawing a portion of it in charcoal. I glanced at Father, who watched her too.

"Now people are copying you. I wish Mother and Lydia were here."

Success can feel strange, the way years of effort open finally to all you've hoped for. When it happens, there is joy, but the moment arrives like every other. I was touched to watch the young student studying my painting, but knew we were more alike than different. Artists do not arrive suddenly—we're always learning. And what of achievement? If I'd ascended a mountain as an artist, Rembrandt had climbed a taller one. Michelangelo's mountain would be so steep few would try. No matter how many paintings I'd sold or how the critics praised my work, when I visited the Louvre with my sketchpad, I felt the same desire and humility I always had.

But the newspapers liked me again. No one was more relieved than I, and after reading two or three reviews, I relaxed for the first time in a year.

"Here's the latest!" called Lydia, a week after the exhibit opened. She was well again, warming herself at a window in the library. She held the newspaper high in the air before her, as though reading for an audience.

> *How can one not be interested, for example, by the studies and works of Cassatt, whose pictures have such grace, finesse, delicacy and, dare I use the word, distinct femininity. The eleven paintings she shows at the independents are all of great interest. Among them I especially like her woman seated outdoors with knitting in her hands. Shaded by a large white bonnet, her face has a lovely tonality that is simple and peaceful.*

"Indeed!" said Father.

"They're praising you again, May," said Mother. "Lydia too."

My family had been reading the reviews aloud since the exhibit's opening. They were mostly flattering, but I couldn't help but wonder how I could be so dismissed in 1880 and so loved in 1881.

"Too much pudding," I said.

By the second week of the exhibit, Edgar finally filled the empty vitrine with his sculpture—*The Little Fourteen-Year-Old Dancer*. I cringed when I first saw it. This was a different dancer than the one in his bedroom, much younger. I thought of the pile of ballet slippers on his floor. How many had modeled for him? How many had he known?

Over three feet tall and made of wax tinted the color of flesh, the piece stunned critics. Edgar had completed the sculpture with real hair tied in a silk ribbon, a muslin bodice and tutu, and actual ballet slippers. Her difficult pose, fourth position, arms stretched behind her back and her head held defiantly high, bothered people. Too brazen for a young girl—a mere *"rat de l'Opéra"*—they said. Her youth, coupled with the public's awareness of leering *abonnés* Edgar depicted in his ballet paintings, only intensified their negative reaction to the sculpture. He portrayed the young dancer's compromise while also revealing her dignity. The critics, not surprisingly, cried immorality.

The sculpture itself, its painstaking detail and modern approach—using real cloth, hair, ribbon, and ballet shoes—was unique. Even I could see that. Was there no artistic medium beyond his reach? No matter how much other artists admired his work, the reviews depressed him. Edgar barely attended the exhibit. He hadn't thanked Berthe and me for rearranging his pictures, and he never brought the other paintings he'd planned to exhibit. I couldn't imagine how long he'd worked on the sculpture. I'd known nothing about it.

By the close of the exhibit, I had sold or had offers on all my paintings. It happened so quickly my parents hadn't realized their memories of Marly had flown from their parlor wall to other homes.

"You sold my grandchildren!" said Mother.

"You know I paint to sell my work—"

"Did *you* know she sold the grandchildren?" Mother asked Father.

"I told her not to."

"Get that painting back, May. These are our family memories!"

I looked at Lydia, who'd lowered her head conveniently to concentrate on her embroidery.

"I can't take it from their wall, Mother."

"You sold it to them. Go reclaim it. Tell them I won't part with it. Give back the money. Some things are not for sale, May."

Mother would not let the issue go. I found it pointless to argue with her. Since Durand-Ruel had assisted me with the transaction, I asked him to help me with my predicament. A month before the exhibit, I didn't know if I'd sell a single painting. Now I was begging for one to be returned.

Durand-Ruel visited the family to explain my situation. Thankfully, the couple who bought the painting had grandchildren and felt sympathetic toward Mother. I reimbursed their money, and they returned the portrait. By the next day, I'd hung the painting again in our parlor. Mother put a hand over her heart and smiled when she saw it. She didn't thank me since she thought I should apologize for selling it. Fiasco resolved. I promised myself to use more models.

Though the newspapers had been kind to me, critics didn't value the exhibition overall. The press made a point of noting artist departures and their return to the Salon. As feared, some read the news as evidence of Impressionist ruin. Though the show was well attended, a few critics called us a sideshow. Edgar's sculpture received the most vehement attention, but predictably, this only brought more people to the gallery to see it themselves. While the press criticized the sculpture, Durand-Ruel said he'd never sold so many of Edgar's paintings. The critical reviews seemed to bolster his sales as much as the kind reviews did for mine.

Soon there were no paintings left to sell—none my family would part with, anyway. Until I could get behind my easel again, I framed some studies I'd made of Lydia at Marly. To my surprise, they sold quickly too. My bank account brimming and a summer of work still ahead, my professional life purred like the cat in my lap.

XXXIII.

My youngest brother Gard, a thirty-two-year-old bachelor, joined us for the summer in Louveciennes, a town close to Marly, at a house fittingly called *Coeur Volant*—Flying Heart. Like Aleck, Gard was not inclined to sit around much during the day. He rode the horses that came with the house every morning and dared me to race him, but I saved the mornings to paint outdoors. Keeping my promise, I hired local models to pose for me daily. The summer carried on and I slowed down, turning my attention to studies I could work from during the winter. Maintaining the frenetic pace of the previous year felt unnecessary. I'd redeemed myself. Father liked to say my stock was up again.

As my bank account was flush, my thoughts turned to collecting art. I loved supporting my friends, but also knew soon enough their paintings would grow in value. Preoccupied with choosing which paintings to buy, I arranged a trip to Paris to meet with Durand-Ruel, and I came home with three paintings from Edgar, Monet, and Pissarro. I saw the purchases as investments—a place to keep and grow my money.

When my carriage returned from Paris to Louveciennes, I couldn't wait to share the paintings with my family. I hurried into the house and saw Gard standing outside the library. He put his finger to his lips and motioned for me to stand next to him.

He was listening to Father consoling Mother. I pushed past my brother, uninterested in eavesdropping.

"Is everything okay?" I asked. Gard came to stand next to me.

Mother motioned for us. "Your sister's vision was blurred again this morning."

"Is she resting?"

"The local doctor came today. Her color was off."

I sat down at the table. Gard stayed standing.

"He has a colleague—" said Father, stopping. "He thinks Lydia may be seriously ill."

"What do they think it is?"

"Her kidneys. Same diagnosis as Dr. Doucet. He wants us to meet with a man who has treated these ailments before. Get his opinion," said Father.

I stood and sat down again.

"How is Lydia taking the news?" asked Gard.

"You know your sister," Father said.

"She's strong. She's sleeping," said Mother. "I wonder if she's veered from her diet?"

"Sounds like the doctor thinks it's more than diet," said Gard. "She hasn't been well since I arrived."

"Too much milk and cream!" said Mother, ignoring him. Gard kept quiet while Father put his arm around her. I left the room.

When I cracked her bedroom door, Lydia stirred, and I tiptoed to her bedside. She opened her eyes.

"You're back. How was your trip to Paris?" she asked.

"Everyone is in the library worrying about you."

Lydia closed her eyes. "I'm doing my best."

"Of course you are."

"Mother thinks I've brought this on myself."

"She cannot bear the thought you are seriously ill."

"And you often talk to me as though my health is a matter of will."

"But some days you are fine—"

"I'm not inventing my nausea and headaches."

"I know you aren't."

"I feel alone all the time." Tears rolled down her cheeks.

"I'm here."

"It's getting worse, May."

I wanted to argue with her, to tell her to fight harder. Instead, I sat on her bed and stroked her hair. Lydia cried quietly. How often did I not listen?

"I'm sorry, Lydia."

She rolled toward me, her arm around my waist, still crying.

I sat with her while she slept. The day in Paris, the new purchases and big plans faded away. For hours, I did nothing but watch light and shadows move along the rugs and walls of Lydia's bedroom. How little I felt like painting. The light turned rose, then gold. The silver vase and yellow roses on Lydia's dressing table shone in the light.

"Will you move them closer to me?" she asked, awake and looking at the flowers too. Her vision had come back.

I placed them on her nightstand, and she inhaled. She'd cut them a day ago, along with the arrangement on the dining table.

"Better?"

She nodded.

"Would you like me to open the curtains so you can watch the sunset?"

She nodded again.

Time creeps during illness. For Lydia, the hours lengthened miserably when she was sick. I did my best to keep her company. Gard sometimes relieved me, bringing cards and games to entertain. Mother read the newspaper aloud and crocheted next to her bedside.

Bright's disease, the doctors finally named her illness. Compromised kidneys deserved another name, anything other than "bright." She could live a long time with the disease. She could have long periods of health mixed with bouts of sickness.

I kept my routine of sketching in the mornings. I also wrote letters to family and friends, updating them on Lydia's health. Aleck and Lois. Berthe. Camille.

Even Edgar. He'd want to know. Within days of receiving my letter, Edgar sent two of his own—one to Lydia and another to me. Along with a request to visit, he wrote, "I know how difficult this must be for you, Mary. I could not be sadder to hear it."

To Lydia, he sent a get-well note with a sketch of a fairy in a hat of light. Underneath the fairy, he wrote Lydia's name. She loved it, of course. Edgar's brusqueness on the outside betrayed his soft inside. I hadn't forgotten our past, but his kindness toward Lydia touched me deeply.

My parents were happy to see him when he arrived a week later, carrying a box of bread and pastries for the family and a new book tied in white ribbon for Lydia. She was feeling better when he arrived, sitting at the edge of the garden with her knitting.

"Just like your portraits. Looking beautiful and industrious," Edgar said as he approached her. Lydia looked up and smiled. She tried to stand.

"No, no. Let me pull up a chair." He placed his hand on her arm as she sat down again. Edgar pulled over two chairs, legs scraping the gravel path as he positioned them. Varying shades of purple and white lavender had grown tall in the garden. Clusters of red zinnias grew in front of the lavender.

"I thought you could use some new poetry," he said, handing her the large volume.

Lydia's expression turned soft as she took it from him. "*Merci*, Edgar," she said, smiling. She read the cover. Walt Whitman.

"An American," said Edgar. "Do you know his work?"

"Yes. He writes poetry without form or verse. Some consider him rebellious. You will like him," said Lydia.

Edgar sat back in his chair, rubbed his eyes, then rested his head in his hand. He had taken to wearing dark glasses, especially outdoors. "Will you read something?" he asked.

"Do you know his work at all?" Lydia asked. He shook his head.

"Select one. Read slowly. *Lentement*," he instructed.

Without looking, Lydia flipped through pages and stopped in the middle of the book. "The title is 'A Clear Midnight.'"

This is thy hour O Soul, thy free flight into the wordless,
Away from books, away from art, the day erased, the lesson done,
Thee fully forth emerging, silent, gazing, pondering the themes thou lovest best.
Night, sleep, and the stars.

Edgar considered Whitman's words before speaking. "There is something kind about the end of the day."

I wondered how Edgar marked the end of his day. Not by sunset or even midnight. He worked all hours. We sat silently with Whitman's words a while longer.

"I haven't yet learned how to part with a day without grasping at it," Edgar said. "He's more at peace than I am. Whitman is like you, Lydia."

Lydia waved his compliment away but stopped. "I know what it's like to grasp at days."

Edgar did not cringe at the sudden turn in conversation. He didn't apologize or look away. He put his hand on the arm of Lydia's chair and sat with her. I didn't have his patience.

"Lydia—" I started.

"I imagine you *do* know what it's like to grasp at days, Lydia," he interrupted.

"Thank you for not trying to console me."

"Read us another?" Edgar asked.

Lydia opened the pages again. Edgar listened to Whitman's words about the War Between the States and its aftermath. I recalled his fond memories of New Orleans, the birthplace of his mother, and he understood the complexity of slavery, emancipation, and its effects on the country. He said Whitman's frank portraits of Reconstruction impressed him— the fate of a mixed-race prostitute living in the South. The grief too many parents felt, losing sons in battle.

"He captures what is, without apology or cloud cover. He writes the way I try to paint."

The truth. Even across the ocean, on another continent, the arts demanded clarity. Ideal gave way to real.

"Everything is changing. The poets and painters are showing us," agreed Lydia.

Perhaps her words were tinged with news from home that President Garfield had been shot at close range a week earlier. The assassination attempt brought vivid memories of the war and Lincoln's death. The violence in our homeland felt sickening even at a distance. How would America survive without the security of its leadership? A vigil in Washington was being held for the President's recovery. We all waited for news of updates on the gunman's pending trial.

Our discussion lasted most of the morning in the sunlight until Gard came to gather us for lunch. He'd returned from a long ride. Edgar stood to greet him.

"M. Degas, how good to meet you finally in person." My brother removed his glove and shook his hand. "My family holds you and your artwork in high esteem."

"Call me Edgar. France would not be the same without the Cassatts. Your parents have always welcomed me kindly into their home."

"We miss them in Philadelphia, but everyone understands why they stay here after visiting France. I'm ready to pack up and move."

"We have room for you, Gard," I said. Lydia nodded.

"I'm afraid I don't have your artistic skill, May."

"And I don't possess your head for business," I answered.

Edgar and Lydia exchanged a knowing look.

"You have more business acumen than any artist I know," said Edgar, as they walked into the house.

"Did Durand-Ruel tell you I purchased one of your paintings from the gallery?" I asked.

"Which one?"

"One of your laundresses, ironing. Red blouse. Laundry hanging in front of her."

"Ah yes. Could I see it?"

"No. I don't want you to take it." I'd heard too many stories of him promising to improve a painting but never returning it.

"I would merely make sure it's presentable. You passed on your own portrait?"

"You portray the laundresses with more grace than you did me in that painting. I can't imagine anyone who would want it. Anyway, Durand-Ruel must agree with me because he took it down."

"You're calling my portrait graceless?"

"Yes."

"And you, Lydia? Do you feel the same way?" She gave us a look of irritation and said nothing.

Anna ladled vichyssoise into shallow bowls as a first course. Father had selected a crisp bottle of Chablis to drink. Mother thanked Edgar for the bread, which Anna served with our soup.

We never spoke again about the vile portrait. I hoped it would be lost somewhere, forgotten in a storeroom.

Lydia was well during the meal and for the length of Edgar's visit. He stayed until evening. After saying his goodbyes, Lydia hugged and thanked him again for his gift. I walked him to his carriage.

"You have my support, Mary." His gaze was direct, deliberate.

"Thank you."

"I know how much she means to you. I know how special she is."

I blinked back tears. "I won't let her give up."

He nodded, then kissed my cheeks before climbing into the carriage. "I didn't have time to see your new work."

"Next time." I waved as the carriage pulled away. I watched it until the sound of the wheels faded completely. The blue evening returned, quieter without him. The gravel crunched as I walked back into the house.

Mother and Father had gone to bed. Lydia, wrapped in a quilt, and Gard with his tie loosened, sat in the library playing a game of chess. "I will not lose to you again," he said as Lydia took his rook.

"Good luck," I said.

"Did you have a pleasant visit?" asked Lydia, not looking up from the gameboard.

"He came to see you, Lydia, but yes."

"He came to see us both," she said, moving a pawn. Gard scratched his head. I knew who would win this game. I wished them goodnight and glanced at my brother and sister together from the doorway before going to bed.

XXXIV.

The summer sketches from Louveciennes lay untouched in my studio for months. I could not bring myself to look at them while my sister suffered. At least when she modeled for me, we were together. My fear had come true; the urge to paint had completely left me again. How could I possibly give myself to work when it took me away from Lydia's side for days? My sister's care became my work. I saw to her meals, following the doctor's dietary recommendations, and made certain she took the remedies prepared for her. Mother relieved me sometimes, but when she did, rather than pick up my sketchpad, I picked up knitting. I wasn't as adept as Lydia and Mother. I chose a soft purple yarn and let stitches drop without going back to fix them.

I longed for ordinary tasks, simple activities. I walked to the *boulangerie* daily for bread and took over menu planning. I watered plants and watched the cat curl in morning light. I wrote letters to my nieces and nephews in Philadelphia, drawing pictures in the margins. I read novels and poetry and took afternoon naps in the chair by the window in Lydia's room.

I felt helpless otherwise and pushed away tears I refused to let fall in my sister's presence. Nothing seemed more pathetic than the idea of my sick sister comforting me. So, I kept a stoic front.

Edgar visited weekly, always with gifts tucked under his arm. Sometimes Lydia was well enough to sit with him in the parlor. He rang with a fresh edition of *Le Figaro* on a cold November evening.

"How did you get it a day early?" Mother asked, scanning the front page. The trial of the President Garfield's assassin, Charles Guiteau, was scheduled to begin the next day. The newspaper probably printed the front page early, knowing little else would take precedence.

"I have my sources."

We gathered around as Mother read aloud about the pending trial. Guiteau claimed God had commanded him to murder the President. He recited poetry twisted with hate and proselytized fear. Americans seemed equally fascinated and outraged by him, which only earned him more space in newspapers. His brother-in-law would represent him during the trial. The press predicted a spectacle.

News from America was a brief respite. The article, while salacious, could not rouse me from worry. I could only glimpse the world beyond our apartment. I would not take my eyes off the task at hand, to get Lydia well and back on her feet.

Edgar tried his best to raise our spirits when he visited. He talked about the latest show at the Opéra and brought new books for my sister wrapped in brown paper. He brought me news from the Impressionists. Even their infighting and differences could not distract me from troubles at home. The next exhibit was only a season away. Though I had mostly sketches, I didn't fret about it as I had in years past. The need to produce good art felt less significant, small.

"Why can't they be happy to be part of a group that allows them an audience and public recognition?" I asked rhetorically, for the hundredth time, when Edgar recounted the latest arguments. I had little compassion for the group's aesthetic disputes. Hearing about the café quarrels then seemed petty and vain. Lydia's health hadn't improved and Christmas was a week away.

"What is this?" Lydia asked when I brought her a package one morning tied with red and green string. Still a few days before Christmas, I said nothing as I opened the curtains and sat in the chair next to her. Lydia struggled to sit up.

"Headache?"

She blinked at the light. Lydia had become thinner in the last few months with her bouts of nausea. Mother and I had made it our mission to have delicious foods prepared that fit within the parameters of her diet. I searched every apothecary in Paris for the best headache tonics.

Lydia untied the string and pushed off the lid. Her eyes shown as she lifted from the box the black velvet pouch cinched with a silk string. She pulled the silver locket from the pouch and opened it immediately. Each half of the locket contained a picture—one of Lydia and one of me—taken when we were children.

"But where—"

"From Philadelphia. Aleck sent me a photograph he'd found."

The locket dangled from a black velvet ribbon, which Lydia tied as a choker around her neck. She fingered the filigreed surface of the heart. We didn't have many family portraits taken. Photography was rare, especially when we were children.

"Oh May, thank you." I was happy to give her something she'd treasure.

"Would you like to walk with me to the *boulangerie*?" I hoped to get her outside.

Lydia shook her head and closed her eyes. "Maybe I'll feel better after lunch." The locket slid along her clavicle when she lay back into her pillows, the metal glinting in the dim morning light.

"Okay." I sat in the chair by her bed and picked up my knitting. Unlike painting, which requires bright light, knitting requires no light at all. My thoughts moved back and forth with the needles. The next exhibit was three months away.

From Lydia's bedroom window, I watched the season turn from snow to puddles of icy rain. Pink and white blossoms burst from bare branches. Sunlight warmed the pane.

I completed a couple of paintings late at night when the house was quiet. The models I'd hired during the summer didn't inspire me like my family, but I finished a portrait of a young woman crocheting. And while attending a performance at the Opéra on a rare night away, I'd sketched two young women in a loge. I imagined they were sisters. One of them holds a fan before her face and the other looks on, a bouquet of roses in her lap. The theater's gilded décor and bright chandeliers sparkle in the background and their white gowns appear soft, made from fine silk. I left the finished canvas on the easel in the dining room.

"Beautiful, May," said Father the next morning. "But where is their joy? Young women out for an evening of music, the loveliest theater in Paris—maybe the world—and where is their joy?"

He was right. The sisters' expressions are solemn. How could I paint them another way? Watching the young women in the Opéra, with their knowing glances and quick whispered conversations, felt like watching younger versions of Lydia and me. My melancholy mood mixed itself into my paint and onto the canvas.

Edgar considered it one of my finer theater portraits. "It lacks sentimentality. You've shown what's real," he said. But I hadn't painted falsely before. I was simply happier when I'd painted the other pictures. Had he ever been happy? The bathers and laundresses. The dancers performing under the gaze of *abonées*. Café singers. Prostitutes.

Edgar changed the subject to the Impressionists, pacing as he talked, shoving his hands into his pants pockets, then waving them in the air to emphasize a point. He rubbed his eyes under his dark glasses and shoved them back into his pockets. Watching him animated, his face turning red then pale again, interested me more than the grudges, the usual disagreements.

"Monet, Renoir, Sisley, and Caillebotte have all returned!"

"But doesn't that strengthen us?"

"Do they think they can come back and take over the group with their landscapes?" Now Edgar had taken aesthetic sides. What happened to his argument that they were a group of independent artists, no matter the subject or style?

"Are you objecting to their art or their return?"

"They outnumber us now, Mary," said Edgar, as if our friends had become enemies.

The power had shifted out of his hands. Edgar had been the Impressionists' unofficial leader for years. He enjoyed issuing invitations to new artists. Monet and Renoir questioned some of his more recent choices. This irritated Edgar, especially since they'd defected and returned to the Salon. His opposition to the Salon hadn't waned at all. Now facing the Impressionists' seventh exhibition, Edgar didn't want opinionated defectors returning *en masse*, garnering press attention for changing their minds, leaning the aesthetic of the show away from paintings of modern life to landscapes. Durand-Ruel had urged the defectors back into the group for the same reason I thought they should be there too—for the strength the group gained with their reputations and professional success. Monet especially had a large following.

"I'm going to quit this exhibit," Edgar said, "And I want you to quit with me. You don't have enough pictures, anyway."

I had only a handful of new paintings, true, but to not show at all after last year's success? How could I walk away? How could he?

"Durand-Ruel will still sell your paintings."

"On what principle would I stand by not taking part?"

"We have crossed a bridge that cannot be retread. There will be no line between the future and the past if we allow the Salon to infiltrate our group. Renoir says the old ways of painting are superior. We've all studied the masters, but we live in a modern age. Life has changed, and it's possible—no, essential—to adapt techniques to fit our times. We're not reinventing painting, only seeing what else can be accomplished."

Edgar stopped speaking, distracted by a gray pigeon alighting on the sill. The bird's wings matched the color of the sky. I imagined him considering how he might capture the movement of the feathers.

"You would never submit to the Salon again, true, but must you hold everyone else to the same standard?"

"A painter cannot hope to please both traditionalists and modernists. How can we move forward while clinging to the past? We would be neither unique nor progressive. We will become what the newspapers have accused us of being from the beginning—a sideshow."

"You feel our exhibition won't be taken seriously if they return?"

He shrugged. "I see it as a question of integrity. Either you believe you have something worthwhile to contribute or you don't. At some point, one must let go of a need for approval from the Salon. Why try to please judges who don't allow for innovation, who won't permit paintings they can't categorize within an artistic lineage? It's an archaic system. Art must adapt to the times."

I considered his comments carefully but questioned his argument about artistic integrity. I wondered if he enjoyed fighting.

"Think about it, Mary," he urged as I walked him out.

XXXV.

"Wretched" was the word Mother used when I asked how she felt that morning. She sat at the small desk in her bedroom, head in one hand and pencil in the other, staring blankly at a list she'd written. Her forehead felt cold. When I reached for her hand to help her stand, it felt clammy. Seeing how my mother struggled, I ordered her to bed at once and asked Anna to bring more blankets and to stoke the fire in her room.

"Please help her undress and send a message to my father at the club," I said. My authority as the family nurse was already well established.

I turned then to check on Lydia, knocking on her bedroom door. No answer. I opened it quietly. Lydia was hunched over and vomiting into the ceramic washing bowl I'd used to prepare cool washcloths for her fever. I'd placed it on her nightstand. I waited for her to stop, but her nausea continued, a jag of relentless heaving. I stroked her bony back through her nightgown. Lydia looked panicky. Her stomach seemed to refuse everything lately, but this was different. Her body was defying her, rejecting her attempts to nourish it. Even the simplest foods. Water.

I set aside my panic and spoke soothingly, but the waiting was relentless. With every heave, I felt more of my sister's strength leave her. Her head fell lower over the bowl and her body grew limp. Finally, by the time Anna had come with another basin of warm water and clean towels, it had ended. I gathered Lydia's upper body in my arms, slack with fatigue, and lay her against the pillows. Already, she slept. I washed and dried her hands. I washed the strands of hair that had fallen out of her braid and into her face, and with my fingers, combed them behind her ears. Then softly, I touched the wet cloth to her forehead. Lydia's pale skin blotched pink. Her breath sounded jagged and shallow.

I pulled the quilts under her chin, exhaled, and heard Anna crying quietly.

"I pray for her every day," she said. She wiped her tears on her apron.

I nodded and thanked her.

"M. Cassatt has returned from the club. He's tending to your mother in her bedroom now. He asked Mathilde to fetch the doctor."

"*Merci* for the care you've given my family, Anna. We couldn't do this without you."

"Are you able to paint at all, Mlle. Cassatt?" The easel had been standing in the parlor untouched for weeks.

"No. My work is here." The Impressionist exhibit had come and gone. I bowed out. Durand-Ruel had been disappointed by my decision. He'd worked diligently to bring everyone together that year, but I couldn't pull myself away from my family. The others might have thought I'd taken sides with Edgar, but I hadn't. Their infighting and aesthetic quarrels were trivial. Such political maneuvering and grandstanding required energy I didn't have. The Impressionists were imploding at the same time my professional ambition seemed to disappear. Lydia's illness clarified all that really mattered to me. My family. I had no artistic life without them. I was indebted to Edgar and the Impressionists, to Durand-Ruel as well, but even without them, I would paint. This understanding came to me in those endless hours near Lydia's bedside. Even Edgar noticed something had shifted in me when he visited, which he still did, often.

"Mary," said Father from the doorway.

"Is Mother all right?" I asked.

His expression hid nothing. He looked at Lydia and back again at me. "She says her arms hurt, and she's having trouble breathing."

"Where's the doctor?"

"Mathilde says he'll be here shortly." Father loosened his tie and leaned against the doorway. His palms faced me as if to ask why. We stared at each other for a few moments while Anna picked up the used washcloths and basin of water.

"Why don't you take my place, Father? Sit with Lydia. I'll go to Mother." Powerless, he took the chair by the window.

Anna glanced at me before leaving the room. "Tea," she said, reading my thoughts. "And cake."

"Bring a cup for Lydia too, just in case."

Dr. Doucet left Mother's room. "Heart trouble. Does it run in her family?"

"Not that I'm aware," said Father, shaking his head. "Is there anything else we can do for her?"

"I've given her a tonic, but she needs rest."

"Would it be too much for her to travel?" I asked, thinking of the house in Louveciennes.

"Getting away to the country might be the rest she needs. And Lydia, how is she?"

"Very sick," I said, voice catching. Father put his hand on my shoulder while I told the doctor about my sister's nausea and the headaches that made her cry out.

"Should I examine Mlle. Cassatt now?"

Father nodded and led Dr. Doucet to her room. I wandered into the parlor, the home's silence in my ears, and stood next to the window. How was it the sun still shimmered on the wet stone walkways while Lydia and Mother were sick? I watched a woman walking in a blue dress, holding her daughter's hand and laughing. Carriages rolled by. I yearned to leave the apartment and become one of the people outside. To get my satchel and walk to my studio, as if any other day. But thoughts of escape felt like betrayal. Was it possible to feel joy at such a time? Could I allow myself an afternoon of painting with the household in crisis? I ran my fingertips along the top of the canvas propped on my easel. Dust. Unbidden words rose inside me. *For dust thou art, and unto dust shalt thou return.* I pushed them away.

So many promises I'd made to Lydia that I would not break. I would be strong enough to carry whatever it was. Lydia would have given her life for me. She should've been healthy enough to help with Mother. We were meant to care for Mother together as sisters. Not like this, I argued silently, a premonition of grief knocking on the door. *Not like this.*

Father reserved the summer house at once. Anna and Mathilde packed their trunks and proceeded to Louveciennes before us. Mother and Lydia mostly tolerated the half-day carriage ride by sleeping. I carried the bag of medicines on my lap. Father and I passed the time with cards. He wore exhaustion like an old coat, except my father didn't own old coats. His wardrobe had always been impeccable. No one could console him like Mother. He was utterly devoted to her, but tending to Lydia at the same time overwhelmed him. I relieved him as much as I could, urging him to spend a couple hours at the club, or to read the newspaper in the library. When he did, he complained he could not harness any real concentration.

In Louveciennes, the green countryside and summer sunlight invited everyone outside. Mother started a new knitting project. Lydia also picked up her needles from time to time, but never made much progress. She was content to lie in the lounge chair I'd cushioned with pillows and blankets, eyes closed, facing the sun.

"Cover your complexion," Mother chided when my sister stopped wearing her hats.

"I don't want to miss one drop of sunlight. Try it." She'd stowed away her need to appease with her hat. She had less patience for trivialities. Her illness seemed to cut through the nonsense she'd carried like a parasol her whole life. For the first time I could remember, Lydia—when she wasn't overwrought with headaches or pain—was living for herself. She began eating more.

I brought home coral roses and *pains au chocolat* from town one afternoon and found Lydia in the dining room, arranging a vase of flowers. She'd felt well enough to cut the blossoms, she said, and was placing them in a polished silver bowl—blue, yellow, and white petals fluttered at her touch. She gratefully took the roses from me and threaded them into the arrangement before placing it in the center of the table. We sat down together to admire her work.

"Shall we have some tea to enjoy with those croissants?"

Mother would never hear of it since chocolate did not fit into Lydia's strict diet. I glanced around to see if she or Father were within earshot.

"You *are* feeling better today, aren't you?"

"Please don't tell me I can't have one."

"I hardly think one croissant will mar your progress." I went to the kitchen to talk to Anna. Lydia crossed her arms over her chest and smiled, satisfied.

"Tell me you've been painting a little without me." The tea arrived and Lydia resumed her role as elder sister, pouring it easily. She tore a corner of the croissant and savored its taste before resting her lips against the steaming edge of her cup, inhaling deeply.

"Would you like to sit for me?"

"I think those days are over," said Lydia, nonchalantly, as though we were talking about a profession she had simply chosen to discard.

"Because you are too ill?"

"Because presently, I am not ill. I don't want to sit for you in a garden. I'd rather sit for myself in a garden."

"I find this change in you baffling but delightful."

"I wonder if I should've put my foot down sooner. I thought I had to be immortalized in your paintings to have any sort of legacy, but I've realized every breath is an opportunity to be immortal, if that makes sense."

It didn't, but I waited for her to continue.

"We only have this tea right now, May. There's no one else is in this room but us. The Impressionists, for all I can tell, don't exist. Not Edgar. Nor Mother and Father. It's only you and me in this dining room with a steaming pot of tea, delicious croissants, and fresh flowers. The sunlight glows in your hair and on this tablecloth. I don't want to live for the future anymore. I don't have a future."

I wanted to argue, tell her not to give up, but her words echoed something I'd been experiencing too, clarity of purpose doing everyday tasks. Until she expressed it, I hadn't articulated how content I'd been simply to live. How strange the realization seemed in the face of Lydia's and Mother's illnesses. Lydia's words came back to me, that she believed she had no future.

"Please don't say it."

"Don't say I will die soon? Surely you've realized this, May. You can't possibly believe the countryside will make me recover. Mother is improving, but I'm not."

"Anything is possible."

"For you, it is. Not for me."

I set down my teacup to demand her to stop, but when I looked into my sister's eyes, I couldn't speak. I saw tenderness.

And a resolve greater than my own. Lydia demanded that I face the truth. She wouldn't look away. I looked down at my lap.

"It's okay," Lydia said.

"But—" She was right. No matter how much I willed her to live and be well again, I was powerless. My anger turned to frustration, then to tears. I wept helplessly.

"I can't do it without you, Lydia."

"Yes, you can."

"Mother. Father."

"They will be fine in your care."

"I fear I've made a terrible choice by bringing all of you here, so far from home."

"We've loved every minute, May. I only wish I had more time, like we planned. Just like this." Lydia picked up her croissant and tore off another bite. "I want to soak up every ounce of this summer."

"I wondered where my girls were."

We turned to see Father in the arched doorway of the dining room with a curious expression. He saw my tear-stained face and glanced at the chocolate croissant in Lydia's hands with the tea service laid before us, like any other morning.

"Come join us, Father," Lydia said. I stood to retrieve another teacup and saucer.

His shoulders relaxed as he ambled in to sit with us.

"How is Mother this morning?" I set a teacup and saucer for him. Anna brought a fresh pot. Lydia's hand rose momentarily to the side of her head, but she quickly placed it in her lap. Father hadn't noticed.

"She's better—well enough for an hour's walk. I was about to search for her, but I know she's been cooped up far too long to keep her here with me."

I imagined my mother in the woods, a basket over her arm, gathering berries or wildflowers—things to make her feel useful again. She would want to walk as long as possible, to build up her strength.

"She's better now." Lydia smiled. Father rested his hand on Lydia's arm. I poured Father a steaming cup of Darjeeling.

XXXVI.

We buried Lydia in Louveciennes.

"May," Mother said, her voice no longer a whisper. Her hand pushed against my shoulder, but I couldn't open my eyes. "Mary?" she asked more urgently, looking for a sign I'd heard her. She sighed and left, footsteps echoing in the hallway.

"Tell M. Degas Mlle. Cassatt is not well enough to see him."

"*Oui*, Madame," said Anna. She turned back to the parlor to deliver the news, heels clicking along the oak parquet floors until muted by Oriental carpet. I imagined his expression, but cared little about what he might say.

My thoughts ran backwards, to the way my mother sat lifeless after Robbie's death. We lived in Germany then. I was a young girl trying to comprehend what had happened. *He was here two days ago, and three weeks ago, we sat by the fire playing chess.* I had been transfixed, wondering where people go when they die. Aleck was too old to play with me, and Gard was too little. Back then, Lydia saw me only as a nuisance, scolding me like a second mother for chasing around the house.

Believing Germany may possess an elixir for Robbie not found in France, Mother and Father moved us to Heidelberg. Learning about different cities in Europe was part of our education, they said, and we welcomed the change of scenery and culture. Heidelberg's stone streets and green rolling vistas carved by the Neckar River looked like pictures from fairytales. My brothers and I knew every inch of the grounds at Heidelberg Castle. We'd try to frighten each other by taking turns hiding in the twisting path to its entrance. Mother registered us at once in a local school to ensure we learned German, and our English lessons continued at home. She instructed us in the evenings after dinner, or if she and Father went out for the night, Lydia oversaw the lessons. Within months of our move, Robbie's health faltered.

Mother did not speak for days after Robbie's death. She wouldn't read the newspaper or pick up her knitting. Lydia made sure we did our lessons every day. She looked after everyone while Father tried to comfort Mother. Sometimes I pretended to roll a ball into my parents' bedroom so I could see her. I longed for Mother to call to me like she always had, to ask me to share a drawing. She might have scolded me for messy hair. My braids were always coming undone, but when I walked in to retrieve my ball, Mother didn't stir or speak. She sat alone. If she glanced at me, she couldn't see me, and the emptiness of her stare scared me. After Robbie's funeral, Mother sat in her bedroom holding a flower, one from a bouquet Father had asked me to put on the grave. I placed the flowers over the turned dirt and looked back to make sure she approved. She must have taken one when I wasn't looking.

Mother's grief was more vivid, easier to contemplate than my own. Robbie's death seemed safer than Lydia's. I couldn't acknowledge my sister's absence, like my mother couldn't bear life without her son running through it. Memories of her sadness showed me how the world can turn dim, and too, how the light can come back again. I needed to fall away from the world for a while, lose myself, to come back. I knew Mother was suffering over Lydia's death, but she seemed stronger having gone through it before. Even Lydia had survived horrific grief. But I was weak. In my lowest hours, I was sure death had taken the wrong sister.

She had been my future. With Lydia, I could live an independent life with domestic tranquility. Without her, my choice to remain unmarried seemed short-sighted indeed. Still, when I considered past affections, only Edgar had held my attention enough to contemplate marriage. I was not meant to have my mother's marriage. Lydia didn't attain it either.

Does one person's life turn on another's? Lydia's presence had wrapped around my life, like skin. I couldn't envision a day without her, but I woke each morning still breathing.

Three weeks after her passing, after the funeral, I received a letter from Camille saying he'd be coming for a visit. I was suspicious, of course. He'd already offered his condolences in person. He and his wife had attended the funeral, so when he walked into our home in early December, I knew he had something important to say.

"Thank goodness you're here," I heard Father say as Camille gave Anna his overcoat, hat, gloves, and scarf.

His cheeks were pink with cold, and his beard was whiter than I remembered.

"All you need is a pair of spectacles perched upon your nose to pass for Saint Nicolas," I said, kissing his cheek.

My parents fussed over him, asking about his children and wife. Father invited him to have a drink in his study after our visit, while Mother and Anna set a table for tea and lemon cake. They left us alone. Camille sat in his chair quietly, warming up while the fire crackled in the stone hearth.

"I love your home like my own."

"You're always welcome—"

He sat silently, watching the fire.

"I'm bereft. I know that's why you're here," I said.

"You need to pick up your brushes again. Find something interesting to paint."

"Nothing interests me now, Camille."

"Then paint that."

"Disinterest?"

"Yes. Or sadness. Love. Your family."

"I don't know if I have —"

"The energy? The Latin root of the word 'suffer' means to carry. You've carried enough for Lydia. It's time to put down the burden, dear friend."

While Camille spoke, a memory of her at the Opéra came back to me. The way she looked. Her flushed cheeks. Her sleeves fitted below her shoulders. Attached to her left sleeve were small roses, one white and the other red with trailing greens. Another red rose tucked into her hair. Her pearl necklace fit perfectly around her neck. She wore kid gloves the same color as her pearls. She shone in the candlelight. My sister never looked more beautiful.

I'd sketched her at the theater, and when I began the painting a few days later, Lydia stood behind me watching. I roughly blocked out her off-center figure with indigo-hued paint. "There will be a mirror behind you," I said. In its reflection, I painted two rudimentary curves that would become the Opéra's balconies.

After I'd finished it, more than a month later, and called my sister to the easel, we stood together assessing it. Lydia didn't speak for a long time, her eyes taking in every detail, every stroke. Finally, she turned to me and reached for my hand. "Because of your painting, May, that night will never end."

A sensation, prickling with heat, arose in my chest.

"Don't let too much time pass before you mix colors on your palette. I understand the temptation to step away from life, but I must tell you, in my years, art has been the balm that healed me. Your sister's spirit surely supports you, even sits with you still."

"Oh, Camille."

He pulled his chair over to mine. I began to cry, deep sobs that filled my chest and spilled small reservoirs onto his suit coat. He tried to give me his handkerchief, but I didn't take it. I leaned into him, and he held me until my tears ran dry.

That's when it happened. Somewhere deep, an ember of old creative desires stirred. A dear friend can remind you of some elemental truth, some rare thing that will restore you. And tears can set it free. My grief burned and shifted shape—as if from black coal to gray smoke.

XXXVII.

- 1886 -

"I am reminded of the days all of us stood at the press," said Edgar. Berthe and I sat at the end of a table in his studio to discuss our three-way agreement to finance the last Impressionist exhibit. We didn't realize it would be our last show together. We rented a five-room, stylish apartment in the gallery district. Four years had passed since the Impressionists had exhibited together, since Edgar had walked out, since I'd been consumed with the care of my sister and mother. It had been more than three years since Lydia's death.

The Parisian art world had changed. Impressionism had lost its avant-garde status. Our paintings were sought by collectors—especially those by Monet, Renoir, and Degas, which sold for premium prices. The growing interest in Impressionist paintings gave us a desire to put on the best exhibit yet. The Impressionists were no longer renegade, rebellious artists, even if we felt nothing much had changed.

"Are you really telling me you'll need more space for yourself, Edgar?" Berthe asked. "You'll leave it half empty."

I nodded in agreement, and he thought better than to argue. Berthe pulled a bottle of wine and a fresh baguette from her satchel. Edgar's maid Sabine carried to the table a tray of meats and cheeses. I retrieved a container of fresh asparagus drizzled with butter and herbs Anna had prepared. Berthe opened the windows, to let in spring breezes.

"I can't help but imagine Lydia with us now," she said, walking back to the table, "Sitting next to you Mary, busy with her handwork, commenting on her latest novel."

I smiled at the thought.

"Did Durand-Ruel tell you that your portrait, the one of Lydia in the loge, has come up for sale again?" Edgar asked.

I longed to see it. "Aleck will surely want it." My brother had built an art collection of Impressionist paintings and prints. He wasn't alone. The demand for paintings grew when Durand-Ruel opened the first Impressionist exhibit in New York. American artists and collectors showed up in droves, buying nearly all the paintings he'd shipped from Paris. Durand-Ruel's influence as an art dealer and our reputation as artists had crossed the Atlantic. I hoped to retrieve Lydia's portrait for my family before it disappeared into another Parisian parlor.

"Promise you won't tell Mother it's available until I'm sure I can acquire it?"

"*Absolument*. I will not tell your mother her late daughter has been sold again to someone outside the family."

"*Merci*."

Berthe laughed. "Which portrait? Weren't there quite a few of Lydia in the loge?"

"The pastel. She wore a pink dress, the color sunrise," answered Edgar, pouring our wine. Berthe passed me a glass.

"I'll visit Durand-Ruel this afternoon," I said, lifting my glass as Berthe made a toast.

"To Lydia."

Edgar nodded, and we took our sips.

"Berthe, I'd like to paint you and Julie together," I said.

"You seem fascinated lately with mothers and children," Edgar noted, reaching for the asparagus.

On very rare occasions, a comment floats above a conversation, like an announcement. My desire to paint family members hadn't waned, but I'd begun seeing in others the same warmth I saw in Lydia, my parents, and my nieces and nephews. I was especially drawn to paint mothers. Child rearing was the labor of women.

In a flash, Berthe's party and the Moroccan fortuneteller came back to me. *I see motherhood in your cards*. Her fingers tapped a card on the table—the image of an empress. The true meaning of her prediction made me shudder. I took a deep breath.

"Are you okay?" Berthe whispered. I nodded, considering Edgar's comment.

"Pissarro sets up his easel in forgotten fields. You loiter backstage with your sketchbook. I'm not free to roam and paint the working class, but I have access to women," I said. "I can make them visible and real. Or would you prefer I add to the world a few more thinly veiled Madonna paintings?"

Berthe smiled at the idea. "I could wear a headscarf. And my most beatific smile."

"Boredom and fatigue are more interesting," I said.

"Now you sound like me," said Edgar.

"There's joy, but anyone caring for a child knows it's hard earned."

Pieces of my oeuvre, not yet assembled, glinted in my imagination. I could still paint Lydia and my parents, my brothers, even myself in the faces of models. I could honor them by revealing the intricate work, passing joy and ennui that come with domestic life. What could be more contemporary than removing the mantle of religiosity from motherhood? Painting actual mothers and children—not stately or romanticized portraits—was as modern as Edgar painting Parisian laundresses. There is beauty and meaning in the unguarded, mundane moments. I imagined what the newspapers would write. *Only a childless artist, who longs for children of her own, could dedicate herself to such a task.* I cringed at the new questions I would undoubtedly be asked at dinner parties.

"Mary Cassatt, patron saint of true maternity," declared Edgar.

"Perhaps it's all figure painting."

"Indeed," he said, tearing off another piece of bread. "One of your strengths."

His support still fanned my confidence, but I realized, nine years after we'd met, how the *artiste mythique* Edgar Degas had taken his place among the other hardworking artists who hoped to create something of value. He had been my lover, but in the end, he remained a friend. For me, familial love was the most stable kind of love. Romantic love brought me grief, an experience I gratefully felt only once. I had not been open to love when I was younger. My ambition would not allow that sort of vulnerability or distraction, and for this, I accepted my life as it was. Still if I could bend time and speak in my youthful ear, I would tell myself this—if you are truly blessed, romantic love can turn into love that sustains you, the kind that extends your family. But I was not born under this particular star.

I had my career and community. We were growing older, and sadly lost Manet, who passed away a few months after Lydia. His departure roiled our social circle. Manet had never refused to take part at the *Salon,* let alone join the Impressionists. His path was his own. New artists were rising through the ranks, breaking into the public's consciousness, testing the boundaries of acceptance with their contemporary notions of illustration. Seurat. Van Gogh. I watched the trend toward greater abstraction while my art reaffirmed traditional lines. I depicted figures sparingly, Impressionistically even, but within the parameters of my training.

Once outcasts, the Impressionists passed through the doors of public acceptance. On the eve of the last exhibit, I thought how odd it was to experience it so quickly.

"This will be one of the finest venues we've secured," said Berthe. She drew an impromptu plan for the exhibit on her sketchpad. She and Edgar bantered over the price of tickets as I sat half-listening.

Robins nested in the white lilac bush outside. The open window allowed the blossoms' scent to waft into the studio with birdsong. I would have climbed into the windowsill to get a better look as a girl, hoping to spy tiny blue eggs among the carefully placed twigs. I was a forty-two-year-old woman, "artist in her prime" the historians liked to say, on the brink of discovering my signature theme, though I'd painted domestic scenes my entire life.

"I suppose I cannot expect people to see through the unfamiliar faces to glimpse the spirits of family and me," I told Camille years later. "Isn't every painting a self-portrait?"

After the twelve years the Impressionists banded together, the Salon no longer held exclusive domain over what was considered good art. Commercial galleries had grown in number, offering more opportunities for artists—including those who pushed against the boundaries of Impressionism with greater abstraction. Would it surprise you to know members of our avant-garde troupe sometimes disproved of these younger, contemporary artists? What is unconventional becomes conventional, but not without people who dare to push the boundaries. The Impressionists were no longer competing only with the Salon.

"Do you have any opinion about this at all, Mary?" Edgar asked when he noticed my distraction. Caught in the act, my interest waning, I admitted the price of tickets didn't matter to me. Whatever price they chose would be fine. Edgar stared at me, eyebrows cocked in disbelief.

"You have no opinion?"

Berthe smiled as Edgar conceded to the lower fare. She wanted to keep the exhibit accessible to students and other artists. She did not know it would be our last.

"Well, we were all once starving," he agreed, then corrected himself. "Except for you both, of course."

So it was that the Impressionists disbanded in the year of 1886. Perhaps as an act of prophetic, last rebellion, Edgar removed the word "Impressionist" from the exhibit catalogue.

The twittering birds reminded me of a different room with open windows and a breeze. Soon I'd return to my studio and begin a new phase of my career in Paris. My easel stood in the corner of the room, next to a small table with a jar of brushes and a paint-stained walnut palette. I could not have imagined the fits and starts, the way my career ambled from friend, teacher, and place. Nothing in my life ever seemed to follow a straight line. Artists flit in and out of the public eye, unnoticed then acclaimed. Gallery owners and art buyers could be unscrupulous, fickle, then generous. There was always work to be done. Hours spent with color and imagination.

I eased my arms into the sleeves of a smock and gazed at the blank canvas. Weeks before, I'd thumbed through sketches from the previous summer, selecting a study of two sisters.

Camille met me often at my studio when he was in Paris. His studio on rue des Trois Frères was a short walk away. One afternoon he brought pastries to enjoy with our tea. We shared news and discussed the latest art exhibits. Durand-Ruel was planning another Impressionist show in New York because he found the American market promising, and so did I. After our tea and conversation, Camille pulled up a chair to watch me work.

The sisters I was painting lived in a village close to our recent summer home. Their mother had given them permission to model for me, and I worked quickly to capture their expressions. They'd never met an artist before. The afternoon sun cast an amber hue, brightening the green grass of the field. I sat in a teak folding chair with my sketchpad as the girls, dressed in summer white, stared back at me.

Standing at my easel with Camille beside me, I brushed highlights into their hair and eyes. Maybe he knew the girls were really Lydia and me, sitting in the open meadow behind our Pennsylvania home. Dogwoods blossomed pink and white against a clear sky. Lydia's dress encircled her, white cotton on spring grass. She plucked purple clover from the field, the longest stems she could find, to make garlands for our hair. I watched her slice the center of stems with her thumbnail, like buttonholes, through which she would thread a new stem and start again. I was too little to manage the garlands myself, though I tried. My stems would bruise and split. Frustrated, I rolled onto my back and pouted.

Lydia giggled. "Practice, May. You'll get it."

My hands weren't as capable as my sister's. I watched Lydia's hands move skillfully over the flowers in her lap.

"I'll make yours," she said. "Don't worry."

Clouds floated above us. Blades of grass moved with small grasshoppers.

"Sit up."

Nine-year-old Lydia placed the crown of clover on my head, arranging it with care. I put my arm over her shoulder, and she smiled. Sunlit strands of hair blew around our faces.

"Magnifique," said Camille.

"Thank you, friend."

AUTHOR'S NOTE

Mary Cassatt first caught my attention in 2008, when I visited an Impressionist exhibit in Frankfurt, Germany. The art museum Schirn Kunsthalle exhibited four female artists—Berthe Morisot, Eva Gonzales, Marie Bracquemond, and Mary Cassatt. I knew little about the female Impressionists then. As an American mother of young children living abroad, I felt drawn to Mary's paintings.

Historical fiction is a mix of fact and imagination. This novel is no different, though I started with the facts. I consider *Mary Cassatt: A Life* by art historian Nancy Mowll Mathews to be the artist's definitive biography. I leaned heavily on Mathews' scholarship while writing this book. I also studied Mary's paintings, placing them on a timeline of her years with the Impressionists. I dove into the biographies and art of Edgar Degas, Camille Pissarro, Berthe Morisot, and other Impressionists. While learning about Mary, and gazing at her artwork, this novel arose in my imagination.

Historians have speculated about a romantic relationship between Edgar and Mary. No correspondence between them has been found, which is strange given the record of letters they wrote to other people. Edgar invited Mary to exhibit with the Impressionists, and they publicly admired each other's work and maintained an on-again, off-again, lifelong friendship. I invented their romance in the novel, but I believe it was possible. Mary's paintings exude a palpable joy during this time of her life, more so than any other. She also worked closely with Edgar in his studio, learning the art of printmaking for the never-published magazine *Le Jour et la Nuit*.

When available, I've used views and direct quotes from the artists. Mary has said she considers the first time she saw Edgar's paintings as a pivotal moment in her career. Edgar reportedly remarked to a friend after seeing one of Mary's paintings at the Salon, "She feels as I do."

Here are a few more facts (among others) in this novel. I pulled Edgar Degas' description of his time in New Orleans from a letter he wrote to a friend while he was there. He reportedly hated the scent of flowers at the dinner table. He produced many brothel prints, which Pablo Picasso collected years later. Berthe Morisot hosted *jour fixe* parties with her husband, Eugène Manet, where artists, musicians, and writers gathered. Mary, ever opinionated, compared Claude Monet's waterlilies to wallpaper. Less is known about Lydia Cassatt, though letters exist between the sisters. It's true Lydia lost her fiancé, Thomas Houghton, in the Civil War and never remarried, allowing her to live with Mary and their parents in a Montmartre apartment still standing today. Press reviews of Mary's Impressionist exhibits are public record.

I offer whole-hearted thanks to my publishing team at Black Rose Writing for bringing this book into the light of day. I'm grateful to early readers, especially Amanda Forsting for (at least) a decade of encouragement. William Boggess provided outstanding editorial support. Kimberley Cameron titled the book and bolstered my confidence during early submissions. Christina Burns listened to me talk for hours about Cassatt, as if I'd been her neighbor in Belle Époque Paris. I'm grateful to Amandine Bandelier for proofreading my French. My desire to write again emerged while on silent retreat—in the exquisite care of Fay Key, Steve Bullington, and Oliver Ferrari. Finally, this novel would not be possible without the steadfast support of my husband Aaron Irvin. With him, I feel I can do anything—including traipsing all over the U.S. and Europe to see Mary's artwork.

A historical novelist weaves narrative between, around, and through the facts, and what a privilege (and riot) to spirit myself into the rooms, art studios, and parties with *les avant-gardes*. I especially loved imagining the hearts and minds of the Cassatt sisters—Lydia and her younger sister, Mary.

-Lisa Groen

Artwork in *The Cassatt Sisters*

The paintings and prints below are listed in order of appearance. All images are in the public domain.

Mary Cassatt, (cover): *In the Box*. Private collection.

Edgar Degas: *Yellow Dancers (In the Wings)*. The Art Institute of Chicago.

Gustave Caillebotte: *Les Raboteurs de Parquet (The Floor Scrapers)*. Musée d'Orsay, Paris.

Claude Monet: *Impression, Solei Levant (Impression, Sunrise)*. Musée Marmottan Monet, Paris.

Mary Cassatt: *At the Theatre (Lydia Cassatt Leaning on Her Arms, Seated in a Loge)*. Nelson Atkins Museum of Art, Kansas City, MO.

Mary Cassatt: *Little Girl in a Blue Armchair*. The National Gallery of Art, Washington, D.C.

Edgar Degas: *In a Café*. The Metropolitan Museum of Art, New York.

Mary Cassatt: *Reading "Le Figaro."* Private collection.

Mary Cassatt: *Woman with a Pearl Necklace in a Loge*. Philadelphia Museum of Art.

Mary Cassatt: *At the Dressing Table*. The Art Institute of Chicago.

Edgar Degas: *Mary Cassatt at the Louvre: The Paintings Gallery*. The National Gallery of Art, Washington, D.C.

Edgar Degas: *Portrait of Lorenzo Pagens and Auguste Degas.* Musée d'Orsay, Paris.

Mary Cassatt: *Waiting.* The National Gallery of Art, Washington, D.C.

Edgar Degas: *Portrait of Miss Cassatt, holding the cards.* National Portrait Gallery, Washington, D.C.

Mary Cassatt: *Lydia Crocheting in the Garden at Marly.* The Metropolitan Museum of Art, New York.

Mary Cassatt: *Mrs. Cassatt Reading to Her Grandchildren.* Private collection.

Mary Cassatt: *Lilacs in a Window.* The Metropolitan Museum of Art, New York.

Mary Cassatt: *Portrait of Alexander J. Cassatt.* Seattle Art Museum.

Edgar Degas: *Little Dancer of Fourteen Years.* The National Gallery of Art, Washington, D.C.

Edgar Degas: *La Blachisseuse Repassant (The Laundress Ironing).* Reading Public Museum, Reading, PA.

Mary Cassatt: *The Loge.* The National Gallery of Art, Washington, D.C.

Mary Cassatt: *Woman with a Pearl Necklace in a Loge.* Philadelphia Museum of Art.

Mary Cassatt: *The Sisters.* Kelvingrove Art Gallery and Museum, Glasgow, Scotland.

ABOUT THE AUTHOR

Photo credit: Busath Photography

Lisa Groen is a novelist and essayist. She is the author of *The Mother's Book of Well-Being*, and her writing appears in the textbook *The Fourth Genre: Contemporary Writers of Creative Nonfiction*. She holds an MFA in writing, and *The Cassatt Sisters* is her first novel. Lisa is a fan of most art—books, movies, paintings, music, and even temporary art, like the sidewalk mandalas she builds with natural materials gathered on her walks. Lisa lives in Utah and shares city and mountain homes with her husband and their dog, George Harrison. Learn more at lisagroen.com.

Note from Lisa Groen

Word-of-mouth is crucial for any author to succeed. If you enjoyed *The Cassatt Sisters*, please leave a review online—anywhere you are able. Even if it's just a sentence or two. It would make all the difference and would be very much appreciated.

Thanks!
Lisa Groen

We hope you enjoyed reading this title from:

www.blackrosewriting.com

Subscribe to our mailing list – *The Rosevine* – and receive **FREE** books, daily deals, and stay current with news about upcoming releases and our hottest authors.
Scan the QR code below to sign up.

Already a subscriber? Please accept a sincere thank you for being a fan of Black Rose Writing authors.

View other Black Rose Writing titles at www.blackrosewriting.com/books and use promo code **PRINT** to receive a **20% discount** when purchasing.

www.ingramcontent.com/pod-product-compliance
Lightning Source LLC
Chambersburg PA
CBHW060534190726
48283CB00003B/718